THE RISE OF THE ALTEREDS

MARISA NOELLE

REVIEWS FOR THE UNADJUSTEDS

"A pacy dystopia that romps along - speculative fiction at its most moreish! I love books exploring questions like this...what does playing god mean? And what's it like when you're the odd one out in the world? Perfect for 12+. Loved the mental health angle too, sensitively handled." – Louie Stowell (Author).

"I loved this book. Great characters and an absolutely brilliant concept! This will appeal to anyone who enjoyed The Hunger Games / Twilight.

The writing was fantastic and the pace was perfect throughout - I was gripped from the first page. The characters were well drawn and I cannot wait to see what happens to them next! I could easily see this being picked up for a film option." – Catherine Emmett (Author)

"As soon as I read the synopsis for this book I was dying to know more. The concept really intrigued me – a world where the majority of the population have altered their DNA? It was such a fascinating idea. When I picked up the book I completely fell in love with this world and these characters, a unique and engaging tale, one that is perfect for fans of Suzanne Collins' The Hunger Games and Emily Suvada's This Mortal Coil." - The Bibliophile Chronicles (Blogger)

"Silver's first-person voice immediately draws the reader in and her appealing personality easily carries us through. It helps that we're given such an incredible plot hook to pull us into the story. (A visceral description as Silver stands in a school corridor and watches a boy die from taking a nanite pill). This sets the tone for the rest of the book which maintains the pace of a thriller without at any time sacrificing the exceptional character development.

Silver is supported by an eclectic collection of characters, including unadjusteds and altered. It's testament to the skill of the author, Marisa Noelle, that I was able to so easily assimilate and track such a large cast. I particularly enjoyed the love triangle between Silver, Matt and Joe and appreciated the fact that, unlike so many similar stories, this was firmly resolved by the end of the book." - Madge Eekal Reviews (Blogger)

"I blinkin' loved it!" – Amazon Reader.

"Though I was a little heartbroken at the end, I just wanted more. Please tell me there's a sequel and I can return to the technicoloured and dangerous world of The Unadjusteds." – Noelle Kelly (Book Reviewer)

"The characters are excellent and imaginative!" - Good-Reads reviewer

"It gave me moments of shock and out-loud gasping." – Amazon reviewer

"*The Unadjusteds* was a well-written, intense and emotional story that kept my attention from start to finish." – Book blogger

"I devoured this book!" – Amazon reader.

"It reminded me of YA heavyweights like *The Hunger Games* and *Divergent*. It would make a superb film!" – Book reviewer.

BOOKS IN THIS SERIES:

For Riley, Lucas and Quinn

CHAPTER ONE

THE JANUARY WIND howls outside the window, banging insistently on the glass, demanding to be let in. It adds to my already frayed nerves. As I look around the room at my friends, I clamp my hands around my mug. How am I going to tell them?

Avoiding questioning stares, I flick my gaze to the empty window and see nothing but snow. My stomach clenches. I'm about to ask the world of them and they have every right to say no. I would, if I had half a chance.

Safely ensconced in the presidential building, we wait for President Montoya. Or Francesca as I'm still allowed to call her. Matt sits next to me and fiddles with a pen, rolling it over his fingers. I take confidence from his presence. He's always been my rock, the one person in my life I know has my back. Not only does he challenge me, he brings out the best in me too, even when I'm not in the mood. I don't know what I'd do without him. Especially with my mother still missing. With his legs crossed, he appears relaxed. But then he knows what's coming and he's the only one who won't be affected.

"What's this all about, Silver?" Erica asks from across the large conference table. Aside from the bulks, she is the one who has changed the most. Not so long ago, she was a fairy and a total pain in my ass. When the cure worked, she lost her wings. Her eyes returned to a human blue, but her hair remained an unusual lavender. Perhaps a side effect. Even though it has been several months since the cure was delivered in the country's water system, I still can't get used to her without wings. They used to change color according to her emotions and now I can't read her as well.

"I'd rather wait for Francesca...President Montoya," I reply. I want to delay the coming conversation for as long as possible.

I glance at my father. He stands by the window with his back to us. A small muscle in his jaw twitches. Right now, the possibility of getting my Mom back is real and tangible. But any one of these people sitting around the table could dash that dream in an instant. If they don't agree. Seeking reassurance, I put my hands in my pockets and find a couple of loose acorns. I circle them in my palm, the smoothness of their skin calming me.

"Is it about the outbreaks?" Paige asks. Her dark hair is longer than ever, cascading down her back. Her emerald eyes have dulled to a warm hazel color, but they hold the same kindness they always did when she had macaw wings. I don't know what I'd do without her, either.

Sawyer's head snaps up, causing his curls to bounce. "What outbreaks?" He asks, around a mouthful of Danish pastry. He still hasn't been able to give up the habit of eating whatever is in front of him. A habit from living on the streets for so long.

Without warning, the door whooshes open and a gust of cold air follows President Francesca Montoya into the room. We stand to greet her.

"Please sit, none of you need to stand on ceremony for me." She smiles and her dark eyes dance with warmth.

Her appearance hasn't changed since her school teaching days, a fact I now find oddly comforting. Although she's swapped her skirts for a trouser suit. Her graying hair and rosy cheeks portray a maternal warmth, but I've learned not to mess with her. Looks can be deceiving. She led the resistance against the altereds and now she's the president of the country that remains.

"Welcome everyone and thank you for coming," Francesca says. She takes the time to go around the room, holding everyone's gaze, then pours herself a black coffee, two sugars.

"I'm feeling oddly nervous." Paige fiddles with a doughnut on a napkin, licking her finger to pick up the crumbs from the table. "Someone please put me out of my misery."

Jacob pats her thigh and leaves his hand there. Like Matt

and me, they've been together since we lived in the caves. We spent several months there, hiding from President Bear and his army of immortal bulks and hellhounds, trying to figure out how to survive in a world where taking nanites was deemed law. After rescuing my father from the President Bear's clutches, he found a cure to turn all the altereds back to their unadjusted selves. But not all of them made the transition.

I'm still uncomfortable with the way they died. Those who took too many nanites couldn't sustain the change back to their human DNA. It was a consequence we hadn't predicted, and now have to live with. Was it worth our freedom? I wrestle with the question. Matt and I often speak of the alternatives. Every single other option left us dead. This way, we get to start again, with a more democratic society, and hope the remaining altereds still out there will see sense, or leave us the hell alone. Francesca's army are hard at work maintaining the new laws and regime, but the threat hasn't entirely disappeared. That's why we're here.

"We haven't all been together since..." Kyle gulps and runs a hand across the back of his neck. He's taller, and somehow even skinnier, not a spare inch of fat on his lanky frame. Even though he doesn't possess the speed ability anymore, he still runs every morning. And he remains fast, even without the nanite. "Well, you know."

"Since the cave," Francesca says. "Since the cure was delivered."

With half the population no longer here, houses stand

empty. Whole neighborhoods. Cars lay abandoned on roads. Entire schools have no pupils. Francesca's priority has been securing a new government. Now she is looking to clean up the leftovers and bring a feeling of positivity back to those who remain. But there is one group above all others who threaten that ideal.

"I don't want to make this any more nerve-wracking than it already is," Francesca continues. "So I'll come right out with it. We've located Earl."

A gasp streaks through the small gathering, but this isn't news to me. Hal's eyes narrow and Kyle punches a fist into the other palm. Even though I'm expecting the words, an icy fear drips down my spine. Earl. He was one of my father's colleagues. A top scientist in the field of genetic modification. He created the hellhounds. The very same creatures who tore off part of my father's leg and attacked me. And he was firmly on President Bear's side.

Francesca places her hands on the back of the chair in front of her. "He's fled to the Sierra Nevada mountains in California and is able to purify his water source."

Sawyer fiddles with one of his curls. "So, he's still an altered?"

Francesca nods. "He is indeed. Along with the others who are with him."

"How many?" Hal turns his chair around and straddles it, his arm resting along the back. I haven't seen him for a while. To begin with it was too painful, every time I looked at him, I thought of Joe. Now, it still hurts, but the pain has eased.

Francesca tilts her head. "We estimate a couple of hundred."

Kyle's eyes light up. "We can take out a couple hundred."

Francesca holds up a hand. "Let's not get ahead of ourselves. We're talking about altereds. Some of the most powerful ones. And they are being organized by Earl." Her gaze drifts from one person to the next. "As powerful as you all used to be, you are now human, and unfortunately, don't stand a chance."

"So, what do we do?" Hal breaks a doughnut in half.

"Can't we just nuke the fuck out of them?" Kyle asks.

A light chuckle eases some of the tension in the room. Sawyer offers Kyle a high five, which he accepts.

"I'm glad you're so eager to help," Francesca says, with a small smile at Kyle. "But there is one other important piece of information. Earl has Dr. Melody. Silver's mother."

I close my eyes and hold my breath. I'm not sure I can face the reactions of my friends. Matt puts his hand on my lap, much the way Jacob did with Paige. I open my eyes and glance at Claus. Leaning on his cane at the back of the room, he gives me a short nod of approval. He's always supported me. He taught me to fight, and even though he's as anti-nanite as the rest of us, I know he is in favor of my forthcoming request.

"So, we need to go rescue her," Erica says, her shoulders

high, her hands splayed, like it's the most obvious solution. I'm surprised it's her who speaks first.

"Of course we do," Hal says. My chest swells with gratitude. "But how? How do we face off against a bunch of altereds? I know President Montoya has her new army and everything, which I'm proudly part of, but we're not bulks anymore, we don't have the strength."

My father steps away from the window and comes to stand next to me. He's been quiet, perhaps as nervous as I am about everyone's reactions.

"Silver and I have a very important question to ask you." Dad puts a hand on my shoulder and squeezes. I brace myself for his next words, all my hope wrapped up in the next few moments. "We will be launching a mission to neutralize Earl and his altereds and to rescue Margaret. But Hal, you're right, we can't do it as humans. Therefore, I am asking you to take back your previous abilities."

Paige's mouth drops open. Both of Kyle's eyebrows shoot over his head and Sawyer's curls remain totally still, for once. Erica chuckles, as if she can't quite believe what she's heard.

Hal half stands. "Are you serious?"

"I'm so up for this!" Kyle's voice pitches high. "I have *sooo* missed my speed. I was trying to figure out a way to ask for it back." He blushes. "I'm in, I'm *so* in."

"Slow down, Kyle. Please. This is…a huge decision. I'm not even sure I would do it if I had a choice. We've been through so much, we've lost people…this is…this is…" My voice trembles and emotion swells through me. I stand and face my friends, my old mission team. I love them all. I'd die for each and every one of them. And now I'm asking them to do the same for me, for my mom, for the unadjusteds.

Matt rubs my back. "Are you trying to talk them into it or out of it?"

A smile steals across my lips and I wipe at my eyes. "It's completely voluntary. We only want you to agree if it's what you want to do. There will be no hard feelings."

"But everyone's normal now," Jacob says. "I mean, wasn't that the point of the cure?"

Erica shakes her head. "Everyone is *not* normal. There are people out there with abilities still. The human ones—"

"Yeah, but nothing serious," Jacob says. "I mean, we can live with a bunch of people who have permanent white teeth and never smell bad, can't we?"

"You forget about the offspring," Matt says. "Born from altered parents, they are unaffected by the cure in the water. We don't know how many are out there, what their abilities are or where they stand on genetic modification. We don't have that information yet."

"Not to mention Earl in the mountains. His people will have the worst kind of abilities," Hal adds.

Matt nods at his words. Frowns and grimaces cloud the faces of the group as they contemplate what I'm asking.

"So, what enhancement will you be having?" Jacob asks Matt, an edge in his tone. "If we're going to be facing off against some big powerful baddies, won't we all need physical abilities? Maybe we should all be bulks."

Back in the day, Jacob had been a nanite junkie, taking anything and everything to further his karate career. Without the added strength, speed and his kick-ass teleportation ability, he is still strong and agile, but nothing like when I first met him.

Beside me, Matt tenses. He was even more anti-nanite than me. But that doesn't mean he is without abilities. Given intelligence in vitro, he's the smartest person at this table, but he'll never add anything else. He won't compromise his beliefs. And I'll never ask him to.

"I didn't take anything additional for our first mission," Matt says through a clenched jaw. "I don't plan on taking anything for this, either. I think my weapon and bomb making skills will do just fine."

Jacob waves a hand. "Sorry, didn't mean to judge…it's just, I never thought we'd be faced with this decision again."

"S'okay." Matt looks at him. "Me neither."

"Providing we go ahead, aren't we going to stand out a bit?" Paige asks.

Behind me, Dad finally speaks again. "No. Silver and I have been working together in the lab. We've figured out a way to give you back your powers and grant you the ability to turn them on and off at will."

An expectant silence winds through the group. Hal grabs another doughnut and Kyle taps out a rhythm on the table.

No one breathes. Wind howls outside the tomb-like room. Tiny sparks appear on the tips of my fingertips. I bury my hands in my lap so one notices and hope I don't accidently scorch my clothes or skin.

The first thing Francesca did when she was elected president was outlaw genetic modifications. Enhancements for the purpose of cosmetics or performance are strictly forbidden. No more bulk genes for football players, no more gills for swimmers, no more speed for runners, no more butterfly wings for cheerleaders, no telepathy, telekinesis, pyrokinesis or mind-control. The list is extensive and unyielding. Any failure to comply is met with the harshest of punishments by the highest court of Central City.

Some genetic modifications are allowed, on a case-by-case basis that fit into the criteria of disease and disability. But each of these exceptions are scrutinized for months to assess the validity of each claim. The case details are presented before the highest court where only a panel of the most supreme judges can grant in favor of the proposed genetic treatment. The rule of thumb is that if you are taking something away; a third eye, scales to be replaced by skin or a disability as a result of the reduction process to an unadjusted state, or if you are fixing something; diabetes, cancer, an organ problem for instance, then the genetic modification is often acceptable and approved. More often than not, they end up in my father's and my lab. But, if you want something added; intelligence, strength or beauty for instance, then it will be refused. Now Francesca is overturning her own laws, for us, so that we might have a fighting chance.

I look at my friends. At Erica and Paige and Hal. They all had abilities that made them stand out. "I appreciate this is harder for some of you."

"I don't claim to understand genetics." Erica leans over the table. "But won't the abilities disappear again as soon as we drink water? That's how the cure works, right?"

"Right, but no," Dad replies. "If Silver and I give you back your powers individually, not through a nanite pill, the markers in the cure won't see your DNA as foreign. Hence why Matt and Silver still have their abilities."

Matt can't turn his intelligence off, it's always there. With me, I can only use my abilities in short bursts, for an hour or so, shorter if I use two or more at the same time. I can produce wings or run as fast as a bullet, or teleport myself a few feet away, any time I wish. I haven't used my abilities so much of late. Occasionally I sprout the wings and take off into the sky, just to feel the wind rushing against my feathers. In a world with no more powers, I try to stay faithful to our new dogma. Now, my shoulder blades itch with the yearning to fly and my core tenses with the need to use an ability, to do something, to fight.

Kyle stands and stretches, like he's warming up for a race. "I'm still in. I want to run again."

Everyone laughs and my shoulders drop a couple inches. Maybe this will work.

"Will it hurt?" Paige asks, her brows knitted.

"Shit, I didn't think of that!" Kyle's eyes fly wide.

"Because when I first got my wings, it hurt like a son of a bitch," Paige says, her hazel eyes fixing on me.

"It hurt me too," I say. "Every ability I gained from each of you hurt every time. But we know it doesn't last. And not all abilities hurt. It's different for everyone. But it is something to consider."

I look at Paige, my best friend. Her indecision is mirrored in her pupils. She is scared. So am I.

"Silver's right," Dad says. "It won't be any worse than taking a nanite. I'll be manipulating each of your DNA individually, so the ability will be more part of you than you've ever experienced. It'll be like muscle memory. I'm pretty sure you won't have any pain at all."

"You don't have to decide right now," Francesca says. "Think carefully before you answer. I'm asking you to take back your abilities on a permanent basis. The effects will be...*finite*. But we do need a quick decision. We want to send a team out ASAP."

"I don't need to think about this." Hal stands, revealing his military uniform. "Of course I'm in."

He glances at me and our eyes lock. Hal will be a bulk again. Joe, his best friend, was a bulk. My chest lurches painfully as I remember his death, and the loss I still feel.

A crow squawks beyond the window, startling me, surprising us all. Matt drapes his arm across my shoulder.

"What's the urgency?" Sawyer asks. "Surely we should

take some time getting used to our abilities again before we charge into an offensive?"

Francesca's lips thin. "Earl has already launched an offensive. An evil, insidious attack that he can observe from the safety of his hideout."

Sawyer blanches. Paige pales under her permanent freckles.

Matt swivels in his chair to look at Francesca. "What kind of attack?"

"The outbreaks," Paige whispers.

Matt frowns and looks at me. Last week, Matt, Dad and I ate together in front of the TV, watching the news. There were reports about a few towns in California succumbing to a virulent flu. Something the world hasn't seen for a few decades, not since COVID swept around the globe. The death rate is high. Could Earl have released something into the world?

"We have vaccines for everything now," Matt says. "Don't we?"

Dad's face turns grim. "Not if you have a determined genetic scientist who wants to mix up a bit of plague, a dash of COVID and a smattering of Ebola in a petri dish. Add an enhanced infection rate, and well…it's nasty."

"The virus is moving. Fast." Francesca says. "It will be here by the end of the week. Maybe sooner. So far there is a ninety-nine percent fatality rate, and we have no idea how to fight it."

No one speaks. Panic swirls in my stomach. The old

panic I thought I'd put behind me months ago. Now it usually manifests in my dreams when I'm attacked by hellhounds and hellcats and can only see their glowing eyes and terrifying jaws before they tear me apart. But the undercurrent is always there. After all, my mother was in prison for two years and then held hostage by President Bear. Now we have reason to believe she's in the mountains with Earl. I won't relax until she's safe. But how will we ever leave the presidential compound with a virus so deadly?

After a few minutes, Erica raises a hand. "What happens if we don't find a cure for it? Or a vaccine?"

Claus steps forward from the back of the room, his cane tapping softly against the carpeted floor. "Then the world as we know it will end."

CHAPTER TWO

WHETHER WE GO to the mountains or not, death is coming. Although I'm terrified of facing another altered as powerful as Bear, I'd rather go down fighting than succumb to some monstrously altered virus. It might be a fast death, but it will be painful, and pointless. And there's something I haven't told anyone else yet, not even Matt.

When I killed Bear with the mysterious power that erupted from my hands, that dark, destructive lightning that reduced his heart to a pile of ash, it came as a huge surprise. I still haven't figured out what those sparks are or where I picked up the ability. Since Bear's death, my ability has been dormant, something I was grateful for, until recently. Narrowing in on my mom's location has thrown my emotions into turmoil, and now little eruptions of the black lightning seem to occur on a daily basis. Sometimes decimating a coffee mug, other times reducing a test tube or pencil to nothing but ash. Each time I clean up the mess and don't say a word. Not to Matt, not to my father, not to anyone. I'm already a big enough freak. If I tell someone, then it will be real, and I'll have to deal with it. Hopefully, it will just go away.

Francesca sits down in a chair at the head of the table. "The reason I called you all to the presidential compound is because since this morning, the virus has levelled every village, town, and city in California, and is on its way through Nevada and Oregon. We must remain in isolation until we can figure out what is going on. Deployed army units are returning to base. Your families are being brought here as we speak."

"Shit," Paige says.

My heart goes out to her. She never found her parents after the cure was delivered. But then she didn't look particularly hard. She says she is sacred of finding them dead, and equally afraid of finding them alive.

Erica turns to her. "It's a whole lot worse than any swear word. This is…this is…apocalyptic."

Paige drops her head into her hands while Sawyer sucks in a sharp breath.

Kyle giggles. "That's just in the movies."

"Not anymore," Hal says, fisting a hand on the tabletop. "But we can stop it."

"How can you be so sure?" Erica asks.

Hal locks his gaze on the ex-fairy. "Because that's what we do."

That's what we do.

He's right. But there's no precedent for this. The fluttering wings of apprehension settle in my stomach. Fear, it's a familiar feeling – the need to look over my shoulder; the low-grade anxiety that's always present, making me jump at a loud noise, making my heart beat a little faster; the dread, the eternal dread accompanied by a bad taste in the back of my mouth.

My fingers tingle. The skin between my thighs warms where I have my hands buried.

"How is it spreading?" Matt asks.

Francesca hesitates and pours another cup of coffee, stirring in two sugars. "All we know is the disease is spread through animal and insect bites and then through the usual coughing, sneezing and touching between humans. Some towns have been infected by mosquitoes, some by rabid dogs, others by maddened birds. Obviously, the animals have been genetically manipulated to attack, that's why the disease has become so widespread so quickly. But the animals die, seemingly after their tenth bite or sting or however it is they are programmed to attack. They dissolve, leaving not even a fragment of bone." Francesca throws her hands in the air. It's the first time I've seen her ruffled. I don't like it.

"Well, I'm not sitting around here waiting to be killed by some virus," Kyle says. "I think the choice is pretty simple. We stay here and die, or we go there and fight."

"I'm with you, buddy," Hal says, swatting the back of his head.

"I'm scared." Paige raises her gaze to meet mine. She gets nightmares too. Every day we talk about them in the reassuring light of morning in the hope that by telling each other, laughing and joking about them, the fear will lose its grip. "I want to help, but I'm scared."

I get up, walk around the table, and hug my friend. The black sparks dance over my fingers and I aim them at the floor, scorching a pea-sized hole in the rug. The smell of burning reaches me, but it's faint and no one else seems to notice. I disentangle myself from her more abruptly than I'd like, afraid I might cause more damage.

Jacob splays a hand on the table. "I'll go. I'll do whatever you need me to do. I'd rather not have any genetic modifications though." He looks Francesca squarely in the face.

"Noted," Francesca replies.

I pray he won't need them. Jacob still competes in the karate circuit and is in top physical condition. But it might not be enough. I'm already loaded with abilities, but terrified they won't be enough to secure a second success. Bear may have been powerful, but he was just a tyrannical president addicted to nanites. Earl is a genetic scientist with a limitless imagination for the cruel and unusual. There's no telling what he might have done to himself. What we'll have to face.

"I'll go too," Paige says, taking Jacob's hand.

"I'm not sticking around here by myself," Sawyer says, running a hand through his curls. He is never the first person to stick his hand up, but he has an internal courage I never question.

It isn't long before we're all on our feet. Everyone agrees to Francesca's plan, though it's undecided who will take back their abilities.

"Can we get a sample?" Dad asks. "If I can't figure out what the disease is then there's no point in us leaving the building. Earl will have won before we've even started."

"We're working on it," Francesca replies, attempting to smooth the creases on her wrinkled suit jacket. Her blouse is equally creased, and dark circles bruise the skin under her eyes. She must have been here all night. She pulls her suit jacket tighter and takes another sip of coffee. "And before I reunite you with your families, I think now is the time to introduce you to some soldiers who are eager to join your mission."

Matt's eyebrows lift in surprise. "Soldiers?"

Francesca nods. "I want our odds to be as favorable as possible. I want you to have as much help as you need."

The door opens and five soldiers in army uniform enter the room. Francesca stands to greet them. "These are the best covert soldiers we have. They'll be joining you on the mission. They've all agreed to take the genetic modification for bulk and any other enhancements that might be appropriate."

The bulk gene; the modification that was favored by

football players and the army, increasing a person's height to at least eight feet, sometimes nine, bulging muscles, and impenetrable, flame retardant skin, speed, strength and increased reflexes. It's a good choice.

The soldiers settle around the table. They look identical; all in the same green uniforms and heavy combat boots, the same shaved, cropped hair. But one of them is different; he is a few inches taller than the rest, wears a black Stetson and tucks into the remaining doughnuts on the table. Dimples flash with every bite. He slouches in the chair, seemingly unaware of anyone else in the room. Until Erica flutters into his focus.

Although Erica is now wingless, the cure didn't affect her lavender hair. It's eye catching. The new soldier notices. I hope he doesn't plan on trying anything. We don't have time for romance, and Erica doesn't need her heart broken again.

Introductions are made. The name of the soldier wearing the Stetson is Sean. Carter and William are twin brothers with bright red hair, who fought against President Bear until they were imprisoned in one of the unadjusted compounds. Although identical, Carter is more muscular and William's smile is more present. The fourth one, Mason, carries an authoritative edge in his eyes and jaw, as if he's used to being in charge. He was a bulk before, fighting on the wrong side, until he saw the light. The last solider, Luis, is shorter than the rest but makes up for it with muscle. He has a soft voice which adds to the lilt in his Hispanic accent.

Francesca sweeps a hand over her disheveled hair. "Without further ado, I think it's time to get you downstairs to the bunker where you can be with your families and settle in. We won't be leaving until we have a vaccine." She looks at Dad, whose face is pinched tight. "But we have the best genetic scientist working for us. It won't be long."

Dad is just a man. Not a god. Not a magician. Not an egotistical tyrant. Just a man. And viruses are complex.

〉〈〉〈〉〈

CLAUS, now head of Francesca's security, leads us out of the conference room. We trudge along the long hallway, down the emergency back staircase for what seems like miles, until we reach the bottom level. I've only been to this part of the building once before; when my father and I accepted jobs to be part of Francesca's genetic counselling team and she showed us around. I remember the statistics she spewed. There's enough room to house one hundred people and supplies to last a year. Completely underground, it has its own air and water supply. It's nuclear proof, although it has never been tested. At the time, I dismissed the details, still riding high from the success of the cure, not believing such a place would ever be needed again. I am utterly wrong. But we should be safe until a vaccine is made.

Inside, Jacob's mother and Matt's family, including Einstein, are waiting for us. That's it. No one else has family left to greet. Either lost in the war or to altered mentalities. Matt's parents and Megan, his youngest sister, rush to embrace him and then turn their affection on me. They express concern over my mother, promising to help locate her. There's little they can do, but I appreciate the sentiment. I suspect she's beyond their help, perhaps beyond my own.

Matt's middle sister, Lyla, leans against the wall by the door. Her eyes wander around the room, taking in every detail, assessing the mood and the people whispering in muted conversation. Something is going on in that pretty, blonde head and I don't think it's going to be anything Matt wants to hear about.

Exhausted, I sit at a table and wait for Dad so we can discuss the modifications ahead of us. The new soldiers have all agreed to be bulks, as well as Hal. Kyle wants his speed back. Surprisingly, Erica was one of the first to say she'll take back her wings, plus a few extras. The others are still deciding.

When Claus crouches beside me, I look up from my notes. "*Daijō desuka*?" Are you okay?

"Yep. I think so." I smile at my mentor. "Is Evan here yet?"

Claus nods to the corner where his partner is bantering with the soon-to-be bulks. Since we moved back to the city, it's Evan who has been training me in karate. He and Claus are equally matched. Well, they used to be, until Claus injured his leg. Now he stands on the sidelines, twiddling his moustache, giving nods of approval or orders in

Japanese.

"We're very close to getting her back." He touches my hand. "You've been waiting a long time."

Tears sting my eyes. "I hope she's okay. That Earl hasn't…" I close my eyes and refuse to finish the thought. Negativity never gets me anywhere.

"*Watashi wa anata no tame ni koko ni imasu,*" Claus says in Japanese.

I look at him blankly. "I have no idea what that means."

He wags a finger. "After all this time?"

"My Japanese is limited to karate instructions. And even then it's a bit hazy."

He smiles. "It means, 'I'm here for you.'"

I dip my head. "Thank you."

I haven't seen my mother for three years. Not since President Bear threw her in prison for refusing to make more nanite pills. Nanites that turned humans into altereds. Altereds who oppressed unadjusteds without compunction. The country became divided. I always stood firmly on the side of the unadjusteds, until I discovered my own abilities, then I existed in the murky gray. But my mother was still in prison and her mental health was fragile before the sentence. I killed Bear, but was unable to rescue my mother before Earl took her away. Now, finally, I know where she is. I can get her back. We can be a family again.

Claus stands, touches my cheek, then moves away to join Evan.

I go back to my notes, but can't focus. I can't stop

thinking about what will happen next. Earl has dozens of powerful altereds at his disposal. There will be a fight. I'm not sure I have it in me to fight again. Last year I got over most of my insecurities about my abilities, but now, if the genetic changes don't work, it will be up to me. I'm the only one who still has powers. All of them. I haven't used them in months and I don't know if I can anymore. Apart from the black lightning sparks. That comes without me asking for it. If I continue to destroy small objects at the merest of anxious thoughts, how will I control it around the people I love? Earlier, I almost singed Paige's hair off. What if next time I can't redirect it to an inanimate object? What if I hurt someone?

Part of me wants to hide in this bunker forever. The other part of me will do anything to get my mother back.

When Matt threads his arms around my waist, I wobble for a moment, wanting to give in to the security he offers. With his arms around me, I am home. It is safe.

"I love you," he says.

I want to tell him the same. But how can I? When I'm keeping such a secret from him? How can I look him in the eyes and tell him I love him and expect him to love me back? There is something dark and dangerous inside me. Something he'll never understand. Instead, I kiss him, and lean into the warmth he offers.

"What about the outbreak?" I voice the fear that's hovering in the back of my mind. "What if she catches the disease?"

Matt rubs my shoulders. "Earl won't let it hurt her. His obsession with her works in our favor." My parents and Earl studied at university together. She dated Earl first, but my father won in the end. Earl has never forgotten it.

I put on a brave smile. "She'll be okay." I say it a few more times in my head.

He takes my hand and kisses my knuckles. "I think you could do with a break."

"I haven't even started."

"Silver, you may have a list of abilities as long as my arm, and Jeez, some of them terrify me, but you're not superwoman. Take a moment."

He is right. He is always right. It's one of the reasons I love him so much. He sees things so clearly. He can cut through the emotion of a situation and always come to the right decision. It used to infuriate me. Now I rely on his ability to filter out the unnecessary.

Walking to the TV in the corner of the room, Matt turns it on. We gather on the couches and chairs and watch the reports of the spreading outbreak. Town by town is destroyed. So quick. As if the virus is an enemy fleet of alien spaceships with indestructible weapons, sweeping across the country.

Matt flicks through the channels. They all tell the same story. The destruction. The death. The symptoms. The virus begins simply enough; a cough, a sneeze, a sore throat. But the progression is swift and merciless. Within minutes muscles are weakened, the afflicted unable to walk. Violent vomiting and coughing fits overwhelm the body until resistance is futile. Veins turn a dark red, eyes bulge, boils and pustules form on the skin, covering eyes and mouth and nose. The organs turn to a liquid mush, releasing an acid that destroys the rest of the host body. Not even a skeleton remains, just a puddle of liquid goo to be washed away by the next rainfall, and maybe a few teeth. Earl has been thoughtful on that account. He found a way to rid the country of decaying corpses. The ordeal lasts about twelve hours from start to finish. It's the quickest viral death in history.

After a few hours, when the reports start to falter and the news reporters run for cover, we turn the TV off again. It reminds me of all those months ago when the altereds went crazy in the streets without the grounding presence of the unadjusteds. Those who had taken too many nanites with animal properties lost their ability to reason when the unadjusteds fled. We are connected, them and us, and everything in between. In a precarious balance. I wonder how Earl is maintaining an equilibrium in the mountains. During the resistance President Bear rounded up unadjusteds and kept them in compounds, purely to keep the altereds sane.

We monitor the situation through the army channels. Rumors emerge of pockets of survivors.

"If there are survivors, then there's immunity," Dad says. He's been so quiet. Since the cure, he barely speaks and some of the mischief has drained from his pupils. But I always know when he's in the room. Although our roles were reversed during the resistance and I was the one to rescue him, I still rely on him for guidance. He is my father. *My father*.

Without him, I would never have learned all the genetics over the last few months. After the reduction process during the cure, some of the previous altereds experienced side effects. My father and I work on those cases, helping to diminish the side effects through genetic manipulation. But he hasn't taught me anything about viruses. This is new territory.

"We can't get a sample if the host animals keep dissolving," Francesca mutters.

Dad's face tightens. "We can't make a vaccine without one."

Kyle frowns. "We can't stay here forever." His feet shuffle around, as if in preparation for taking back his speed ability.

"Give it some time." Lyla's blonde hair is swept up in a high ponytail and swings with confidence. The confidence of someone who has no idea what it's like to face down a man as ruthless as Bear. But I have to give her credit, she survived an unadjusted compound. "Silver and Rufus will sort it. Just give it time."

Kyle sighs. "We've only been in here a few hours and I already miss the sun."

"Dismal, much," Sean, the Stetson-wearing solider drawls. "I've still got a sunburn, kid. And we're not just going to live in the sun, we're going to *dance*." He grins as he twirls Erica into a reluctant pirouette.

"*Arriba! Arriba!*" Luis smiles, clapping his hands as Sean breaks into a decent imitation of *La Bamba.*

Matt chuckles. I rest my head back on the couch and try to forget about all the obstacles ahead of us. At least we can work on the genetic modifications while we're waiting for a virus sample.

Francesca leads us to the living quarters. Civilians, army and mission team are lumbered together. Steel framed bunk-beds line one wall. There is a common room with a TV, left blank, a pool table and board games. A kitchen is stocked with fresh and canned food. Separate male and female bathrooms containing toilet and shower stalls. Tomorrow Dad and I will begin work on the modifications. One by one, we will give my friends back their abilities, perhaps with a few added enhancements to even up the odds.

Matt's parents take up station in the kitchen and cook up a meal of spaghetti and salad for the group. Attempting to maintain an air of normalcy, they even manage cup cakes and cookies for dessert. Not that anyone feels like eating them. But then again, I reason as I take two cupcakes that Megan iced, this could be the last time for a long time that we have access to such treats. Appetite be damned. Shame there isn't any ice cream in the freezer.

Sean, the Stetson-wearing cowboy, locates a crate of beer and cracks it open, then instigates a competition on the pool table. Leaning against a wall to watch and licking the icing from my fingers, I wish for my guitar that's back at my house propped against the leather couch in the living room.

Hal stacks the balls with little clickety-clack sounds. He grabs a cue and breaks into the balls with violence. A belly-laugh erupts from Sean's mouth as he snakes an arm around Erica's wrist and twists her to face him. She frowns, splutters, gives him two furious eyebrows and prods his chest with a jabbing finger. Unperturbed, Sean laughs again. I can tell Erica is wishing for her wings; she performs the little leap she always used to do before taking to the air. Sometimes she forgets the wings are gone. They'll be back soon enough. She manages to free herself from the cowboy's advances and flees across the room. Sean chuckles, watching her retreat with amused eyes, and takes another swig of beer.

Hal offers me the cue for the second game. Smiling, I walk to the pool table and break. The balls split with a satisfying *crack*. I manage to scrape the felt with the cue. Horrified, I pull out my healing power, hoping it will work on an inanimate object, but the black sparks erupt over my fingers and widen the rip.

"What the hell is that?" Lyla says in my ear.

I shove my hand behind my back. The pool table bears a noticeable, scorched rip in the green felt. "I haven't played much. I ripped the felt."

Sean rolls his eyes at me and the other soldiers laugh.

Hal takes the cue away from me before I can cause more damage.

I walk away from the pool table, with Lyla hovering at my side. "Not the scratch. Those little black things on your fingers? What was that?" She searches my face and heat rises to my cheeks.

"I don't know what you're talking about."

"Don't lie to me, Silver."

I scan the room. Everyone else is busy and I pull Lyla into a quiet corner. "I don't know what it is."

She inhales sharply. "A new power."

I shake my head. "It can't be. But I have no idea what it is or where it came from. I think it's what I used to kill Bear."

Her eyes widen. "Does Matt know?"

My silence speaks for itself.

"You have to tell him."

"No, I don't," I hiss. "It's under control."

She smirks. "You call tearing a pool table with black electricity under control?"

"Lyla," I say, my irritation spiking. "Just give me a freaking minute, okay? You can't tell anyone."

She places her hands on her hips. Her blonde ponytail swings as she narrows her eyes. "That depends."

I resist the urge to growl at her. "On what?"

She glances over her shoulder. "I want to go with you. I want you to give me an ability too."

I glare at her. "What the...? No. *No*. Lyla, I can't. You

have no idea what you're getting into. It's far too dangerous, you're far too young."

Lyla scoffs. "I'm almost fifteen. Not far off your age when the resistance started. I had to sit on the sidelines then and watch you and Matt leave the cave, never sure if you were going to come back. I can't do that again. I can't sit around and wait. I have to be there. I was tormented every day at school for being different, for being an unadjusted. I have to *do* something. I have to fight back for myself." Lyla's hands form fists at her sides, her voice an angry whisper.

"Lyla…"

She crosses her arms. "Or I'll tell."

I look her fully in the face and try to avoid those mesmerizing blue eyes that run in her family. Determination rests there. She is strong. Physically. She dances for hours every day. I sigh, and against my better judgement say, "I'll talk to Matt."

She grins. "I knew I could count on you."

I touch her shoulder. "Lyla. It's dangerous. This isn't some joyride. You need to think about this carefully."

She tosses her hair. "Says the girl keeping secrets from my brother."

CHAPTER THREE

MY FATHER and I sit in the lab going over our notes, triple checking everything is in order. The mild scent of disinfectant fills my nose, mingling with the vanilla candle I just lit on my workbench.

"I can't believe we're giving people abilities," I say.

Dad looks at me and waits for me to continue.

"I mean, it was only a few months ago that we were in a battle to stop this very thing." So much has changed in such a short time. Like my black lightning power. But so much has remained the same too. Like Matt and me.

"How do you feel about modifications now?" Dad asks.

My gaze falls to my hands. Inside me, there are a plethora of abilities, some of them I haven't yet discovered. I have the unique ability of gaining a person's power if they touch me. President Bear touched me, and I have no idea how many nanites he took. I'm still discovering some surprising abilities. "I think they have their place."

Paige grew wings so she could fly away from her problems. Matt gained intelligence as a side effect to a brain operation. Joe and Hal were football players, Sawyer just trying to cope living on the streets. These people are my friends, and most of them took nanites with good intentions. So, I get the positives. I get how they can help. But I never want to be in a situation again when the president of the country insists everyone have an ability.

"I live in the gray now. Everything is gray. Life, death, modifications, power, friendship, love—"

"The mountains in the Sierras," Dad says, an amused smile playing on his lips. "It's not all gray, Silver. There's color too."

I nod. "There is. There are rainbows. But with regards to genetics, we're in a situation where we might be fighting for our lives again. So, we need every advantage possible."

"No more weak spots," Dad says.

I blink against a memory. Joe died because of the weak spot at his throat. Bulks have largely impenetrable skin, apart from the four weak spots. One of them is at the base of the throat. That's where the hellhound managed to bite into Joe's neck.

"Maybe you can make us all immortal while you're at it," I say. The thin layer of fear that found me in the conference room, again invades my spine. My fingertips tingle, with what I now associate as a precursor to the black lightning coming. I put my hands in my lap just as a tiny bolt streaks out, scorching the edge of my shoe.

As if sensing my worried thoughts, Dad places a gentle hand over mine. "This is going to work." A light dances in his eyes. One I haven't seen for a while. He's actually excited by the challenge. After all, genetic modification is what he built his entire career on, before it all went to hell.

The lab door swings open and Hal enters the room. The rest of the soldiers file in behind. They laugh and jostle each other. Sean twirls his Stetson round a finger.

"Are you ready?" Dad asks.

Hal gives a curt nod and tenses his jaw. "As I'll ever be."

Mason's cautious eyes dart around the room and Luis jiggles a leg nervously. The twins, Carter and William, stand in identical poses, leaning toward each other, as if leaching confidence from the other.

"Hot diggity dawg," Sean drawls, cracking a grin. "Ready to be superpowered."

I'm tempted to poke some seriousness into Sean. But then I suspect humor is his defense mechanism. I look at them all. "Are you sure?"

Hal nods. Mason's Adam's apple bobs as he swallows hard. The twins both say 'yes.'

"Don't need to go putting no downer on it," Sean says. He's still smiling, but the spark is gone from his eyes.

Luis doubles over and pukes into a trash can. He stands, wipes his mouth, and puts some steel into his gaze. "Despite the hurling, I'm ready."

The others laugh. Hal slaps his back and Carter lands a noogie on Luis' dark head. He blushes as the others tease him and explains it's his stress reaction. He always pukes when he's nervous. Smiling, I make a mental note not to sit with him on the long ride west.

Dad lines them up on stools. I pick up the first needle with contents made especially for Hal and inject him. Then I prick the others, each with their own individual cocktail of genetics.

Hal opens and closes his fist a few times, as if trying to pump the new DNA around his bloodstream faster. William manages a smile, and hugs his brother, while Mason's serious expression doesn't change.

Luis pukes again. He's never had a modification before. "What's going to happen now?"

Dad spends the next half hour going through the side effects again and showing them how to turn their abilities off and on at will. When the modifications take effect, Hal demonstrates changing from bulk to human several times. Seeing him as a bulk again brings back a plethora of memories and emotions. They shudder through me and my fingertips tingle. I wish I had a puke reflex like Luis, even if it is embarrassing, rather than the black lightning.

Luis gives it a go, grows two feet and pukes a third time.

The others laugh, but help him and show him how to get accustomed to his new mass.

After they all adjust to their new modifications, they prepare to leave.

Sean looks over his shoulder when he reaches the door, flexing a bulk bicep. "It feels different to what I thought."

"How so?" I ask.

He clicks his tongue and fiddles with this hat. "I know I'm physically stronger, but I just don't feel it inside."

I know the feeling, but don't speak of my doubts. "You will."

He tips his hat at me and leaves.

For the duration of the afternoon and the next two days, we give the mission team back their abilities. Most of them, anyway.

Erica regains her wings, and adds a shrinking ability, bow and arrow included. Dad secured Erica a top of the line bow and quiver set that is fabricated from a material that binds with her skin and can take on whatever ability Erica uses. It's how the invisibility pill also affects our clothes. Kyle gets his speed, and the grin on his face as he leaves the lab makes everything worth it, almost. Sawyer, more nervous than I thought he'd be, reclaims his telekinesis, and adds a dash of pyrokinesis too. Now he can set things on fire just by thinking about it. It's not an ability I possess and add it to my lengthening wish list. The pain comes as a crushing headache, and while I'm bearing it, the black lightning flashes over my fingertips. I concentrate on breathing, but one of the bolts escapes. It steaks across the lab and breaks a glass beaker in two.

"What was that?" Sawyer asks.

"Nothing," I reply, too quickly.

He spends a few extended seconds staring at me, then lets it go.

Jacob doesn't come near the lab, insistent on going without any modifications. Which leaves Paige as the last to regain her wings.

When Paige enters the lab, she is ashen faced, and lingers at the threshold.

I pat the seat next to me. "What's the matter?"

"It feels weird, taking back abilities." A fragile smile wobbles on her lips. "I thought I was done with all that."

I touch her shoulder, where her wing used to be. "You don't have to, if you don't want to."

Her hazel eyes lock on mine. "Yes, I do. I can't sit around here worrying about all of you."

Out of all the abilities I possess, the wings I gained from Paige are still my favorite. It's the one ability I still use sometimes. After a long day in the lab, there's nothing better than sprouting my wings and taking to the sky. Flying above it all. From up high, the world looks so perfect, so untouched, and I can pretend the scars the resistance left behind aren't there.

"When you get your wings back, let's fly together," I say. "I miss flying with you."

Her smile turns genuine. "I do miss it. Half of me has

been afraid of how much, wondering if I needed some kind of support group."

I chuckle. "They were part of you for a long time. Of course you miss them. And, Paige, this time you can turn them on and off, like I do."

She nods. "Let's get this over with." Paige presses the heel of her hand to her eye and lets out a shaky breath. "Are they still going to be green?"

"Yes." Without wanting to drag out the moment, I inject her arm with her personal cocktail. "Is there any news on your parents?"

Paige shakes her head. "I assume they died when they were exposed to the cure. I mean, I think that's better than them being alive and not even bothering to look for me. Maybe." She swipes at the skin under her eye. "I think. I don't know. It's not like I want them to be dead, or anything."

"I know." I kiss her cheek. "There's always the possibility that they're in the mountains with Earl."

Her eyes widen. "I hadn't thought of that. I don't know…if I want them to be there…"

"You don't need them," I say. "You have us."

The members of the mission team were given accommodation within the new presidential complex. Not everyone works for Francesca's new administration. Kyle chose to finish school and Erica went to college. But we all live in a row of houses near each other. Matt and his family next door to my father and me. Paige, Jacob and his mother on my other side. We are a family. All of us. Even though we don't get together in one big group often, we all know we can rely on each other. ·

"We have each other," she says, circling her shoulders. "I can feel it coming back."

Her eyes change color, to the startling emerald green they were when I first met her. I smile. "It's working."

Lyla storms into the lab. "You said I could have an ability!" She marches up to me, lands a pose, and crosses her arms.

Paige shoots me a look.

I hold up my hands. "Whoa! Calm down, Lyla. I said I'd talk to Matt."

She glances at Paige, then at me. "I'll tell."

"Tell what?" Paige asks.

I take a breath and stand to face Lyla, cursing the fact that she's taller than me. "Lyla, if that's the kind of attitude you want to go on a dangerous mission with, I'm not sure you *should* have an ability."

Now I feel like a parent. I hate it. But I can't afford for people to bring all their baggage with them, their shitty attitudes and emotional scars. I've got enough of my own to deal with.

Her frown becomes Grand Canyon proportions. "Then I'll tell my brother."

"Tell me what?" Matt asks, as he comes though the doorway.

. . .

An expectant silence falls on our small group. Paige's gaze darts between me and Lyla, who stands with her hands on her hips. Matt's smile slips as the tension in the room builds. The white of the lab becomes too bright and I feel the sparks on my fingertips, which are hidden in my lap.

Lyla points a finger at me. "Why don't you ask Silver."

Inside, anger surges, dwarfing the nerves. I've always had a soft spot for Lyla, admiring her determination and grit, but right now she is pissing me off.

Intending to splay my palms and protest my innocence, I release my hands from between my legs, forgetting about the black lightning. It erupts from my hands, little streaks zooming in all directions. Paige yelps. Matt ducks and Lyla stifles a shriek.

Glass shatters, all the beakers and test tubes lining the back worksurface. Dad's computer monitor implodes, and a few of the syringes in front of me turn to ash.

"What the hell is going on?" Matt asks, huddling with Paige and Lyla under the workbench.

It's my lightning. I stand and watch, knowing it won't hurt me. I'm half mesmerized and half terrified of what I've done. But if I can reduce Bear's heart to a pile of black ash, then of course I can decimate a few glass items in a lab.

When the glass settles and stops tinkling, I look at my friends. "It's me," I say in a small voice.

Matt and Paige crawl out of the space under the work surface. Lyla remains, tears streaming down her face.

"What's the matter?" I ask her, a thread of impatience still lining my tone.

She looks up at me with her big blue eyes and removes her hands from where they cradle her shin. Along the length of it, stretching about three or four inches, is a hideous burn.

"Lyla!" Matt crouches to inspect her leg, then chucks a glance over his shoulder at me. "Silver? What's going on?"

Paige backs away, using her hands to advance along the work surface like she's afraid of me. "What did you do?"

Tears well. "I didn't do anything. I didn't mean to."

"I'll get help." With a flutter of green feathers, Paige runs from the room.

Swiping at undeserving tears, I crouch to look at Lyla. "I'm sorry. I'm so sorry. I don't know what's going on with me."

Matt turns to me, his blue eyes half sympathetic and half doubtful. I've never seen doubt in his expression before. "You did this?"

I nod and bring my shaking hands into the open. "With the power I used to kill Bear. I don't know what it is or how to control it." I look at him, imploring him to understand. Lyla cries softly.

Matt reaches for my hand, firmly wrapping his fingers over mine. It's a small gesture, but one for which I'm eternally grateful.

"Lyla." I raise my hands to show her the absence of the black lightning. "I'm going to heal you."

Far too trusting, she nods. What if the lightning comes out again? Just because I'm irritated with her? Why do my abilities have to be so tied to my emotions? Sometimes, I long to be numb, to feel nothing, so I can't hurt anyone and never feel fear again. But then who would I become?

I place my hands around the edges of her burn. It smells, bad, of burned flesh and unnaturalness. I breathe deeply, calling on the healing power, willing the warm glow to replace the darkness so recently used.

"You can do it," Matt whispers in my ear, then kisses it.

But I can't. I sit there for over twenty minutes, pleading with myself, with my abilities, with the one power of goodness I possess, to come and heal Lyla. Nothing happens. My emotions churn and disappointment swells within me. I'm in danger of invoking the wrong power, so I remove my hands.

"I'm so sorry, Lyla, I don't know why it's not working." My hands tremble.

Matt rises and pulls her to her feet. He lifts her into his arms as if she weighs no more than one of her treasured ballet slippers.

"I'll take her to medical." He kisses my cheek.

Tears stream down my face. "Matt, I'm so sorry. I don't know what happened."

"It's okay." His blue eyes hold such warmth that I'm afraid to trust it. "It's okay. It was just an accident."

"But what if I...?" I trail off, not wanting to voice the

thought aloud. I killed president Bear. I'm more than capable of killing many more people.

"Don't go there," he says, as if reading my thoughts. He is always so in tune with my fears. "And let's keep this to ourselves for a while."

He leaves and I am left alone in the lab, miserable. How can I have done this to someone I love so dearly? Will she ever forgive me? Can I forgive myself? How can I go on a mission to fight Earl if I can't save my friends, if I unintentionally hurt them instead?

My thoughts are derailed when my father and a few soldiers burst through the door. It slams open and bounces off the wall. Francesca bustles through after them. One of the soldiers carries an inert shape bundled in his arms. It's wrapped in several layers of plastic.

Dad looks at me, triumph flashing across his face. "We got a sample. A dog."

My heart lifts.

Despite the several layers the dog is wrapped in, a reeking stench disperses into the room.

"One of Earl's creations," the soldier says. "The disease has spread to Kentucky, we found it in a ditch there." He dumps the dog on a workbench behind me.

"Everyone out," Dad says. "I don't want to put anyone at risk while I work on the vaccine."

The room empties until it's just Dad and me. Through the plastic sheeting, I look at the dog. Its flat black eyes stare at nothing. Its open jaw reveals sharply pointed teeth.

Dampness matts the skin around its jowls and jaw. It twitches. I jump.

Bracing myself behind my desk, I wait for the dog to move again. Behind me, Dad's shallow breath tickles my ear. Five minutes tick off on the digital clock on my desk.

"Just a death throw," Dad says.

"Sweet Jesus that was scary."

Dad turns to look at me. "You okay?" His gaze floats to his broken monitor and the broken beakers. It reminds me of the time we purposefully trashed his lab, so no one could recreate what he'd started. "What happened in here?"

No way I'm telling him what just happened. My guilt is unbearable as it is. I wave a hand. "Just a little bit of experimentation going awry." I try a smile on but it doesn't take.

Dad hugs me and I almost cry again.

He holds me at arm's length. "You look tired. I can handle this on my own if you want to get some rest."

"Are you sure?" There's nothing I want more than to crawl into a bed and forget the events of the last hour. But I don't want to leave Dad alone to deal with this. Or maybe I should. If the black lightning comes back, I could hurt him, I could...

"I'm sure." He ushers me to the door and tells me to eat something.

I take the elevator to the living quarters. At this late hour, most people are asleep, but some of the bulks play pool in the common area. Keeping to the shadows, I sneak along to my bunk, noting with a guilty heart that Lyla and Matt's beds are empty.

I crawl into my own bed, pulling the covers up high, hoping I can shroud myself in an emotion besides guilt. I tell myself Lyla's leg will heal, she will be okay. She might have a scar but it's nothing her ballet tights won't cover up. And if my healing ability comes back, I can finish the job.

Focusing on the larger threat, I pour my energy into trying to predict Earl's booby traps. I know he'll have something besides the virus, he is a careful man. And he has my mom. My thoughts whizz all over the place, too scattered to settle on one area for long.

I don't know what I expected after the resistance. I was mildly surprised we won. Now, my mother is on my mind constantly. While Dad and I work every day, we talk of her, wondering where she is, *how* she is. Her absence hangs like a dark shadow over our efforts to try and maintain a positive outlook. Now it's my chance to get her back. But with the black lightning emerging again, the odds of success seem greatly reduced. As I lie there, a thread of unease winds through my limbs. The old panic lingers at the periphery of my senses. I haven't had a panic attack in months, but I have a feeling they'll be back soon.

Needing reassurance, I release my knife from my belt. I haven't used it since the caves, but can't seem to stop carrying it around with me. I grip the handle, then rotate it around my fingers, feeling its weight. When I lived in the caves, its presence was the only thing that calmed me. With it, I can face anything. Anything Earl can dream up. I'm ready.

In the middle of the night, Matt and Lyla enter the sleeping quarters with their parents. Her shin is wrapped in a thick bandage. Matt carries her to her bunk. She's out cold. While her parents tuck her in, he creeps to my side and sits on my bed.

"You okay?" He asks.

I shrug one shoulder. "More importantly, is Lyla okay?"

"Lyla is fine. The burn wasn't too deep. The doc treated her and gave her a sleeping pill." Matt touches my arm, rubs it gently. Tears well in my eyes again. "I'm more worried about you. What was that, Silver?" Even in the dark his bright blue eyes shine. They usually comfort me. But right now I find them scrutinizing.

"I'm not sure if I have the energy to go into it right now," I say.

Understanding, his chin bobs, and he lies down beside me. We both look at the slats of the bunk on top of us. He raises an arm to touch them, his fingers playing over the wood. "I love you, Silver. You know that, right?"

I swallow against the emotion in my throat. "I do. I love you too."

"Together, we can face anything. Together." His hair tickles my cheek. I long to stroke it, but I'm worried what my fingers might do.

"In the past, when I've taken on a new ability, it hasn't taken me long to understand how it works." I pause, thinking of how the team have adapted so well to taking their abilities back. "I mean, even with Sawyer's new pyrokinesis, I absorbed that. I can throw fireballs with my mind. It's easy. But this black lightning thing…it's something else. I used it to kill Bear. That was months ago, and I still don't have a clue how it works. It's as unreliable as my healing power."

"Maybe they're connected," Matt says.

I scoff. "How can they be? One is filled with everything good. The light of the world, the ability to heal, to bring peace. The other is nothing but darkness and destruction."

Matt lowers his hand and laces his fingers through mine. "Yin and yang. Everything in balance."

I ponder his words. It kind of makes sense. But if the healing power represents all that is good in me, what does the lightning signify? Feeling a tingling in my fingertips, I let got of his hand. "I don't want to hurt anyone again."

"You won't."

Rolling on my side to face him, I stare at his beautiful face. "You don't know that. You don't know what it feels like inside me. How it wants to destroy. You have too much faith in me."

Matt takes my tingling hand and lifts it to his lips, kisses my fingers. The tingling sensation fades. "You're stronger than you think."

There are so many things I want to say to him, that I want him to understand. I'm not strong. Not at all. Not emotionally. But my powers are stronger than I'd like, stronger than I can deal with. I don't know how to make him see how dangerous I can be.

He falls asleep beside me, his arm dangling over my stomach. I manage to catch a few hours too, despite my cycling thoughts. Early in the morning, I get up and wander over to Lyla's bed. She's still out cold. I place my hand on her shin, but the healing glow still won't come.

Her eyes open, and they take a moment to focus on me.

"Does it hurt?" I ask.

Ignoring the question, she sits up and winces. "You owe me an ability."

I sigh as the rebuttals go through my head. But I know she'll end up stowing away if we don't let her come with us. And if she's going to come with us, she needs to be protected.

"Come on," I say. We grab Matt on our way out of the living quarters and head to a smaller lab near where my father is working on the vaccine. Inside, the three of us sit around a work bench discussing ideas. Lyla has already convinced him and her parents that an ability is the right way to go. That she might have been able to protect herself from my burn if she'd been 'powered up.'

I pour coffee into three mugs and hand them out.

Matt tilts his head and rotates his mug in his hands. "She was about to turn professional before the resistance, in her dancing, despite never having taken a modification. These last few months she started training again, but I think that future will be different for her now. She has many natural abilities that I think, if enhanced, could be an asset to the team. I don't know what her future will be now, but she needs a purpose."

Lyla arches a blonde eyebrow. "I'm right here, you know."

"Sorry squirt," Matt laughs. "Right you are."

Thinking, I purse my lips, trying to picture Lyla on a mission, what she will do and how she'll be. I run my quaver pendant up and down its chain, the one Matt gave me for my sixteenth birthday. "Lyla, are you sure? There's no room for doubt on a mission like this. You can't distract Matt, or me, or the rest of the team."

Her other eyebrow pops up. "I'm sure." She slaps down a printed document on the work bench. "You'll see the signatures of President Montoya and both my parents. They've all agreed I can have an ability and I can go on the mission."

She works fast. I wonder how long she's been campaigning for this.

A headache pulses at my temples and I massage the area with my fingers. "I can't wait for the day when I never have to speak the words *genetic modification* again."

"Right?" Matt says. "But first we need to finish the war."

"I know."

He taps my pendant. "We're in it together."

"I know," I say again. I turn to Lyla. "This isn't a game, Lyla." I point to the document with the fancy signatures.

"This is a matter of life and death. There will be...casualties...on our side too."

She looks at her bandaged leg and heat rises to my cheeks. "I just want my chance at vengeance too."

Her slight stature belies the fierceness inside. Perhaps I'm not giving her enough credit. She's always been Matt's younger sister. The one who dances and doesn't take life too seriously. I see now that she's changed. We all have.

Before we can decide on an ability, Paige and Claus enter the room. Paige's green wings are extended and she wears a tentative smile on her lips. "Thought I better get some practice in."

With his arm tucked in Paige's, Claus taps his way to my workstation. I look between the two of them and a blush rises to Paige's cheeks.

I swallow. "What did she tell you?" I ask Claus.

Paige holds up a hand. "Please don't be mad. I was worried about you." Her emerald eyes plead with me to understand.

I remind myself that she's my best friend and we've never had an argument before.

Claus pats Paige's arm and then moves away from her. He looks down at me on my stool, his thumb rubbing the handle of his cane. "Paige tells me you're having a little trouble with your abilities?"

I nod. There's no point denying it. I can never lie to Claus.

"She burned my leg off," Lyla says, pointing at her

bandage. "But I'll be okay," she adds, when Matt shoots her a stern look.

Paige's wings rise and circle us, as if she's protecting our small group. Claus sits next to me and leans on his cane. "It's to be expected."

"It is?" I ask.

He twiddles his moustache. "Your powers have always been connected to your emotions. And now you are concerned about your mother, are facing a deadly virus, and will have to travel to the mountains to defeat someone who might be more powerful than President Bear."

My stomach clenches. Paige's lips wobble.

"But you can do this," Claus says. "It is all in your training. You just need to find yourself."

I understand what he's saying. Half of our karate training isn't physical. It's mental. We spend many hours in meditation together, a skill I'm a long way from mastering, but Claus would never lie to me. If he thinks I can handle this new dark power, then I will.

"My thoughts exactly," Matt says. "But I do want to add, some of the others may not be as understanding. I think we should keep this between us for now." Matt never keeps secrets. He likes everything out in the open, which makes me think he's putting on a brave face, just for me. "Are we all agreed?"

"Do we have to do like a pinky swear, or something?" Lyla smirks.

"Agreed," Paige says, putting her fist in the middle of

the group. Matt places his on top of hers. Then Claus, then Lyla, and lastly, my own. Even though the action won't save us from the virus or a fight with Earl, I find it strangely reassuring.

While Dad works on the vaccine, I don't see him. He sleeps in the lab and calls late at night, sometimes in the middle of the night, to update me on his progress. He's developing something, adding an increased multiplication rate to the antibody production. If it works, we could be leaving in a matter of days.

Matt, Lyla and I spend the next couple of days settling on an ability and changing her DNA. She opts for gills. We'll be crossing a lake near the mountains and the gills could come in handy if we send her ahead as a scout. When Matt takes her to test her new abilities in the swimming pool, I stay in the smaller lab and try to get a handle on the black lightning.

I sit on my stool, staring at my hands, willing the little bolts to appear. Nothing. I focus on the healing power instead, thinking I might use it to heal emotional trauma, but I won't have enough power for that. The warm glow won't appear either. I evoke my bird wings, butterfly wings, move objects with my mind, light a fireball in my palm and turn into a bulk. All my other abilities work perfectly. Disheartened, I drop my head into a hand. Only then do my fingers tingle. This time, I take out a stack of paperwork and have to use the fire extinguisher on the burning embers.

I tug on a thin pair of fleece gloves. I'll have to wear

them at all times. Thankfully, it's winter, cold underground. I shouldn't get too many suspicious questions.

The radio in the room squawks as I finish wiping up the frothy remains of the fire extinguisher.

"I've got it," Dad says. "I've got a vaccine."

CHAPTER FOUR

DAD MADE A VACCINE. Now I can get my mom. I push my doubts away and allow the trickle of excitement to flow through me.

"I'm going to test it tonight, expose myself to the virus. Then I'll be sure," Dad's voice crackles down the radio waves.

"No, Dad," I say. "If it doesn't work, no, just no. Let me do it."

"You're too valuable, Silver."

"So are you."

There is a pause as we both listen to each other breathing. Or maybe I'm holding my breath. Thanks to one of my abilities sometimes I forget to breathe.

"Trust me, Silver. Have I ever let you down?"

"Never," I say. And that's that.

Dad exposes himself to the virus and I go back to the

living quarters, cradling a walkie-talkie in one hand and my knife in the other.

Hal leaves the others at the pool table and approaches me.

"Is there any news about the outbreak? My mother?" I ask, knowing Hal is always the first to have news. He is one of Francesca's most trusted soldiers.

"Nothing. On either count." Hal places a hand on the arm of the couch I'm sitting on.

"I can't stop thinking about her." I drop the walkie-talkie and fiddle with the quaver pendant hanging at my collarbone.

"It's because we're so close." He scoots close, folding his leg into the couch to face me, and props an elbow on the back of the couch. "Knowing where she is. Knowing she's in reach, it would make anyone anxious."

Fearful the lightning will come back, I push thoughts of my mother away and bury my hands in my pockets with the acorns. They're harder to feel through the gloves. "How are you holding up?"

He opens his mouth, about to speak, then stops. He looks at me, as if weighing up some decision. "I'm scared shitless."

"That's good," I say.

Hal snorts. "Good?"

"It will make you cautious."

"We've lost so many already," Hal says, under his breath. His shoulders drop and he rests his chin in a cupped hand. Joe. He is thinking of Joe. He should be here, with Hal, with the soldiers, taking back his enhancements. And being my friend.

A stab of sadness squeezes my chest. "Do you miss him?"

Hal's face tightens as he runs a hand over the back of his neck. "There isn't a day that goes by that I don't think about him, wonder what he would be doing now if he was still alive."

"Me too." I touch Hal's hand. "He'd be with you. He would have joined Francesca's army."

"I like to think so." He interlaces his fingers in mine and closes his eyes for a moment. "We'll start again, Silver."

"Again, again," I say. "We've done it once already."

"Again, again," Hal echoes. "We'll do it again."

We sit together for a few minutes, sharing the loss of one we both dearly loved, until Sean sends a pool ball flying in our direction and the moment is broken. Hal picks up the ball, then throws a glance over his shoulder at me. He gives me one, brief nod; he is in this to the end.

)0(0(0(0(

THE NEXT DAY Dad calls us all to the lab. The vaccine has worked and it's time for us all to receive a dose. The twins, William and Carter, volunteer to go first. They hold hands as the nano patch is administered, much to the laughter of the rest of the group. It's good to laugh, even if it's only fleetingly. Within a few minutes, the rest of us are wearing dissolving nano patches that contain the vaccine. It will take twenty-four hours to dissolve, and then we can go to the mountains. There are no side-effects, apart from Sawyer. Later that night he gets a fever and his cheeks turn chalky white.

Mason, the bulk who never smiles, finds me and asks me to help. With trepidation I crouch beside Sawyer's bed. He offers me a weak smile.

"I'm okay," he says.

"Let's try healing you all the same. Can't have you feeling like this tomorrow."

I place my hand on his forehead. The heat rolls off him, making my hand damp. I hold my breath and count to ten. The warm glow of the healing power seeps from my fingers and into Sawyer. Relieved, I let out the breath. I feel Matt's presence behind me. He squeezes my shoulder. So much is communicated in that gentle touch. He believes in me.

Color returns to Sawyer's face. He sits up and gives me a hug.

"Impressive," Sean says, and lets out a whistle. "The great Silver Melody."

I blush under the praise. Then the group strike up with the freedom song.

We are the sun, we are the dawn,
We are the voice that urges you along.

Cast your eyes to the wreckage, the oppression, and the
pain,
Lift your sights to the horizon—learn to live again.
We are the pain, we are the tears,
We're the voices that were lost over all these years.
But when our hearts burn quiet in the darkness of the night,
We won't bear to keep this silence—we will stand, and we
will fight.

As the song dies down, I look at Dad. "Let's go get Mom."

His smile turns sad. "You go. I have to stay here."

My world spins, like I've swiveled on one of the lab stools. "I don't understand?"

"There's something I need to tell you."

Matt holds my hand and a look passes between them.

"Do you know?" I ask Matt. My heart stutters in my throat. "Do you know something?" I snap my attention back to Dad. "What's wrong?"

I'm tired of dodging curveballs and I have the feeling this is going to be a big one.

"As much as I want to, I can't go with you. I'll only hold you back."

"You're not that old—"

Dad holds a hand up. "I have a heart condition."

The words are meaningless. No one has heart conditions anymore. "I don't understand. Since when? There are pills for that."

"Not for this." Dad touches my arm. "Any more modifications and my heart won't take it."

I stumble back a step. "But it's okay to experiment with a dangerous vaccine?" I can't keep the anger out of my voice.

"It was worth the risk." Dad replies. "When the virus gets here, most people will die. I had to take the chance."

I look at Matt, the empathy in his bright blue eyes, and choke on a sob. "Are you going to die?" I ask Dad.

He shakes his head. "It's not serious. I'll be fine. But I can't go galivanting across the country." He steps closer and puts both his hands on my shoulders. "I would give anything to be there to rescue your Mom. But I'd rather be alive for her when she gets back. I need you to be brave. For both of us."

I nod, but tears well in my eyes and the old panic flutters in my chest, squeezing it tight. "I thought we'd be together this time. Like in the woods, before you got captured."

"I wanted that too." Dad moves his hand to my chin. "But you've got Matt, and all your friends. It's going to be okay."

"I don't know if I can do this without you." When both my parents were held prisoner by President Bear, I felt so alone. I had Matt then too, and the rest of his family, but it wasn't the same. Now, only a few months since I killed President Bear, I'm not sure I've healed enough to embark on a new mission. I carry scars. Nothing physical; they're all buried inside. Life is fleeting.

I'm scared to leave Dad here. But I know I don't have a choice. "But I'll try."

Dad wraps me in a hug. "It's hard for me too. This isn't the world I wanted for you, Silver."

Breaking the embrace, I blow my nose and hurl the tissue at the trash can. "We need to go soon. Earl must know we're locked down. I don't want to wait around here to see what his next wave of attack is. I'm sure he means for us all to die."

"I'm sure he does," Dad says.

While Dad checks on the nano patches on the rest of the mission team, Matt leans into me, resting his forehead against mine. I thread my arms around his neck, breathing him in. He wipes away a tear under my eye with the pad of a thumb. "We'll get her back."

One more night until we leave for the mountains. I spend the evening with Dad, soaking up his presence until I can't have him anymore. Eventually he pleads exhaustion. He didn't sleep for the three days it took him to make the vaccine.

Matt drags me to bed, saying I need to rest. I snuggle up to him, encircling him with my arms, desperate for his warmth to leach into my own shivering body. I long for something more than body heat to seep into me, something to make me strong and dependable and capable of saving the world. The thought of hiding under a rock somewhere crosses my mind.

CHAPTER FIVE

I SQUINT into the January sun, my eyes struggling to adjust to the natural light. The snow is crisp and untouched. The virus has swept across the country, killing most, isolating the rest.

Einstein woofs and dances around the snow, leaving a trail of paw prints. I take a deep breath, sucking down the fresh air and the scent of purity.

"It's too quiet," I say.

"It's the birds." Claus flips his fur-lined hood back. "There aren't any."

"Or anything else for that matter." Matt shoves his hands into padded gloves.

It isn't just people who've been wiped out, but animals. Every single species. The world waits, unnaturally still, for the next thing to happen.

Claus walks with me a little way from the gathering

team. His cane makes potholes in the surface of the snow. "I'm sorry I can't come with you."

I dip my chin. "You need to look after Francesca. I understand. If Earl tries anything else, you need to have people here too."

His hand drifts to my cheek. "Remember everything Evan and I have taught you. Trust your instincts."

"Even when they're different to everyone else?"

His moustache twitches. "Even then."

"Claus?" I look over my shoulder at my father. He's talking to Francesca, his hands tucked into his armpits. "Look after my Dad."

"Of course." He bows.

The blaring of a distant car alarm penetrates the muted conversations of the group. It seems louder than it should, magnified into a piercing scream that sends most of us covering our ears with our hands. It's the last clinging reminder of humanity as we know it. The car, the noise, the surrounding silence marks a change in the world. A before and after.

I hug Claus and then crunch my way through the snow to the line-up of army jeeps. The first jeep will be driven by Matt, once again the mission leader, along with Hal. In his jeep are Sean, Erica, Lyla and me. The five of us climb into the jeep and take our seats.

Dad stands outside the vehicle and reaches through the window for my hand. He smiles at me and kisses my cheek.

"I have a present for you." He looks at me, then at Matt. "For both of you."

"A present?" Matt asks.

Dad pats his thigh and Einstein comes running. He sits by Dad and looks at us expectantly, his pink tongue lolling playfully.

"Not only did I give him the vaccine, so he could go with you, but I increased his intelligence too."

Matt does a double take. "You did what now?"

Dad smiles. "He can understand you. Anything you say."

I look at the dog, who is eating the snow by Dad's feet. "Einstein, do you want to come with us?"

He barks once.

"One bark for yes, two for no," Dad says.

"That was just a coincidence," Matt says. He turns to the dog. "Einstein, can you beat Earl for us?"

Two barks. We all laugh.

After a few more questions, Einstein proves his intelligence. Matt shakes Dad's hand in thanks, and then beckons the dog into the jeep. He claims a position between Matt and me in the front.

Dad squeezes my hand through my glove. We don't talk about anything deep and meaningful, and keep the conversation light. I place a hand on his chest. His heart beats steadily under my palm. Strong. He'll be okay.

"Take care of Claus," I say. "His leg isn't what it used to be."

"He'll be fine," Dad says, patting my hand.

I grit my teeth against nerves. "And Matt's parents. And—"

"Silver, I love you too."

Dad raps the side of the jeep and Matt starts the engine. My stomach flip-flops. This is the moment of no return. Not that we have a choice in the mission; Earl is coming for us and if the virus doesn't defeat us it will be something else he sends our way.

Francesca and the remaining civilians gather and wave us off. We lock eyes in the rear-view mirror. There are many messages in her pupils, and I choose to latch on to hope.

As I settle into my seat, the images of the news reports concerning the virus circle back. I was able to put them out of my mind while performing the modifications. But now, out here in the world, we'll be seeing the devastation the virus has left behind. Crazed animals rampaged through the streets trying to flee the inescapable. Ravens with demented eyes, black dogs with dripping fangs, mutant insects twice their original size. They all bite. Or sting. They all infect. Or have been infected. There is always pain. I hold on to the hope that the infected animals may have died out, that they've all inflicted their tenth deadly blow and have simply dissolved away.

Two of the other bulks, William and Luis, take to the second jeep with Paige and Jacob. The supply truck is the next vehicle in the line-up and is driven by the other two new bulks, Mason and Carter 'the Rock' Harris, as he likes to be called. Carter is the burliest of the bulks, even bigger than his twin, and he's discovered he can crush rocks in the crevice of his bulk elbow. The last jeep is driven by Hal. Kyle and Sawyer ride shotgun.

Each bulk carries an automatic machine gun. Matt and Paige are given automatic pistols. Since the time we spent in the cave, Paige has become friendly with a double-barreled sawed-off shotgun, her personal favorite. She calls it Tallulah. She modified a backpack to make a holster of sorts for it. Reaching behind her head, she can pull it from the backpack and aim at her target in an instant. My best friend, a fragile beauty with green bird wings and emerald eyes, has become an expert marksman.

I keep my knife in my belt. I finger the familiar hilt, covered with green cord, now molded to fit the grip of my hand perfectly. It's been through hell and back with me.

The tires crunch over the snow. Those staying behind wave until we are out of eyesight. The main gate rolls wide. I contemplate leaping from the jeep and fleeing into the wilderness. A deep determination pins me to my seat.

"When you hear the lone wolf howling," Lyla sings from the back seat.

A chill rushes up my spine as the familiar words float around us.

"When sky comes crashing through." Erica joins in with Lyla, and Matt squeezes my knee. They are the words of my freedom song. A song I wrote while I lived in the caves. A song that gave people hope and courage. A song that everyone in the cave learned and became our anthem.

"What you singing now?" Sean asks. "Is it *the* song?"

"You'd do well to learn it," Erica says, but she's smiling.

Matt and I open our mouths and finish the chorus with Erica and Lyla.

> *With all the hellhounds growling,*
> *If it ends, just me and you*
> *Just close your eyes and breathe in deep,*
> *Look to the new sun's sky.*
> *Because our voice is freedom,*
> *And they will hear us cry.*

"Hot damn, if I didn't just get a chill." Sean pokes a finger into the corner of his eye. "I like it, Silver. I like it a lot."

I hear the people in the other jeeps take up the song and teach it to our newest members. Pretty soon the whole team are singing, and a steely determination settles in my bones. God, I need that.

When people fall quiet, we creep quietly onto the deserted highway. I grimace as the chomping tires signal our presence. But there isn't a person or animal within miles to hear us. Earl won't have any idea we're coming. After all, he doesn't have a magic crystal ball, just genetics.

I pull my hooded, winter jacket tighter as we gain speed on the highway. A few cars litter the sides of the road, abandoned, but not enough to impede our journey. By the time the disease reached this far east, most people stayed in their homes and died in their beds. Matt's jeep has been fitted with a plow to move any obstructing vehicles out of the way. Claus advised we'll need to turn off the highway eventually as the abandoned cars become thicker.

We drive in silence, each of us taking in our new country, or what has become of our country. Only Sean is undisturbed, snoring faintly beneath the Stetson he's draped over his face, sleeping off last night's beers.

I look for signs of, well, something, anything. It's eerie. Not a person in sight; no angry honks, no fumes billowing from traffic jams, no people walking along the sidewalks, no dogs barking. Just us and silence. Like we've trespassed on sacred land.

My uneasiness heightens with every mile we travel. Out the window, the world streaks by. There are no bodies. No bodies anywhere. As if there was some mass alien abduction. But there is something else instead of bodies; several puddles of a green goo.

As we travel they became easier to spot. Some are on the sides of roads next to abandoned vehicles, others in the drivers' seats of said vehicles. The hospital we pass is the worst, the largest green puddle outside the chained entrance doors. People who desperately tried to seek help after the hospital shut its doors, died enmasse, and left behind the tell-tale green, tacky substance of death in their wake. There are rumors of survivors. Where are they hiding?

My thoughts turn to the mountains and Earl. What will we find there? A monster surely. On this mission there was no briefing about what obstacles we might face during our journey or what trials we may encounter. Claus, Francesca, and the army simply don't know. As a result, we travel forward, blind, hoping we have enough skills, enough abilities and enough courage to face the monsters we know are waiting for us under Earl's command.

"We're coming, Mom," I whisper, as the deserted country rolls by.

"Woof," Einstein barks gently. He rests his head in my lap, his soulful eyes demanding a pat.

Absently playing with Einstein's floppy ears, I scan for movement. Hopeful to find a survivor, but watchful for whatever it is that Earl may have sent our way.

Meandering through abandoned cars, it takes two hours to reach the outskirts of Central City. Another two hours to dip into New Jersey and drive halfway across Pennsylvania.

"Look." Lyla points out the window, into the sky. "A bird."

A lone pigeon lands on the field neighboring the highway and pecks at the frozen earth. More birds fly from surrounding trees to join the one in the field. Einstein's ears prick up.

Matt slows the vehicle. "Perhaps there'll be other animals."

I lean out the window. "If they're pecking at the ground

there must be worms." Birds. Worms. Survivors. I cross my fingers, hoping we find more.

Sean stirs in the back seat. Pulling her furry hood around her face, Erica molds herself into the corner. Lyla sits between them.

"Are we nearly there yet?" Sean drawls, grinning at his own joke.

"I think I preferred it when he was asleep," Erica mutters, glaring at him with one raised, scornful eyebrow.

"Aw, shucks, don't be like that. There's good times to be had." Sean winks at Erica and throws his arm around Lyla.

Lyla shrugs out of his embrace and Erica turns her head to examine the birds outside.

"Shall we turn on the radio? Have ourselves a little sing-a-long?" Sean asks.

I turn in my seat. "Seriously? This is not a frat-house road trip."

Matt chuckles. "What were you doing before the resistance, Sean?"

"I was a rodeo rider, the best in Texas." A smug grin curls his lips.

Typical. Should have seen that coming. Didn't the Stetson and accent give it away?

"Of course you were," Erica says.

Sean makes a noise in his cheek. "Know how to ride the meanest of bulls and not get shaken off. It's taught me a lot about life. When to push hard, and when to back off."

Erica smirks. "I'm not sure you've learned that well enough."

Sean throws his head back and laughs.

The walkie-talkie crackles to life. "Shall we make a pit-stop?" Hal's voice. "We've been on the road a few hours now, I think people are getting hungry."

"Roger that," Matt replies. "There's a picnic area two miles ahead, we'll pull over there. Over."

A few cars dot the parking area of the picnic area, like scattered dominoes. A Ferris wheel stands in the field, its metal buckets squeaking in the slender wind. Other rides, equally vacant, take up most of the flat field. Bumper cars. High swings. Even candy floss and popcorn stalls. Portable toilets. Everything empty. Like the set of a slasher movie. We wander through the vacant rides. Sawyer digs a hand into the vat of popcorn and releases its buttery scent. Kyle opens the door of one of the toilets. A puddle of green goo bubbles over the step and onto his shoe. "Yuk!"

Einstein wanders around, sniffing the rides, raising a leg here and there. Movement catches my eye. I grip my knife.

"What is it?" Lyla asks, shrinking into her winter coat. For all her bravado and bluster at the compound, fear now deflates her.

I frown. A spinning teacup swings back and forth in perpetual motion. That's all. "Nothing. It's nothing." I let go of the knife.

"Let's crank it up! Go for a ride." Sean jumps onto the

platform of the teacup ride, looking for the central console and flicks a switch. Music blares from the speakers. Lyla cover her ears. Einstein woofs and runs around the perimeter of the ride. The music dies just as suddenly, cut off, out of power.

"Bummer," Sean says, jumping back down.

"Enough mucking around." Hal carries bags of food to a picnic table and spreads out the sandwiches and fruit. Fresh stuff first. I know the self-heating packet noodles and canned peaches will come in time.

Einstein refuses to eat, but stands alert, watching the landscape at our back, his nose twitching.

We eat the food with minimal banter. I keep my gloves on, but I'm not the only one. Paige shoots me a sympathetic look. With our hoods pulled up to shelter us from the cold and wind, conversation is difficult. Can't say I feel up to talking much, anyway. My thoughts are torn between my father and the mountain. I gratefully accept a cup of hot tea Matt hands me. The steam rises to my face, defrosting my frozen nose.

"Look." Carter points to a field beyond the fairground.

A dog stands in the middle of the field. A big, black, shaggy dog.

"More survivors," Matt says. "Bigger animals. That's a good sign."

"And bugs." Sawyer slaps at his neck, causing his curls to bounce. He pulls his hand away revealing the remains of a squished bug and a few droplets of blood.

"I'm not so sure." Hal stares at the dog. He drops his sandwich. "It looks, *off.*"

The dog sniffs the air, perhaps trying to catch our scent. It raises its snout and barks, once, twice and then lets out a growl.

Einstein growls back. His hackles rise and he backs up until he bumps into a jeep. Surprised, he snaps at the tires, then turns his attention back to the black dog.

"What's the matter, boy? It's just another dog." Matt rubs Einstein's neck. Einstein refuses to be calmed. He barks and barks. Louder and louder, spittle dripping from his jaws, lips raised to show his teeth.

The black dog takes a step, then another, gaining speed. It trots toward us. Faster. Faster and faster until it reaches an all-out run.

"Paige?" Jacob whispers. She stands next to me, watching the dog.

"Hmm?"

"Get your gun out," Jacob says. "Quickly."

Hal unholsters his own gun. Matt moves behind me. I grip my knife. Paige reaches for her shotgun. The dog growls, arching its back, spraying spittle. Close now. Too close. Close enough to see the madness in its eyes, the white saliva dripping from its mouth, its ears flattened in aggression and its fur matted and covered in something wet.

"It's blood." Matt reaches for a gun. "It's covered in blood."

No more hesitation. As the dog leaps into the air ten feet

before us Hal, Matt and Paige simultaneously pull their triggers, letting forth a volley of ammunition.

Bang. Bang. Bang. Bang. Bang.

The dog's body bucks and kicks and jiggles its way to the ground as bullets punch through its head and torso. It lands near my feet, dead, along with a couple dozen spent shell casings. The acrid scent of gunpowder fills the air.

Lyla steps closer, examining the dog. "Wow."

Einstein woofs and wags his tail, but doesn't venture any nearer.

"It was infected." Matt kneels in front of it. "Or sick."

"Same result either way." Hal nudges a black paw with his boot.

"Stand clear." Sawyer steps up, throws a fireball with his mind, and disintegrates the remains. Hal leaps away from the sudden heat. I haven't practiced much with the pyrokinesis ability yet, as my energy has gone into controlling the black lightning, but Sawyer's demonstration shows how powerful it can be.

"Good riddens," Lyla says.

"Pit stop over, let's get going." Hal scans the far fields. "There could be more."

We climb back into the trucks and continue along the highway. Matt moves his gun from his holster to the bucket between our seats, accessible. Einstein growls from his position at my feet.

We crawl along the tarmac, the roads now thick with abandoned cars, impeding our progress. Soon we'll have to turn to the smaller roads. The ball of unease in my gut grows hard.

"Erica, when we get back, we're gonna go on a date, yeah? I'll take you to this nice little seafood restaurant I know on the coast. The best clam chowder around. There's a guesthouse next door too." Sean sets his Stetson on Erica's head.

Erica removes the Stetson and throws it into his lap. "Shut-up Sean."

"Aw, Jeez, that's no way to talk to a soldier, fighting for his country. Just feeling a little lonely and looking for some human companionship." He twirls the Stetson around a finger.

"Shut-up, Sean." Lyla elbows him in the ribs as Erica shrinks to humming-bird size. It's an awesome new power, one that will come in handy when we need to scout ahead. Or lay an ambush.

Sean does not shut-up. He keeps up a running mono-logue of jokes that are not laughed at and come-ons to Erica that are met with stony silence. The guy seriously can't take a hint. But then we all have our own ways of coping. When I gave him his bulk ability, he told me about being in the compounds during the resistance. There are scars on his torso to match his story.

I looked into his eyes and saw the sincerity there. He's capable of sensitivity, and tact, but now he chooses not to employ those particular traits. Now, he chooses the bravado act; the fully masculine, unshaven, tobacco-chewing, phlegm-hoicking, balls-out approach. And let's not forget the twinkle in his eye and the swagger in his step. I imagine it was the same when he came face-to-face with a bull in his rodeo days. Bravado and confidence, even if it is fake, is the only way to deal with two sharp horns on the end of a two-ton weight running at you at thirty miles an hour.

Late in the afternoon we reach the western border of Pennsylvania and a wall of abandoned vehicles. It's time to leave the highway. Matt picks up the walkie to communicate his intentions.

"Roger that," Hal replies. "I was going to suggest we stop anyway. There's something wrong with Sawyer. Over."

CHAPTER SIX

WE PULL off the highway and park along the side of a smaller road. I jump out of the jeep and run over to Hal's vehicle.

"What's up with Sawyer?" I ask.

I expect to hear he's cold from the non-existent heating system in the jeeps, or has a headache, or some other minor ailment. Instead, I find him lying in the back of the jeep, his face drained of color. He shivers violently, despite the blankets piled on top of him, and he is barely conscious.

"How long has he been like this?" My breath plumes in the freezing air.

"It started soon after lunch." Kyle stamps his feet on the ground and wraps his arms around his waist. "He said he didn't feel so good and was going to lie down in the back. I thought he was being all man-flu about it." Guilt crosses his face. "Then when I checked on him..." he turns to his friend. "Shit, dude, I'm so sorry..."

Sawyer doesn't respond.

"We thought he was sleeping," Hal adds, blowing on his hands. "We didn't realize he'd gotten so bad until just now."

Paige joins my side. "Is it...could it be...the virus?"

Sawyer's body convulses. His eyes bulge and the veins in his head rise like slithering snakes trying to escape the confines of a too-tight skin. Almost like a nanite death.

Paige takes a step back. Kyle whimpers and the rest of the team hover at my back, their unease almost physical.

"I don't know. Maybe his vaccine didn't work." When I healed him last night, I thought it was side-effects of the vaccine that made him unwell, but maybe it didn't work to begin with.

"Heal him, Silver." Lyla looks at me, a challenge in her eyes.

Irritated, I yank the glove off my hand. I will not let her rile me, and I will not let the black power win. I place my hand on Sawyer's head. He's hot, way too hot. Sweat dampens his corkscrew curls into straight lines and the faint stench of stale body odor rises from the tangle of blankets. The cold air seeps into me and I lean into it, calling on its freshness to keep me focused. I close my eyes and picture the disease inside his body. The benevolent light warms my hands. It flows into Sawyer's body, the familiar glowing luminescence connecting my hands to his skin. I imagine the infected cells shrinking, dying, leaving his body, to be replaced by healthy new cells.

"Come on, Sawyer," I mutter.

After a few minutes I sense a change. Sawyer stops shivering and his forehead no longer radiates heat. He opens his eyes.

"Water," he croaks.

Paige hands him a canteen. I remove my hand. Inside, a flicker of triumph warms me. My black power did not appear. I turn to Lyla and offer her my glowing hand.

She shakes her head. "Don't touch me," she whispers, backing away.

I can't blame her reaction, but I don't like it. She's two years younger than me and she makes me uneasy. Maybe because she shines a light on my failings.

"What infected him?" Matt asks. Einstein sits by his feet, pushing his head into Matt's thigh, seeking attention.

"I think it was the bug, at lunch, the one that bit his neck." I watch Sawyer carefully, making sure he's really healed.

Hal chews on his cheek and scans the horizon. "The disease is still out there."

"We need to be careful, especially as we now know that Sawyer's vaccine didn't take." I turn to face the group. "We don't know who else might be at risk."

The group exchanges wary glances. There isn't even a wise crack from Sean. Luis pukes on the side of the road. This time, no one laughs.

"Can we put another nanopatch on?" Paige asks.

"No, if you have the antibodies, the overdose might trigger the illness, and if you didn't develop the antibodies the first time, then you won't with any subsequent vaccine. I don't have the equipment with me to decipher who has antibodies and who doesn't. But please keep in mind that it's very rare that a vaccine doesn't work." *Where is Dad when I need him?*

"Yeah, but this is an untested, new vaccine, and the first one that your Dad created." Mason rests a hand on the gun at his hip. Casually. Like it's simply another appendage. Maybe it is to him. He was a solider in President Bear's army too. "No offense."

The group falls silent. There's nothing more I can say to reassure anyone. Mason is right. It's the first vaccine Dad created. It's possible he made a mistake.

"We'll make camp here tonight," Hal says, kicking snow off his boots. "It's getting dark anyway and Sawyer could use the rest."

Matt makes a fire and we cook hamburgers and hotdogs on the flames. Einstein lies at his feet and begs scraps from the group.

"Wish we had some graham crackers and marshmallows." Jacob pokes at the fire with a long stick. Paige nestles into his side and lifts her fur-lined hood. Her face is pale, paler than usual and her permanent freckles seem to hover on her translucent skin. I hope she's not worrying about my black power.

"We've got chocolate." Hal breaks off cubes and hands them out.

I drum a tune on my leg, missing my guitar. I'd give anything to feel the strings under my fingertips. It helped me manage the anxiety while I lived in the cave. Now it might help ease the guilt over Lyla's injury and control the black lightning.

"Ignore her, Silver." Matt leans in close and ruffles Einstein's ears. "I've noticed how Lyla is with you. She'll get over it."

I sniff. "No one else burned her leg."

He takes off my glove and kisses my hand. The fool. I shrug out of his grasp and put my glove on. "It's too dangerous."

He eyes me carefully, a muscle in his jaw pulsing, but doesn't say anything else.

"I'm sorry," I say. "I'm just…scared."

He nods. "Me too. But we'll figure it out."

"We have to. Before we get to Earl. I can't be malfunctioning when we reach Earl."

He takes my hand again but doesn't pull off my glove. Maybe he was being brave before. Maybe he is actually scared of me. He should be. Everyone should be. Maybe I shouldn't have come.

Not wanting to dwell on something I can't fix, I turn my attention to the group. Sawyer sits between Mason and Carter, telling a story of a card trick he performed on the streets, his eyes dancing with life. He glances at the bonfire and the flames leap impossibly high, stretching into the dark sky. Small spirals of red and orange hang in the air before winding their way back to the leaping mass of heat. I lean my head against Matt's shoulder, enjoying Sawyer's pyrotechnic display.

Sean puts his Stetson on Erica's head again. This time she leaves it on, but she turns her back on him and listens to Luis tell a story. His soft voice is hypnotic, his Hispanic accent adding a lulling quality I could fall asleep to.

"You're not the only person I'm worried about." Matt juts his chin in Paige's direction where she sits in Jacob's arms, wrapped up in a blanket against the cold. In the dark of the night and flickering light of the fire, it's hard to tell, but her face looks completely drained of color. As white as my lab coat hanging back in Central City. Her eyes are closed and her raven-black hair unusually lack-luster. I'm not the only one who noticed.

"You don't think..." I can't bear to voice the thought.

Matt gives Einstein the end of a hotdog and then pulls me close. "No, she's been unwell for a while, before we left. If it was the virus she'd be dead by now."

Possibilities race through my mind. She could be tired. Afraid. Cold. Like the rest of us. I can't bear to think of my best friend in danger. "Maybe it's just a case of the normal flu."

"Maybe." Matt accepts a mug of steaming coffee from Hal. "Maybe."

The night passes restlessly. I dream of old-fashioned

armies on a battlefield; knights dressed in armor fighting it out with swords and maces. Severed heads, hacked limbs, spurting blood. Horses run wild with wide-eyed fear and flaming arrows cause sporadic fires to ignite throughout a dry grass field. I toss and turn in my sleep, trying to find some comfort on the hard, frozen ground. Despite the thick quilting of my sleeping bag I'm left bruised and sore. I wake in the pre-dawn light, exhausted from my fight with sleep. Inside my gloves the fur is burned. As the first rays of sun break the horizon, soft, crunching footsteps sound nearby.

I roll onto my side and peak out of my sleeping bag. Jacob, his hair long and ruffled in the wintry air, walks a little way from the camp and faces the rising sun. Leaning on an elbow, I watch his graceful movements. He begins his Tai Chi ritual with a 'Salute to the Sun.' Quietly, he is joined by Carter and Paige. They fall in step behind him, mirroring his movements, exhibiting a peacefulness I haven't felt in months. Their movements are slow and precise, reminding me of an ancient dance passed down through generations.

Since the resistance, while competing in the martial arts circuit, Jacob opened his own dojo to teach kids. They love him, every single one of them. For himself, he focuses on Tai Chi and the peace it brings him.

Paige moves with a graceful fluidity and her green wings rise from her back. Her breath plumes in the cold air and her cheeks turn rosy. Perhaps she isn't unwell. Perhaps the cold affected her last night. And there's the stress of the mission that hovers around each of us, but no one will talk about. What will happen to the world if we fail?

With Sawyer completely recovered, we pack up camp and load the vehicles. The main highways are littered with abandoned cars and ominous piles of tacky, green goo. I spot the odd lump of misshapen bones, none of them recognizable. People. This is all that is left of them in their desperate attempt to escape a deadly virus.

Before we left, there were rumors of survivors, but we've seen no sign of human activity. I assume those who are left are in hiding. *If* there are any left. Perhaps we won't encounter another living soul between us and Earl.

CHAPTER SEVEN

MATT and I glance at Paige. It's our third day on the road and we've pulled over for a pit-stop. Paige is puking her guts up in the trees a few yards away. Jacob rubs her back. The rest of the group paces, talking in short sentences, and blow warm breaths into cold hands.

"What do you think is wrong with her?" Matt whispers. His frosty breath plumes between us and warms my cheeks. Concern emanates from his depthless blue eyes.

Ordering my thoughts, I pick at a hangnail. "I'm concerned it might be the virus. I know she started looking pale before we left Central City, but the vaccine could be slowing down the effects." Saying the words aloud feels like a betrayal, but I'm grateful not to have to think about my black lightning. "If it was a normal flu strain she would be feeling better by now, and she wouldn't have periods when she seems completely well."

Jacob and Paige exchange a few heated words and then Jacob marches out of the woods toward us.

"Silver, Matt, Hal." He beckons us over.

We huddle in a small group, heads bowed, waiting on Jacob's news.

"I know you've all been concerned," Jacob says, toeing the frozen ground. "Paige knows she can't hide it any longer. She's not sick, she's pregnant. At least she thinks she is."

The information hits like a knee to the guts. Not that being pregnant is a bad thing. Under normal circumstances. When the world hasn't gone to hell and we aren't on a mission to take down evil itself and save the world like some comic-book heroes. Then it would be fine, then it would be great. Then we could have a party and toast with champagne and the men could break open a box of cigars.

But the fact of it is, we *are* on a mission to save the world, we *are* going to fight the most evil being in the history of the universe and his army of equally hideous minions, and we need Paige to do it. We need her healthy. It's too late to send her back.

We can't leave her here. We *need* her. *I* need her. With her wings and ace marksmanship, her presence adds a serious advantage to the team. Plus, she knows about my dark power. Her friendship is one of the few things that reduces my anxiety.

Matt watches Paige. A deep frown crosses his forehead.

"This...is *not* good." The one person who always knows what to say is speechless.

"How long?" Hal asks, pulling at his chin. "Do you know how far along she is?"

Jacob cocks a shoulder. "Maybe six weeks."

"Okay, she's going to be fine. It's just morning sickness. I remember when my girlfriend went through it..."

Hal had a kid? Where is his kid?

"...they're both dead," Hal says before anyone can ask. "Anyway, she'll be fine. It's going to take us a few more days to reach the mountains, if we're able to continue with the vehicles. Let's give her plenty of rest in the meantime and she'll be good to go when, if, we need her. And Silver, we've always got you." He looks at me. He knows nothing about the darkness trying to consume me. "You've got her abilities too."

Tension rips through me, but I can't avoid the responsibility. I sigh, then nod at Hal. The *ultimate weapon*. There will never be an escape from it. But I need to figure out how to use it without hurting anyone.

Hal approaches the rest of the group to give them the news and I meet Paige in the woods. I pick up a couple of acorns from the ground and circle them in my hand. The scent of pine and fresh air surrounds us, while a cold wind nips at my cheeks.

Tentatively, I touch her shoulder with a gloved hand. "Congratulations?"

"Thanks." She smiles weakly, spreading her hands help-lessly. "I'm sorry. I know the timing sucks."

"It's okay." I pull her in for a hug. "We'll manage. As long as this baby doesn't change your abilities—"

"No, everything's working fine, better even. I feel better when I'm using my powers." As if to prove her point, her green wings sprout from her back and lift her in the air. "I'm beginning to think the baby may be developing powers of its own. When we saw that black dog, I felt something stirring, something trying to control it, but then it slipped away."

"That would be something," I reply, as I steer her back to the jeeps. "Plenty of rest for you." I wrap her sleeping bag around her.

"You okay?" Matt asks, as I clamber into the seat beside him. The question is loaded.

"Yeah." I zip my jacket all the way up and snuggle my chin inside, ignoring the meaning behind his words. "You?"

"Yeah." He turns the key. "Let's go."

"Let's go," I echo. Neither of us is willing to discuss the sudden shift in mood that's affected the group. The news of a baby ought to make people joyous and happy. Instead, I feel deflated, as though it's yet another notch against us, one more complication that we have to deal with in a mission of the unexpected.

The mission has been going well, so far. It's early days. We've driven half-way across the country with no major mishaps. The sense of foreboding that's lurking around is because I know, deep in my gut, our luck is running out. I'll be expected to save everyone, if and when it comes to that. No one has said as much, but isn't that what I'm here for? Little do they know I won't be able to.

I know I have tremendous power. But what if I fail? The more people who rely on me, the greater the potential to screw up. And this isn't a job where an "I'm sorry, I'll do better next time," will suffice. Look at Lyla's leg. This is life and death. I'm sixteen for God's sake, I shouldn't have to deal with this.

Einstein woofs gently and lays his head in my lap.

"I know, I know, stop feeling sorry for yourself, Silver, and just get on with it," I mutter to the dog, to myself. I huddle deeper into my jacket and pull Einstein closer to me as Matt guns the engine and propels us onward.

That night we reach the Colorado border and the temperature drops below freezing. Tents shield us from the wind, but not the noise or cold. While the others gather around a fire, I spend an hour away from the camp with my gloves off trying to bring the healing glow to my fingers. I manage a couple of times, then push it away again. Then the black lightning appears and cracks a tree in half.

A shape darts out of the shadows and tackles me to the snow just as the tree comes crashing to the ground, inches from where I was standing.

"Stay down!" Luis covers my head with a bulk arm.

The tree lands, kicking up snow and pine needles. We remain on the ground, just breathing.

"Thanks," I say.

He helps me to my feet. I can't read his expression in the dark, but I don't think he saw my lightning sparks.

"I wouldn't venture so far from the group." He looks over his shoulder as we head back to camp. "Lots of dangers out here."

"What about you? Why are you out here?"

He smiles sheepishly. "I needed to puke again."

I stop walking and put a gloved hand on his arm. "Are you okay? I mean, it's okay if you're not."

He shivers. "I wouldn't be anywhere else." He makes the sign of the cross. I haven't seen anyone do that for a while. "What about you? What were you doing out here? How did you crack that tree in two?"

"You saw that?"

He nods.

I look at my gloved hands. "I was practicing one of my powers." It's the truth, but I feel deceitful.

He offers me a fist bump. "Glad we've got you, Silver."

I tap my padded knuckles against his. "You too, Luis."

We return to camp and settle into our respective tents. My sleep remains fitful; I'm sure a tornado is about to blow through our camp and sweep us all away. The night is bad to Paige too. She wakes pale and sickly. We'll have to make a pitstop for medication.

We break camp early, eager to be rid of the cold ground. There is only one road that traverses the Colorado mountains, and that is an interstate highway.

Progress is glacial. Un-plowed snow covers the road. It's prime time ski season and abandoned vehicles litter the blacktop. Matt uses his plow to push the snow and some of the smaller vehicles out the way. Other times the bulks have to switch on their ability and move the vehicles off the road and down the mountain. Relishing the opportunity to test their powers and flaunt their newfound muscles, they welcome the physical work. But along with the cars that are shoved down the mountain, are the ominous piles of green goo, glaring reminders of humanity lost, of what the world was.

Einstein sniffs the snow, and a few times Matt and I remove teeth and bone fragments from his mouth. Not his own. Human leftovers. It makes me shudder every time.

We weave our way through the narrow mountain road and come across a small village atop a snowy summit. The scent of pine overwhelms everything else and brings clarity to my thoughts. Snow clings to roofs and car tops, covering everything in a white blanket. Christmas lights hang across the small main street, flashing multiple colors over the desolate town. The door to the local diner is smashed and hangs askew. A large puddle of green goo flows out of the restaurant and seeps into the frozen snow. A radio hisses from an apartment over a small hardware store. Nothing but static. The snow crunches under our tires as we creep forward. As we drive through the small town, I spot a drug store.

"Matt, stop." Erica lays a hand on Matt's shoulder, also

spotting the shop. "Let's check out the pharmacy, they might have something for Paige."

The convoy halts and I motion for Paige and Jacob to follow me. The others get out to stretch their legs and pull on their gloves. Sawyer throws a snowball at Kyle. The two engage in a lighthearted snowball fight which Kyle is winning on account of how fast he can throw. Sean crafts a simple snowman and sticks his Stetson on top. Einstein finds a lamppost and turns the snow yellow.

A bell jangles as I open the door of the pharmacy, startling us. As I step over the threshold, a wolf howls in the distance. But it's close enough to send shivers down my spine. Violent images explode in my mind of the time my father and I were trailed by wolves and attacked. I smother the memories back down into their bottle and try to cork it.

The door slams behind us. I brace myself, waiting for a presence. Someone. Anything. I hold my breath, but no one appears. The bell settles into silence. We inch toward the back of the store, dodging the odd pile of green remains, and step over boxes and vitamins and sleeping pills that fell off their shelves.

"These poor people," Paige mutters, holding on to Jacob's elbow. "If only they'd had your Dad's vaccine, Silver."

"I wish he could have saved them too," I say.

The metal security shutter is closed and locked. With my abilities it poses no problem. I inhale a focusing breath and turn into a bulk. Snapping the lock with two fingers, I raise the shutter. Then returning to my smaller, unadjusted self, I clamber over the serving shelf.

"What am I looking for?" I ask Jacob.

Jacob bends over the counter. "Anti-nausea for pregnancy. Hal says it's a blue bottle."

A green tinge colors Paige's skin as she leans against a wall. Fearing she might collapse, I rummage through the pill bottles. I find antibiotics, antidepressants, Vicodin and other pain meds. Hoping we won't need them, I pocket a few bottles of codeine and tramadol. Finally, I find the anti-nausea pills. Hal said the relatively new pills were effective for his girlfriend, better than any previous anti-nausea medication. Before I climb back over the shelf, I grab a bottle of pregnancy vitamins and some iron tablets. Hopefully the combinations of drugs will return Paige to her healthy self.

"Got them!" I announce as I shove them in my pockets and jump down from the shelf.

Jacob and Paige stand unmoving, eyes focused in another direction, twin looks of horror on their faces. Beneath his olive skin Jacob turns as ashen as Paige. Fleetingly, I worry that maybe Paige isn't pregnant. Maybe Earl has sent a second virus in our direction and one of them has caught it. But that's impossible. Earl can't know we're coming.

A low growl rumbles from my left. Confused, I look for Einstein's wagging tail. Then my gut clenches as I recall an animal Earl is responsible for creating, hellhounds. With my heart knocking against my ribs, my hand flies to my knife. I picture vicious fangs and claws and powerful, invincible muscles. I've killed a hellhound before. I can kill one again.

Looking toward the end of the aisle, my gaze settles on a wolf blocking our exit. I back up toward Jacob and Paige, but a second wolf blocks the other end of the aisle.

One is completely black, the other gray and white. They both have matted coats and the whites of their eyes have turned yellow. They are skinny, too skinny, with lolling tongues and rumbling growls. Hungry. And sick. Infected? Blood from a recent kill covers their muzzles and flanks.

I glance outside the storefront window. Matt sits in the driver's seat of the jeep, a map spread over the steering wheel. Sitting in the back, Sean smokes a cigarette. Half her normal size, Erica scowls at the fumes wafting over her. Hal and Luis stand by another jeep, sharing a joke. They are unaware the wolves have entered the store. Or were they always here, lying in wait?

Only Einstein is aware something is wrong. He paces in a small circle, barking, trying to get Matt's attention. Matt, unused to Einstein's new intelligence levels, shushes him and clicks his fingers, trying to get him to heel.

With creeping fingers, I release my knife from my belt. It's the only weapon we have. Paige left her shotgun in the jeep.

They attack simultaneously. The first wolf leaps toward me. At the other end of the aisle, Paige screams and Jacob's legs turn into a blur of karate kicks.

I raise my knife as claws and teeth and frothing saliva fly through the air. Instinct takes over. The images of the fights I endured last summer tumble through my mind and help hone my reflexes. Ducking under the leaping wolf, I raise my knife above my head. I slice through its belly as it sails over me, showering myself in the blood and guts and the insides of the wolf. It lands in a heap between me and Jacob and Paige.

Paige has stopped screaming and stands with her wings high above her shoulders. Jacob's mouth is gaping open.

"Are you okay?" I call.

They don't answer, and I follow their eyeline to the second wolf laying on its back at Paige's feet. The wolf whines submissively. She stares into its sick, yellow eyes a few more seconds before looking at me.

"I think we're good," she says, sweeping her raven-black hair behind her shoulders.

Wary, I stand straight. "How do you know?"

Her chin lifts. "There's something inside me. Something new, from the baby, like I told you. I think it can communicate with animals and I told it not to hurt us."

I inch toward her and the inert wolf. "You can control it with your mind?"

Paige's hand drifts to her stomach, covering the new human inside. "I think so, but I don't want to stick around here to find out."

I back away from the wolf, slipping in blood and entrails, not quite trusting Paige's new ability. The animal remains on the floor, head cocked in confusion, whining for attention. Jacob and Paige retreat and meet me at the front door.

"I thought all the mind control nanites had failed," Jacob says.

"I did too." My gaze falls to my hands at the dark power that is stored there. There is no tingle, but I know it's there. Waiting.

Paige and Jacob leave the store, but something catches my eye on a shelf near the door. A shelf of pregnancy tests. I grab two boxes. Better to be sure. I step outside into the snow and shut the door firmly behind me. The wolf remains on its belly, looking at us mournfully as if it wants us to come back and give it a belly rub. No thanks.

"We thought we'd take shelter in that café." Matt points across the road after I join him at the jeeps. "Maybe we can rustle up some decent hot food for us all." His eyes widen as he takes in my bloody appearance. "What happened?"

"Wolves, diseased wolves," I reply, climbing into the jeep. "We can't stop here. I'm sure there are more."

Matt hands me a towel and a bottle of water. Wishing for a change of clothes, I clean the bloody grime from my face and hands. Expecting more of the vicious creatures to materialize, I scan the mountains. Instead, a chorus of lonely howls echoes across the mountain top. Are they lamenting the loss of a member of their pack? Or is it some kind of warning?

"Let's go." Matt says to the group and finds his place

quickly beside me. He pecks my cheek. "I'm sorry. Are you okay?" He looks at my gloved hands.

"I was in control," I whisper.

"Hey, Silver." Sean calls from the back seat as we pull onto the mountain top road. "You missed a bit. A little bit of wolf guts, right there, on the back of your neck."

I pour more water from the bottle onto the towel, dab at the nape of my neck again.

"A little to the right...a little more...a little more—"

"Shut-up Sean," Erica and Lyla say in unison.

CHAPTER EIGHT

THAT NIGHT we find shelter in an empty ski chalet. There are enough beds for most of us and the remainder use sleeping bags on the floor. After checking all the rooms, entrances and exits, Hal locks us up against the night and whatever creatures, modified or diseased, lay in wait beyond the dark windows. William builds a fire, which Sawyer lights with his mind, and we circle around the blazing heat warming cold fingers and toes. We drink cups of hot chocolate laced with something a bit stronger and feast on hot pasta Matt finds in the kitchen.

I attempt to ignore the random puddles of human remains dotted around the chalet, but there is a luminescence to the green liquid that attracts my eye, enticing me to look and imagine what once existed. Einstein sniffs at them and backs away, his hackles raised, until he finds a rug by the fire to settle on. Thankful to find hot water in the tank, I take a shower and scrub the remaining wolf guts from my body and hair. I throw out my dirty clothes and dress in my spare army combats, t-shirt and a thick, black fleece.

When I'm clean, I hand Paige one of the pregnancy tests. "You need to take the test."

Paige frowns. "I already told you I'm pregnant."

"I don't want to leave anything to chance." I stare at my best friend, who is already defensive of the life inside her. "Prudency dictates we confirm. We need to make sure you're pregnant and not—"

"Not sick with some new disease that's going to infect everyone else." Paige finishes for me.

I don't take my eyes from her emerald ones. "Too many mistakes have already been made. I've made too many mistakes. My powers—"

"Alright. Alright." Paige lifts a hand and edges toward the bathroom. "But it's only going to tell you what I already know."

Despite the circumstances, I manage a smile. "I hope so."

Five minutes later, the pregnancy is confirmed. It doesn't change the battling emotions inside. The tension between my shoulders remains hard and unforgiving.

We settle down by the fire for the night. Every time it dwindles, Matt or Hal add a log and Sawyer throws in an extra fireball. Luis manages not to puke all night and Mason pours over a map, tracing our remaining journey. Lyla sits on the far side of the room. After changing the bandage on her leg, her gaze alternates between the fire and me. She's still mad at me.

After performing a couple speedy laps of the chalet, Kyle sits near me, repeatedly slamming a fist into his palm with his speed ability.

I put a hand on his fist. "You're going to give yourself a bruise."

He offers a sheepish smile. "I just want to get there."

"We will," I say, staring at the flames. "Whether we're ready or not."

Kyle casts me a curious glance. "You were born ready. Look at the way you took out Bear. Did you ever figure out what power that was?"

My hands tremble and sweat dampens the inside of my gloves. "Nope."

"Bummer," he says, leaning his head on the back of the couch. "That was awesome."

In the morning, we wrap up against the cold and climb into the jeeps. Our goal is to reach the bottom of the mountain today. A journey that normally takes two hours, but with the dense trail of vehicles abandoned on each lane, will take much longer. At least at the end of it, when we arrive in Utah, we'll be one state closer to California and the Sierra Nevada Mountains.

Not long into the day the supply truck, driven by Carter, poses a problem. It is the largest and hardest to maneuver of the vehicles in the convoy. Thick layers of snow and dense lines of abandoned vehicles prove to be larger obstacles than it can deal with. The truck holds our food supplies and weapons.

With the morning sun warming our backs, we unload the supply truck and re-pack the essentials into the jeeps. Matt sweeps a reluctant hand over the box of rocket launchers and shoves as many as he can into his backpack. I pray we won't come across anything that will require them. Carter and Mason join Hal, Sawyer and Kyle in the third jeep.

A box of noodles rests between Matt and me. Erica and Lyla each sit with a twenty-gallon water canister at their feet. Erica builds a wall of ammunition between her and Sean.

"How am I gonna pass the time now, when I can't see your pretty face?" Sean drawls, trying to maneuver a peep-hole in Erica's wall.

Shrinking, Erica turns her best scowl on him. "What a shame." Her comment is laced with enough venom to make a hellhound look like a domestic pet.

I glimpse Sean in the rearview mirror. "I'd give it up if I were you."

He winks. "Good thing you're not me."

Erica shoots him a thousand daggers with her steely gaze, but as she turns her head away, I catch a smile on her lips.

As the sun slips behind the mountain peaks, we descend the last of the slopes and arrive on flatter ground. Miles of barren land stretch out around us as we drive. The ground is devoid of snow and instead, covered with scrubby grass and orange rock and the beginning of a desert landscape. Even the air smells different. Dusty.

The road is one long pencil dividing the land in two. Free of cars, Matt guns the engine and we pick up pace. Wind tousles my hair and anxiety gnaws at my stomach. A superstitious fear. Part of me is amazed we've made it this far without loss of life. Not that it can be avoided forever. There will be death. There always is on a mission like this. To hope otherwise is foolish. The further we travel unscathed, the larger the fear grows in the pit of my stomach, spreading up my esophagus until it thickens my throat. There isn't anyone in our convoy that I'm willing to lose. Thinking about who it might be, and how, twists my guts into a painful ache. I haven't had a panic attack yet, but it hovers nearby, ready to land at the most inopportune time.

The sun dips lower and brings night on its heels. Within the night, darkness lives. Shadows flicker over the barren ground. Shadows and darkness and fear. Fear I thought I got a handle on. Since I developed abilities, I learned to trust my instincts. But with the black power showing up whenever I feel ruffled, I can't trust them anymore.

With the mountain at our backs and the stars in the sky, we follow the highway until we reach a bridge.

We climb out of the jeeps and stand by the edge of the road. The bridge expands across a deep valley with a churning, white water river two hundred feet below. It's also missing a huge chunk in the middle making it impossible to cross. It's gone.

Hal scans the length of the road and the expanse of the collapsed bridge. "Weird."

"Has there been an earthquake? Or something?" Lyla asks.

"Nothing reported before the virus." Matt checks his travel laptop with satellite signal. "And according to this, not since either."

Einstein woofs and dances by the edge.

"So, what then?" I ask, as my spirits deflate. "What could cause this?"

"There's no cars on either side. Or in the river below." Hal stands by the foot of the bridge looking through a pair of binoculars. "This has been done on purpose."

"Maybe something to prevent the virus spreading?" Erica says.

"Whatever." I point to Matt's laptop screen. "It doesn't matter why. What matters is how we get across."

Sean lights a cigarette, the small glow illuminating his wary expression. Some of the others gather around him and a hushed conversation ensues.

Matt consults the map. "There isn't another crossing for a hundred miles in each direction."

Hal's lips purse and he rubs at the back of his neck. "It's too far for the jeeps. If we tried to jump it, they wouldn't make it. Besides we don't know how weak the bridge is."

"What about telekinesis?" Matt touches my arm. "Silver, could you and Sawyer move the supplies across? Maybe even the people?"

"I can try. I don't know the range of the ability, but we can give it a go."

I beckon to Sawyer and explain what we're going to attempt.

"I don't think I can do that," he says.

"I'm not sure I can either, but we have to try, right?"

His face tenses, but he nods. Together, we step onto the broken bridge. Bracing against a whipping wind, we walk a hundred yards before the ground wobbles under our feet. The wind gusts through the valley like a steam train, blowing my hair into the sky and causing stinging whips to lash my face. My clothing flaps wildly. One glance at Sawyer confirms he's struggling to control his balance too. If the bridge collapses, I can sprout wings and fly away, unharmed. But Sawyer doesn't have wings.

I set the box of noodles at my feet. "Ready?"

He nods, his blonde curls flopping against his forehead.

Feeling our combined power is stronger with contact, I take his hand, but don't risk taking off my glove. Together, we lift the box into the air with our minds. We raise it a small distance above our heads and push it forward, with the wind, across the bridge. Buffeted by the elements, the box reaches the broken section quickly. Sawyer frowns and tightens his grip on my hand. With sweat pooling in the small of my back, we nudge it further. The box hovers halfway across the gap, then further. It bobs jaggedly toward the other side as though it's a small inflatable boat riding the waves of a turbulent storm. The strain pulls at my muscles.

"You can do it, Silver! Sawyer!" Erica's shout reaches me.

Tension tugs at the edges of my mental leash. *Come on. Just a little further.* The box falters, dropping a couple feet, then regains its altitude. There is a moment of release, as though a heavy backpack has been lifted from my shoulders, when I realize the box is out of reach and no longer within my control. The momentum of the box carries it on a few more feet, but I can no longer reach it. It's like trying to hold on to someone's hand with fingers coated in Vaseline. My grip keeps slipping, grabbing, slipping, until the box is completely beyond my mental control. It plummets to the river below. It almost made it. Only another ten yards and it would have been across.

Sawyer lets go of my hand. "This isn't going to work."

"What are we going to do?" I whisper.

He looks at me, but says nothing.

Sawyer and I retreat from the wind and the bridge, our sense of failure a hard rock in the stomach. How will we get across the bridge?

Walking toward the group, their concerned expressions add another layer of guilt to my insides. There isn't another crossing for a hundred miles in a either direction. Through littered highways and infected animals. We don't have that kind of time. Not if we want to use surprise to our advantage.

I lift my face to the darkening sky, gazing at the approaching stars, appreciating their twinkling beauty despite having no answers for the group. If we're going to try anything else we'll have to do it now, or camp out here for the night, in the open, vulnerable to whatever might be out there and the wolves that suddenly don't seem so far away.

"Okay, plan B," Hal says as I meet him on solid earth.

"There's a plan B?" I ask, feeling a small measure of relief.

He eyes our pile of belongings. "I'm thinking we can zip line across. We've got a rope that's just about long enough. I've got a pulley with a handlebar. But I don't have any safety harnesses. They were in the supply truck."

"No safety harnesses?" I question.

"What choice do we have? We don't have time to go around." Matt taps my arm. "It'll be just like those outdoor camps we used to go to in the summer."

I smile, remembering when we were eight and Matt fell out of a tree, breaking his wrist. But this time, if someone falls, it will be a hell of a lot worse than a broken bone.

I grit my teeth. "This is a nightmare."

Matt walks to the cliff edge, glances at the bridge, down at the river, then at the other side. He trots back to us. "We can fashion a seat out of a couple of belts, attach it to the pulley and then we would have our hands free to pull ourselves along the rope."

"Silver, can you fly with the rope and tie it off on the other side of the bridge?" Hal asks. "I can set the rest up from here. Then I want you to keep your wings, if anyone starts to fall...you can grab them."

I can grab them? That's plan B?

"Is there no other way?" I try to take a deep breath, but it gets stuck midway in my chest somewhere, causing an uncomfortable tightness. The distance from the bridge to the frothing, foaming river below is at least two hundred feet. A fall will mean certain death.

"I can't think of another way across," Hal replies, his eyes searching mine. "If we try to find another crossing it could take us weeks. There are too many abandoned vehicles. And if we did find another bridge, it might be broken too. We would have wasted weeks to be in the same situation."

"But what if I can't—"

"Silver." Hal puts a hand on my shoulder. "I've been on a mission with you before. I wouldn't ask you if I didn't think you could do it."

I gulp. But his words help. They are the mental slap I need.

Matt jerks a thumb at Hal. "What he said."

Hal is right. We can't drive up and down the country looking for an accessible crossing only to be met with the same fate. Not that it matters, but I still can't figure out why the bridge was broken in the first place. The virus spread so fast there wasn't time to attempt isolation or quarantine. There was only time to run. Which leads me to my second hypothesis. Earl must be responsible. Which is even more nuts. Because he would only tamper with the crossing to stop an advance. To prevent a mission team from taking him out. Which implies he knows we're coming. And not only that we're coming, but which route we've taken. Which is impossible. Isn't it? Genetics can't predict the future. It can't make a crystal ball.

"What about Paige and Erica?" Matt asks. "They can fly too."

I shake my head. "Erica's wings are too delicate, and neither of them can use bulk strength if something goes wrong. It has to be me."

I push thoughts of my friends falling out of my mind and focus on the task at hand. I struggle to find the confidence I felt on the last mission. The bravery, the boldened daring, is strangely elusive. I still have confidence in me, my powers, my abilities. The normal ones, anyway, not the black power. That is the crux of it. I don't know how to control the black lightning. I hurt Lyla. I might do worse. The whole situation scares me.

Hal gestures for the group to huddle close to him. Against the bursts of deafening wind, he explains his plan. Most accept the idea in mute silence.

"I'll go first." William's beady eyes dart in all directions, not quite resting on any one member of the group. His red hair catches the last of the dying sun. "I'm one of the heaviest. I can make sure it's safe for everyone else."

No one counters his request and his gaze shifts in the direction of the bridge.

A few rogue rays of sunlight creep over the distant mountain peaks and illuminate the swaying bridge. Hal ties off the rope on our end of the bridge, then attaches the pulley mechanism and the seat made from a belt with an additional coil of rope. Handing me the other end, Hal instructs me how to tie off on the other side of the bridge.

I wrap the rope around my wrist a few times. Taking a breath, my spine ripples and parts and I sprout my blue wings. Lifted by powerful new muscles, a flicker of elusive confidence blooms in my chest. *I can do this.*

"Only essentials." Matt drops to his knees and rifles through his backpack while Einstein sits at his side. "Take anything you don't need out of your backpacks."

"Sawyer." I take him aside. "I need you on the bridge too, just in case."

He grimaces but makes his way across the bridge and anchors himself on a handrail.

I carry my backpack, now only containing medical supplies, nanite pills, a lightweight sleeping bag and a few rations of food. Leaping into the air, I flap my wings. The wind tunnels under my feathers and pushes me into the air. I rise five feet, ten feet, twenty feet. Hovering, feeling the strength and power in my wings, I adjust to the feel of my extra limbs.

I cycle my legs a few times, adapting to the thermals and then take off across the bridge. Once I rise above the valley and draw level with the bridge, a blast of wind blows me twenty feet to the left, down river. I hold tight to the rope as it goes taut, anchoring myself in the air. Battling with the more vicious wind levels, I inch my way across the valley. I offer a confident smile to Sawyer and William as I pass, but it probably comes out more as a panicked grimace.

Reaching the other side of the bridge without incident, I dump my backpack on the ground. With my wings fluttering over my head, I remove my gloves and tie off as Hal instructed. Putting my gloves back on, I wave to indicate the zip line is ready. As William clambers into the make-shift seat, I fly back across the bridge to assist him.

His gaze shifts, never resting on any one thing for too long. His red hair gleams in the twilight and his hands twitch on the makeshift harness, double and triple checking it's secure. Every few seconds, his gaze darts to the raging water below. The noise of the thunderous rapids makes conversation difficult. Carter, his twin brother, hovers at the edge of the bridge, calling out encouragement.

"Don't look down," I shout, as I flap alongside him.

William shakes hands with his brother, then sets his gaze on the horizon and begins to pull himself across the rope, hand after hand, painstakingly slowly. The wind turns the harness into a swing, causing him to stop repeatedly with squeezed-shut eyes and a white-knuckle grip on the rope.

"Take a deep breath." The wind buffets my wings. Spray from the water dampens my feathers. Using abilities always saps my energy, but fighting the elements takes all my strength. Already exhausted, I worry how long I'll be able to maintain my position.

William gains speed and reaches the middle section of the bridge. We pass Sawyer and he offers a small wave. William lifts his face and grins at me, but that small action unbalances him. His hand misses the rope. Reaching forward, he grasps nothing but air. He tips forward, the motion propelling him out of the harness. His body slides from the seat. As I fly toward him, against the wind, his hands scrabble for the harness.

But it's too far away. He slips out of the harness but manages to clutch its seat. He hangs there from one hand, two hundred feet above the raging water.

His fingers slip.

Struggling against the wind, I glance at Sawyer. He shrugs helplessly, his telekinetic ability out of range. I focus on my own telekinetic ability, but struggle to fly close enough to use it.

William's fingers slip another notch and he screams. Now he holds on with only the tips. I shift his weight with my mind, trying to help him gain a better handhold. The wind knocks me back, out of range. I drop the telekinesis and flap my wings furiously to draw level with William again. He shifts into his bulk form, perhaps thinking the added strength will help him clamber back into the harness. His skin ripples as his armor takes over, and his arms and legs stretch, lengthening as the muscles become large and defined.

Now, he is heavier. His eyes widen.

Paige appears beside me, her green wings tangled in the wind's currents.

William's fingers slip. Yanking off my gloves, I reach out with a bulk arm as Paige attempts to get closer. His terror-filled gaze locks on mine.

"No!" I shout into the wind.

I grab his hand, but the weight pulls me down too. With the wind pounding on my wings, I can't hold us together in the air. Paige is still too far away. Her panicked wings refuse to beat to her will. William's fingers slip down my arm, past my hand. Hanging from my fingertips, he glances below. My hand tingles and the black lightning flickers over my fingers. It shoots out, into William's hand, making him flinch.

He lets go and plunges toward the river. Bringing my wings close to my body, I tunnel after him hoping I can somehow help him land safely if I reach the ground first. Black lighting shoots all around me, taking chunks out of the rocks as I descend.

William is a bulk. He falls fast. The wind holds me in the air. I arrive in time to hear the loud thud and the crack of bones as he lands brutally on the rocks abutting the river. Although his bulk skin cannot be cut, cannot be penetrated by knife or bullet or rock, I can only imagine what a mess his bones and organs are inside. There is nothing to protect a bulk from an impact like that.

William's eyes cloud over. The river tugs at his boots,

pulling them closer until he's dragged into the water and washed away by the rapids.

My hands tremble. The lightning bolts remain, jumping from one finger to the next. Tears stream down my face. I killed William.

I sit on a rock, watching his body disappear, watching his head sink under the water forever. Paige lands as he drifts downstream. The lightning fades. She sits next to me on the rock and holds my bare hand.

"It's not your fault," she says. She's trying to be kind.

"Of course it's my fault. He let go because my dark power hurt him."

She sandwiches my hand with both of hers. "He would have fallen anyway. He was already slipping."

I look at my friend. Sympathy whirls in her emerald eyes. "I know you're trying to make me feel better. But it *is* my fault. I could have held on it if it wasn't for..." I shake my head. "I'm going to be the death of everyone."

"Silver," Paige says. "I can't deny I'm terrified of what we're going to find in the mountains. My parents could be there. We might all die. The baby inside me is doing...weird things. I don't know what he's going to be like. Will I survive the pregnancy? Will the baby? There are so many questions. So much fear. But I know you. You tried your best. You always do. This isn't your fault." She kisses my cheek. "I wouldn't say that if I didn't believe it."

I lean against a green wing. "Thanks, Paige. I needed that."

I sit for a few minutes, my heart rallying against the injustice of his death. I squeeze Paige's hand and compose the words I'll say to the rest of the group. Shoving the guilt of William's death away, I vow to protect the others. I won't let anything happen to them, and the dark lightning is just going to have to get used to that idea.

"There was nothing we could do," Paige says, her wings covering mine.

"I am so damn angry." The anger dwarfs my sense of failure, making my vision blur.

"Hold on to that." Paige stands. "We'll need it."

We fly back to the group and greet the line of grim expressions. Breaths plume in wispy clouds and Sean's cigarette glows like a star come down to earth. Carter turns his back and hangs his head. Lyla backs away into the night. Luis pukes in the snow.

I glance at Matt. The message in his eyes is clear. We still need to make the crossing. We have nowhere else to go.

CHAPTER NINE

I LAND on one knee and fold my useless wings into my back. Carter walks a way into the darkness while Erica throws an arm around Lyla as tears run down her face. Sawyer and Jacob stand with arms dangling at their sides. Kyle, for once, is still, his courage yanked out of him faster than a rollercoaster can plummet to earth. Matt and Hal dip their heads in a quiet conversation. The rest of the bulks group together, mute.

Hal is the first to address the situation. "Silver, Paige, it's not your fault. It could have happened to any of us."

"You did everything you could." Sean fiddles with his Stetson and then pulls it low on his forehead.

My friends look at me with expectant faces, but I have no comforting words to make the loss more bearable. Despite what Paige says, my black power is partly responsible. If I dwell on that, it might undo me, so I push the guilt away. Matt steps forward and enfolds me in his arms. Everything drains out of me in that moment and I'm left freezing and exhausted. He shelters me from the still brutal wind and I wish he could shield me from my own sense of failure.

"We'll camp on this side tonight," Hal says to the group. "It's dark now and the wind is stronger. We'll try again in the morning."

A respite. Brief. But needed. The morning will bring light but won't change our situation.

Leaving the rope and harness dangling, we board the jeeps and drive a couple miles around the corner of the mountain, out of the wind tunnel. We park in the forecourt of a deserted gas station. Luis and Mason go inside and return with armfuls of candy bars and hot chocolates.

We sit in the jeeps sipping the hot liquid, warming ourselves against the frigid night. Our breath plumes and rises in the cloudless sky. Removing my gloves, I blow on my stiffened fingers and wriggle them to bring some feeling back. I'm not worried about the black power right now. It's already performed its worse. Quietly, we wrap ourselves in sleeping bags and hunker down for the night.

The wind whips around the corner of the mountain, ghostly and loud, reflecting the discordance I feel inside. Leaves rattle in the nearby trees as they stand in battle with the elements. If I strain my ears, I can hear the howl of the wolves on the mountain. I shudder and finger the hilt of my knife.

In the back seat, Erica slumps against Sean's shoulder. Lyla props herself against the door, a sweatshirt rolled under her head.

As the rest of the group sleep, I sit through the night stroking Einstein's head and whisper to Matt.

"Did anything happen?" he asks, looking at my hands.

I shake my head. There's no point revealing the whole truth. William is dead. Admitting my black power played a part won't get us anywhere. Plus, I'm not ready to talk about it. I can't say, out loud, what my power actually did. Matt would look at me differently, maybe even treat me differently. I can't deal with that.

Matt drifts off to sleep, but I can't close my eyes. I see William's face. Which then melds with Joe's. His loss is still raw. My fingertips ache from where William held on. My mind flinches from the startled look in his eyes when he slipped away.

While Matt sleeps, a panic attack rolls through me.

"Here it comes," I mutter. It was only a question of time.

Adrenaline courses through my veins and bile rises to my mouth. I squeeze my eyes tight and clutch my gloved hands together, desperate to feel something solid and real. The only way to get through a panic attack is to breathe through it. Dad taught me that. I wish he was here.

My fingers tremble and my vision blurs.

Breathe, breathe, breathe.

Slower.

Breathe...breathe...breathe.

I can pretend everything is okay. Everything *is* okay. We're just sitting in a jeep in the dark, not being attacked by lions or anything. It's just a stupid anxiety disorder. Superstitious thinking. Foreboding thoughts. I have the complete package. I ought to take the damn nanite pill for it. But I can't justify it. I see the benefit of some of the alterations, and I've learned to love my wings, but every time I contemplate something new, I see Diana's face. It's enough to harden my resolve. She was my best friend, and she died, because her parents forced too many nanites on her.

Taking deep breaths to dispel the nausea and dizziness, I refuse to let the fear overwhelm me. I can't afford to fall apart right now. I have to stay strong. Please let me be strong. *Please.*

Restless, I climb out of the jeep. I walk around the corner of the gas station along the deserted road and into the barren scrub land. Breathing. Sometimes I think I won't be able to. The pressure in my chest gets so tight that it's hard to suck in a mouthful of air. But I force it in, trying to focus on something else. The stars, the cold, the feel of my fleece gloves. Anything tangible to distract my mind from my racing heart and the feeling that my body is fatally malfunctioning.

Taking off my gloves, I dig for the acorns in my pocket and circle them in my fingers. Smooth, hard, real. Eventually, my legs stop trembling. I raise my face to the sky and gaze at the twinkling stars. So full of hope and possibility.

My mother is under this same sky. Can she see the same stars as me?

Shivering, I head to the service station. I push open the door and blink against a strobing fluorescent light. Carter sits at the service desk, a box of pencils in front of him, systematically breaking each one with two bulk fingers.

"Couldn't sleep?" I ask.

He doesn't look up. "Nope. You?"

"No." I grab a pack of M&M's and haul myself up to the counter.

Snap.

"William?" He asks.

Snap.

"That. And other stuff." I don't have the energy to go into the details of my anxiety. Although most of the mission team know I suffer from it, it's not something I like to admit to. "You?"

"William." Carter pauses to throw a can of soda through a glass container. The glass cracks, shatters and cascades to the floor. "Our whole lives we've never spent a day apart. We were in the compounds together, during the resistance."

Snap.

I rip open the pack of M&M's. "I didn't know that. What did they do to you there?"

Carter pushes himself away from the counter on a wheelie chair and faces me. "We were experimented on. Blood was taken. Things were injected. We were tortured, abused, starved. But we had each other's backs." He pulls at his jaw as if the pain of the memory is stored there and he can simply rub it away.

"I'm sorry." I want to touch him. But I don't know him all that well.

Carter waves a hand dismissively. "We got through it." He laces his fingers behind his neck. "Did you know William played the violin?"

I shake my head.

"Beautifully." His eyes mist and he uses a thumb and forefinger to pinch the bridge of his nose. "He played every night."

I think of my guitar and how the music evokes such primal feelings in me. Comforting words are inadequate, so I stay quiet.

He picks up two of the broken pencil ends. "We both decided to enlist in Francesca's army to stop any more of Bear's bigoted ideas. We looked out for each other. Now he's gone—" His voice breaks and the pencils fall to the counter and roll off the edge. "I didn't look out for him. I couldn't help him." Carter drops his face into his hands and weeps like I've never seen a grown man weep.

The guilt rolls over me as great heaving sobs escape his body. His torso shudders under the strain of sorrow. I wrap my arms around him, shushing him like a baby; it's the only thing I can think to do.

When Carter pulls himself together and wipes his tears away with the hem of his shirt, he looks up at me with a weak smile. "I'm sorry."

"Don't apologize," I say.

One pencil remains unbroken. Carter twiddles it around his finger. "We weren't just brothers, twins. We were best friends. Soul mates. How do you fill the hole that leaves behind?" His gaze drops to the broken pencils strewn across the counter. He brushes a hand over his closely-shaven hair.

"You don't," I say, thinking of Joe.

"I don't know what I'm going to do without him." Carter meets my eyes. "He was the one who knew how to laugh at life, how to not take things too seriously. I needed that."

I give him a heavy nod. "You'll find it again. You have it in you. You're stronger than you think."

A weak smile wobbles on his lips. "I wish I had your confidence."

I smile back. "I'm only confident about other people." I hesitate. He has a right to know how his brother really died. I tell him about my black power. I ought to tell everyone, otherwise I'm putting them all at risk. I tell him how out of control I feel, how the lightning played a part in his brother's death.

He stares at me. I can almost hear his brain processing what I've told him. Did I reveal too much? Should I have kept it buttoned down? Will he ever forgive me?

"You tried to save him," Carter says finally. He's far too forgiving. "You would never hurt anyone on purpose. You're Silver Melody."

His words touch a nerve, in a good way, and some of the

burden of William's death lifts, but much of it remains. William may not be the only victim of my power if I don't learn to control it.

"You may not feel it now, but you have every right to hate me. I would, if I were you." I check my own tears. This isn't the place for them. "I just want you to know that's okay. If you need to hate me. It's okay."

"I could never hate you," Carter says. "Seriously. You've done more good for this world than anyone I know. You're the bravest person I've ever met."

I laugh at the absurdity of his comment, but his serious look tells me he believes it.

"If you want to blame anyone," Carter says, "blame Earl."

"That I can do."

Carter offers me the last pencil. I snap it in half with a bulk hand.

"Carter?"

He looks up.

"We're still a team, Carter. Everyone here. We all look out for each other. You still have us." I mean every word of it.

Carter nods. "And, Silver?"

It's my turn to wait for words of wisdom.

"No one is perfect. No one expects you to be perfect either. So maybe go a little easier on yourself."

My lips twist. "Any idea on how to do that?"

He splays his hand. "Just keep being you."

I nod. *Keep being you.* I don't know what to do with that.

I jump off the counter. "You going to be okay?"

"Who knows?" He picks up a broken pencil. "I'm just going to sit here for a while."

"Okay." I pour myself another hot chocolate. "Goodnight, Carter."

"Night."

Returning to the jeep, I snuggle next to a sleeping Matt. I hold onto him as tightly as I dare without waking him. Einstein warms my feet and whimpers in his sleep. The conversation with Carter has compounded my exhaustion. Sleep tugs at my eyelids and I give in to the numbing wave, to the escape, and to the dream world where reality can't reach me.

XXXXXX

I WAKE JUST BEFORE DAWN. But I'm not the first. Erica, Paige, Lyla, Carter, Mason and Luis all follow Jacob in his morning Tai Chi ritual. He's started quite a following. Perhaps they're looking for some internal stillness after the emotion of William's death. Anything that can prepare them for the physical obstacles we'll face crossing the bridge.

As I roll out the kinks in my neck, an idea flutters. I use my super speed to run the two miles back to the broken bridge. The wind's stinging tendrils and freight-train screams has abated and leaves a silence in its wake that's almost deafening in itself. The supplies we emptied out of our backpacks sit in a loose pile by the bridge. There's no reason I can't carry them across. But today I won't use my wings.

Grabbing a box of ammunition, I adjust to its weight in my arms. I walk onto the bridge, but I don't unfurl my wings. A flea is capable of jumping more than fifty times its own body height. It's an ability I acquired in the cave and only used once before. I cradle the box in my arms and start to run. As I near the broken section, the bridge wobbles under my feet. I plant my feet on the bridge and push off, soaring into the sky. A gentle breeze plucks at my hair, nothing compared to the whipping I experienced yesterday. My stomach flip-flops as I descend.

I land. On solid ground. On the other side of the bridge. Grinning, I almost drop the box of ammo. I plan to jump most of our supplies across, and everyone's backpacks. Conscious of draining my abilities too much, I move as fast as I can and spend a half hour on my task. When the group appears around the corner of the mountain, I've made a pile of backpacks, ammunition and food rations on the far side of the bridge.

My success in transferring our supplies gives the group the morale boost they need. They throw smiles and thumbs up across the bridge.

"I don't suppose you could jump or fly us all across?" Hal asks.

I shake my head. "I don't think I could get you all across

before my abilities are sapped." If I fatigue halfway across, the results would be catastrophic.

"Okay, listen up." Hal addresses the group. "William's loss yesterday was a tragedy. It's devastating that we've lost a member of our team, especially to an accident like that. But the fact remains we still have to cross the bridge."

The group hang on Hal's every word, trusting him, believing in him to do the right thing, to say the right thing. Just like Joe did before. As Hal talks, I stare at the brightening horizon, breathing deep to ease the stab of grief in my chest.

"The wind is gone." Hal points at the sky. "That was a huge obstacle for us yesterday. Now, it's just like a playground zip line. I'm sure you all remember those."

There are a few chuckles from the group.

"Let's get to it." Hal holds up a motivating fist. "Don't look down. Pull hand after hand."

Matt steps away from the group. "I'll go first." He stares at me and I force myself to meet his gaze. Matt. *My* Matt.

Ignoring the rise in my heartrate, I retrieve the pulley and make-shift seat from the middle of the bridge where it hangs limply. Matt climbs into the seat. I unfurl my wings. I'm not sure they'll help, but it gives me the sense that I'm doing something. If someone slips, I might have just enough power left to add in some bulk strength and retrieve them from their fall. With the lack of wind, it's easier for me to maintain a position next to the person in the pulley.

Matt swings out over the river. One hand in front of the

other, again, and again. He doesn't look down, not once. Instead his gaze remains fixed on the rope, ensuring every handhold is secure. After only five minutes I help him onto the far side of the bridge and tell myself to breathe. He grins and embraces me. His fear is only betrayed when his knees buckle as he takes his first steps on solid ground again.

Next comes Luis, the smallest of the bulks. The rope sags as he approaches the middle section. Hesitating, he looks down briefly, and manages to retain the contents of his stomach. The water roars below and the air carries the scent of desert dust and dampness. He shudders, then readjusts his gaze to the task at hand.

When it's Lyla's turn, I expect her to be a whimpering mess, but she climbs into the harness with a gutsy determination.

"I'm not sure I want your help, Silver." She looks at my hands.

I keep my distance, but make sure I'm close enough to help her if it's needed. She whips her ponytail over her shoulder and sets her gaze on her brother. She crosses the fastest.

Then Paige. She flies across. Jacob, Mason, and Sawyer. Before Sawyer attaches himself to the harness, he spends a minute throwing up over the edge. I hold my breath as he passes, worried he'll pass out and fall. I encourage him along and he makes it to the other side.

Then Carter. He gives me a brief nod as he climbs into the harness. He's pulled himself together.

Sean, with his Stetson firmly on his head, goes next and Erica flutters across on her butterfly wings beside him. Her wings cycle through hues of red and purple, colors I know she reserves for special people, special emotions. Has his tactless charm finally won her over?

Kyle wastes no time and crosses in a blur of speed. When he gets to the other side he runs circles around the group, leaping into the air and whooping with triumph. He nabs Sean's Stetson and puts it on his own head. Sean tries to chase him, but Kyle is too fast for him.

Amidst the jostling, Hal, the last member of the group to cross, arrives safely on the other side.

We are high-fiving and congratulating each other when I hear the 'woof.' I turn back to face the bridge. We've forgotten Einstein. After folding my wings away, I leap back over the bridge. I ruffle the fur on his flank and look into his soulful brown eyes. Einstein isn't capable of pulling himself across a zip line.

"How are we going to get you across?" I ask him. After moving all the supplies and using my wings for the better part of the morning, I'm not sure I have the energy left to get him across. But I can't leave him here.

"Woof."

He'll be the heaviest load I've attempted, but there is no other way. If I use some bulk strength with my flea ability, I know I can get him across. But using two abilities at the same time will drain me faster.

I tell him what I'm going to do, and we walk together to the end of the broken bridge. Pushing some bulk strength into my limbs, I gather the dog in my arms. He's heavy, at least seventy pounds. He adjusts his weight in my arms, then licks my ear.

Urgent shouting barrels across the bridge. Hal waves. Matt raises an arm in the air, palm out, in the universal gesture of 'stop.' I don't have time for arguments, I can already feel my power draining.

Ignoring them both, I run with Einstein and leap into the air. For a moment, a tiny split second, my body hangs in the air, not rising, not falling, and I think it might all be over. Just like that. But then I cycle my legs and take off over the bridge. I land heavily on my feet and fall to my knees, tearing a hole in my combat trousers. Einstein chuffs and jumps out of my arms, then turns back to nuzzle his face into my body.

The bulk strength leaches out of my arms and I know I won't be able to use an ability for the rest of the day.

"Hey, buddy." Matt ruffles Einstein's fur. "Glad you made it." Without glancing at me, or offering me a hand up, he turns on a heel and walks away.

After briefly examining the cut on my knee, I push myself to my feet. "That's it?" I call after him.

Matt swivels back and looks me up and down. "What do you expect me to say?"

"*Thank you*," I yell. "*Or here, have some water*. Maybe some sign of appreciation? Is that so much to ask?" Joe would have understood. Hell, Joe would have helped. I squeeze the unkind thought from my mind.

"What you did was really dangerous," Matt hisses. He hates public arguments and his eyes turn cold. "I know you were tiring. You took a huge risk." He lowers his voice. "And what if your black power came out? You're not even wearing your gloves."

I frown. "We couldn't leave him behind."

The group start packing up the supplies I carried over while Einstein winds between them looking for pats.

Matt's face tightens. "He's a dog. He's *my* dog. And yes, leaving him behind would be shitty. But your dad increased his intelligence. He'd wait for us. He would have been fine."

I march toward him and poke a finger into his chest. "Matt, he's so much more than that. He knew the black dog was infected and if you'd paid any attention to him on the mountain you would have realized he was trying to warn you I was in trouble, in the drug store, with the wolves."

Matt has the decency to look embarrassed.

"He's an asset to this team. One that I have a feeling we'll need again." I cross my arms over my chest. "Something's coming. Something bad. And we need every advantage we've got."

"We know what's coming, Silver." Matt's legs are planted wide and his nostrils flare. "Earl."

I shake my head. "Something more than that."

He looks at my hands and I narrow my eyes at him.

"That's not fair," I say.

The fight leaches out of his voice. "Are the gloves even helping?"

"Yes," I reply. "I don't know. I think so."

"I'm not sure if that's good enough. How do we stop it coming out at the wrong time?"

I haven't even told him about William. "You've changed your tune. What happened to all your faith in me?"

Matt has never doubted me. He is the one person who always has my back. I don't know what to make of his uncertainty.

He sighs and his blue eyes light up. "I still have faith in you. But I'm scared."

"You're never scared."

"Of course I am. I just don't talk about it." He steps close and tentatively wraps his hands around mine.

"Will you help me?" I ask. "Will you help me figure this damn power out?"

"I will."

CHAPTER TEN

OUR FIRST PRIORITY after crossing the bridge is to find suitable vehicles to transport us all. Paige remains quiet and sickly despite the medication and our pace slows. Carter carries her backpack.

"I'll stay behind," she says to me for the fiftieth time. "I don't want to jeopardize the mission."

"I don't want to hear that kind of talk." I grab her hand and squeeze. "Not only do we need you, but I'm not leaving you out here alone. Pregnant and unwell. Nope. Not going to happen."

We walk along the roadside, checking car doors, looking for keys, following it into Utah.

Matt jimmies open the door of a Range Rover. The alarm blares instantly. He dives in the front seat, pulls the wires out from under the dash and disconnects the alarm.

"Ugh." He comes away from the car covered in green goo. "Let's not take that one."

I peer into the driver's seat. The bulk of the green, luminescent goo covers the driver's seat and floor. The back contains two child seats. My heart lurches as I notice the two smaller puddles of green goo. If only my healing powers extended to beyond the grave.

I sigh. "Next one."

Every possible car or jeep we find has the same puddles of luminescent goo in the driver's seat. No one wants to sit in the tacky remains to drive a vehicle.

"We'll try five more. If we don't find something suitable we'll abandon the search and continue on foot," Hal says.

Each abandoned vehicle is the same. Feeling desperate, we attempt to clean the green puddles, but they are sticky and resistant. It clings to whatever material it comes into contact with, as if in a last desperate attempt to hold onto the world, wanting the universe to remember these puddles were once people. Talking, breathing, laughing people that need to be mourned and remembered. Just the thought is enough to drive most of us back to our feet with a new vigor.

The crisp winter air helps bring color back to Paige's cheeks, but she needs to rest frequently to keep the dizzy spells at bay. It's cold standing still and the rest of the group grow increasingly restless during each pit stop.

Finally, Luis turns bulk and plucks Paige off her feet as she walks. He places her on his shoulders and tells her to hold on. After that we pick up speed. Mostly we march in silence, aware our destination is becoming closer with every passing hour. Einstein bounds by my side, woofing gently when he wants to communicate.

After three days on foot our food supplies run out. We haven't seen a service station for miles. At night we build a fire and boil water for tea and coffee. It's all we have left.

"Woof." Einstein pulls at my hand and leads me to my backpack, sniffing.

"I know, I'm hungry too." I pat his head.

He slumps down beside me, lays his head in my lap and whines.

"Quiet," Matt says, raising a stern finger.

Einstein moves his head to his paws and goes to sleep.

We break camp in the morning, hoping today will be the day we find food again. A gas station, supermarket, something, anything so we can replenish our stock. Water isn't a problem. Several streams and lakes crisscross our route and allow us to refill our canisters. When they disappear we melt the piles of snow heaped by the roadside.

Hour after hour we trudge onward, our stomachs grumbling, our conversation non-existent. The sun sits high in the cloudless sky, but its rays seem unable to penetrate the frozen earth. Einstein pads to my side, pulling at my hand. I spot a lone deer, a doe, only two hundred yards away. It stands outside the tree line, staring at us.

"Erica," I whisper. "Can you make it?"

Erica lifts her bow and nocks a single arrow. She closes

one eye. As she exhales, she releases the arrow. It sails through the air with barely a *whoosh*. The deer doesn't see it coming. One moment it's sniffing the air, looking for our scent. The next it's laying on its side, the arrow through its heart.

"Good shot!" Sean exclaims, twiddling his Stetson around. "I didn't quite believe the rumors."

Erica smirks. "You ain't seen nothing yet." She mimics his drawl, setting her violet eyes on him. But her wings shimmer a deep purple under his praise.

The group find a new energy as Sean sets off to retrieve the deer. Luis collects sticks for a fire and when they are gathered, Sawyer ignites the pile of kindling with his mind. Hal skins and fillets the deer while the rest of us salivate and wait. We sit around the fire, roasting venison on small sticks, filling our ravenous stomachs. It reminds me of when Joe trapped squirrel and roasted the meat for me. The further we travel, the more I think of him.

"I haven't seen a deer since we set off, back in New York, in the fields near Central City," Lyla says. "Do you think they're going to go extinct?"

Kyle tears into a chunk of meat. "We need to eat."

"To the extent that we might wipe out another species?" Lyla's head tilts questioningly.

"*We're* almost wiped out," Sawyer says around a mouthful. "And if we don't stop Earl, then who knows what will happen."

The flames leap higher and flush my face with heat. The

aroma of the cooking venison makes my mouth water, and I devour each chunk of meat, licking the juices from my fingers.

Lyla doesn't say anything else. She nibbles at the meat, not eating nearly enough to fill her stomach. Although I agree with Kyle and Sawyer that we need to eat, I hope we haven't killed the last of a dying species.

"I'm sure Francesca's making plans." Hal rests a kettle over the fire. "She's back in Central City right now trying to re-build the country, to reach out to the world."

"The world? What's happened to the rest of the world?" Sawyer asks.

Hal turns a tin mug in his hands. "The virus, it spread everywhere. People boarded planes and carried the virus around the planet."

"The whole world's wiped out? It's not just us?" Carter unzips his jacket and leans toward the fire.

"Afraid not. But there are survivors in other countries. That's what Francesca is working on, trying to contact everyone and bring them together. That, and developing a plan for our future." Hal removes more mugs from a backpack and spoons coffee granules into them.

"What future we have, if any," Kyle mutters.

"Let's try and stay positive," Matt says. But he's met with a stony silence, the campfire revelry suddenly extinguished.

"Positive, but serious," Hal says. "We're not just on a

mission to save our country. We're on a mission to save the world."

No one replies. Everyone stares at their feet or the crackling flames. Matt hands out more meat. We roast in silence.

"Damn!" Lyla loses her chunk to the fire. Kyle, using his speed, retrieves it for her, unharmed.

"Thanks." She reattaches the meat to her stick.

The silence continues until Sean burps and releases an ice-breaking giggle. Then the stories begin. Stories of our former lives, tales of the resistance. I'm made to recount my killing of a hellhound three times.

"We are the sun, we are the dawn,

We are the voice that urges you along.

Cast your eyes to the wreckage, the oppression, and the pain,

Lift your sights to the horizon—learn to live again," Hal sings loud and clear.

The words of my freedom song wind through the group.

Sean claps his hands, licks his fingers and takes up the chorus.

"When you hear the lone wolf howling,

When sky comes crashing through.

With all the hellhounds growling,

If it ends, just me and you... " He winks at me. Everyone joins in, but I remain silent, listening to my friends. It is a powerful anthem, one that's been adopted by many, but it reminds me of loss too.

"Just close your eyes and breathe in deep,
Look to the new sun's sky.
Because our voice is freedom,
And they will hear us cry."

Matt throws his arm around my shoulder. The whole group is singing now, eyes shining, smiles wide. My hands tremble as I listen. Shadows cast by the clouds move across my palm. My fingers tingle, but the black lightning doesn't appear.

A few of the bulks sing the song again, from the top, at a more subdued volume. It is our song. The song of the people. It belongs to all of us.

After we eat, Matt takes my hand and pulls me to my feet.

"I miss you," he whispers.

We haven't spent any time together alone. I didn't expect to. But it's still hard. Since we moved out of the cave and into the presidential compound, we spend most of our time together. Inseparable. Making up for all the lost time when I didn't realize how I felt about him. The events of the resistance and cure taught me to be honest, to say how I feel, to let it all hang out there, no matter the consequences. *Carpe diem* and all that. But ever since the virus, we've been running from one obstacle to the next. Perhaps now, even if only for an hour or two, we have the opportunity to slow down for a while.

"You too," I whisper back.

"I think it's time to test that power of yours." Matt leads

me into the field where the deer was shot and into the tree line beyond. Our heavy boots crunch over the frozen leaves and brittle twigs. In the trees, hidden away from the world, it feels warmer. Safer. But we're not alone. Lyla has trailed us from the fire.

"Silver, I want to talk to you." She looks at Matt for approval. He nods.

I sigh. "You've done nothing but give me a hard time. What do you want?"

"Give her a chance," Matt says.

Lyla sucks in her lips. "I was coming to say sorry, but if you're going to be like that." She turns on her heel.

I sigh again. "I'm sorry. Stay."

She looks at me squarely. "I'm sorry for giving you a hard time."

Away from the sunlit road the forest is full of shadows. I take a step toward her. Stumbling, I grab for a branch to steady myself. But it's too late. I fall hard, landing on my right knee. The same knee I gashed jumping Einstein across the bridge. A sharp pain stabs through my knee and down my leg.

My wail shoots out through gritted teeth. Reaching for the ground, I sit and inspect the wound. A sharp rock to my right, covered in my blood, proves to be the culprit. The hole in my trousers widens and flaps open, letting in the icy air. Gently, I poke at a two-inch gash under my kneecap oozing blood.

"God dammit!"

Dark lightning streaks from my fingers. The electric bolts whizz through the forest, singeing Lyla's hair and burning a hole in Matt's coat. Whole branches fall from the canopy and we duck.

"For fuck's sake, Silver!" Lyla yells, with her hands over her head. "I'm starting to think you have it in for me!"

"It's not you," I yell. It's everything.

The tingling abates from my fingers and the black lightning disappears. Matt dusts Lyla off and pulls her to her feet. Most of her ponytail is missing.

"Go back to the camp, Lyla," Matt says. "I'll deal with this."

She throws her hands skyward. "My hair!"

Matt frowns. "Just go!"

Lyla pivots away from us and marches back the way she came.

"Are you okay?" Matt crouches beside me, taking my leg in his hands, and wipes the blood away.

I can't respond. A flood of emotion makes speaking impossible.

"Silver?"

"I almost killed you," I whisper. "I almost killed both of you."

"Your powers have always been connected to your emotions. What were you thinking about?"

"I'm so tired. I'm scared. I'm worried about my mom. If anything happens to her..." I look over my shoulder as I voice my biggest fear. "I'm worried about Paige. I'm worried what the destruction of the bridge really meant. And I'm positive that Earl has invented more trials for us to face and I can't prepare for what I don't know." Now it's all out there; the jumble of worries that has occupied my mind for the duration of our journey.

"We've been here before," he says, staring at my hands.

"I didn't have this stupid power before."

"So we have to control your emotions."

I laugh. Hysterically. The thought is absurd. Lightning flickers on my fingers again and Matt ducks out the way.

"Go back to the group, Matt, and let me try and figure this out."

He comes out from behind a bush and gets to his feet. "I want to be here for you."

I lock my gaze on his. "You can't. You can't help me with this."

"I love you."

"I know."

He sidesteps away and follows his sister's footsteps back to the group.

Ignoring my bleeding knee, I stand and survey the damage I've caused. Several silver birches bear scorch marks on their trunks. Countless branches line the path and forest floor. Large patches of snow are now ash. I need to get control over this.

Tentatively, I place my hand on the nearest tree. The trunk under my hand warms and starts to spark. Lightning flickers across my fingers and up and down the length of the trunk, scorching the bark. Feeling a growing heat under my fingers, I quickly remove my hand. The electrical sparks race back to my fingers, leaving the tree in peace.

I look at my hand. The lightning bolts dance, much like the flames of a fire, stretching and growing, warming the air around me. They don't travel anywhere, but jump from one fingertip to the next until all five are involved in an electrical light show. Fascinated, I stare at the black electricity. I've never seen anything like it. Sparks are normally white or blue or even orange. But these are completely black and little puffs of dark smoke rise into the air.

Something whispers in the back of my mind. A voice. But not my own. It belongs to the power. An external, intangible presence, something that probes the thoughts in my head.

The ordeal only lasts a few seconds. The probing fingers in my mind abate, the lightning on my hand diminishes, until there's nothing left but the pink, fleshy palm I was born with.

There is something about it that is just plain *wrong*. When I killed Bear with this power, I pulled his heart right out of his body and held it in my hand, the black electricity reducing it to a pile of ash. Something so powerful can't be good. I feel this power has intention, that it wants me to give in to its enticing sparks, to listen to its lures. It wants to be used. But I can't. It's too much, too powerful, too...*evil*. I'm finally able to admit that. There is evilness inside me. I am tainted.

It appears Earl and his monsters aren't the only obstacles we will face. Now, there is something bad inside of me too. More worryingly, there is a part of me that enjoys the feeling when the lightning escapes my hands. It thrills me, all that power. I stuff that thought down deep.

Matt waves from the campfire, indicating that we're leaving. Putting my gloves back on, I limp across the snow to join the group. I gained a measure of control over this dark power in being able to invoke it and push it away again, but I have a long way to go before I consider myself safe to be around.

When I stumble twice and fresh blood leaks from my knee, I pause to see if I can heal myself. Healing is one of the most difficult powers to master. Just like the dark power, it relies on emotions. The concentration it takes often leaves me with a headache. Conflicted, worried and full of self-doubt aren't quite the right emotions to focus on when I'm trying to heal myself. But I can never shake them off.

With the range of abilities I possess, I should be able to save anyone and everyone and the whole world while I'm at it. *The ultimate weapon.* But I can't. My abilities just aren't that good. I fatigue too quickly and every failure pulls me farther into a world of insecurity. Especially when I know whatever this blackness inside me is, will cause more pain. I'm supposed to heal people, not hurt them.

Taking a deep breath, I place my hand on my knee. I close my eyes and focus on all the good I've done; saving Lyla from the compound, killing Bear, rescuing my father.

These are things to be proud of. Events I played a huge part in, that may have not been possible without me.

When I remove my hand the gash across my knee has knitted itself together. There is a small scar in its place. Not perfect, but it will do, and I don't need to limp anymore.

CHAPTER ELEVEN

PUTTING MY GLOVES BACK ON, I return to the group. I fix a smile on my face as I approach.

Sean grins. "Silver, your hair's looking a little tousled, did you have a good time in the woods?"

Kyle giggles and socks Matt on the arm.

I arch an eyebrow at Sean. "Oh, please, as if I have time for that, and on frozen snowy ground for that matter."

"Didn't think you were quite so fussy." Sean tips his stupid cowboy hat at me. "Who said you need ground to do it anyway?"

Matt chuckles. I stomp over to my backpack, shoulder it, and march down the road with Hal and Carter, but not without making Sean stumble first. I trip him with my mind and he lands flat on his face.

"Idiot," I mutter under my breath as I draw alongside the bulks.

"Hey, play fair," Sean shouts after me. A small smile of satisfaction tugs at my lips.

Late in the afternoon, as the claws of darkness tackle the sun behind the mountains, we find a gas station. Food! Glorious food. My mouth salivates at the thought of the candy bars and cans of soda that will be stacked neatly on the shelves inside. I imagine cookies and pots of instant pasta, cakes and pastries, hopefully not gone too stale. We can camp inside the shelter of the store tonight, use the facilities to freshen up.

Einstein barks, pacing back and forth in a small area outside the gas station. He ate a share of the venison. But we didn't eat large portions. Hal thought it best to package it up and use it as rations in case we don't find more food.

I'm practically drooling when Hal and Matt rush inside, weapons prone. After a few minutes they emerge from the small store, heads low, disappointment written on their faces.

"It's empty," Matt says. "Looks as though someone beat us to it." Without warning, he drops his gun and raises his hands in the air.

The cock of an automatic weapon sounds behind me. Another click to my left, two more to my right. Surrounded. Einstein woofs again, he was trying to warn us, not point out the store. A group of ten men surround the small circle my team has formed.

Survivors.

One of the men calls out. "Lower your weapons."

Hal hesitates. One hand on his gun, the other held at chest level. These men might be survivors, but are they the *right* kind of survivors? Our mission is essential to the survival of the unadjusted human race. If we are to be taken hostage now...

Wind whips a snow flurry around our heads, howling gently as it tunnels down the road. On Luis' shoulders, Paige clutches her stomach. Matt keeps his hands high.

"Lower your weapons." The ten guns are aimed at our group. If a shootout ensues, not many will make it out alive. Not enough to complete the mission.

Sean flexes a bicep, as if readying for a fight. Einstein barks. Continuously. An arrow rests in Erica's hand. The wind pulls strands of lavender hair loose from her ponytail. Hal finally relinquishes his weapon to the snowy road and raises his hands. The rest of the team follow suit.

A woman emerges from behind the gas station. "Who are you and where are you going?" Long, dark hair flows over a thick sheepskin coat. Her face, wrinkled and weather beaten, is typical of the indigenous people who live in the area.

"We're just a bunch of survivors, on our way to California," Matt calls into the wind. His hand twitches near his holster.

The woman walks up to Matt. Slowly. Eyeing the group as she moves. "Why California?"

"We have family there, alive, waiting for us," Matt says.

Not that far from the truth. I think of my mom, held

hostage within Earl's domain. Although, strictly speaking, our mission isn't top secret, we don't want to volunteer any information about Earl until we know more about these people. Are they friend or foe? Could they have been sent by Earl?

The woman considers Matt's words for a moment. She cocks her head to one side, inspecting him. I hold my breath. The arrow in Erica's hand trembles. Out of the corner of my eye, I watch Sean's hand turn bulk. But it's just his hand. Not enough to arouse suspicion. Einstein circles up to Matt, sniffs at the woman, and sits down. Finally, she gestures to her men to lower their weapons. Hal sighs and Matt drops his hands.

"I guess you'll be needing a place to sleep tonight." The smile transforms the woman's face, revealing a cracked front tooth but a well of kindness in her eyes. She holds out her hand to Matt. "I'm Koko."

Matt takes the offered hand and begins making introductions, pointing at each member of the group as he says our names. When Luis nods at his introduction, Koko's eyes tighten and her lips compress into a thin line. Carrying Paige, he is still in his bulk form. As far as the world is concerned, altered abilities are no longer legal, or possible.

After a warning look from Hal, Luis plants Paige on her feet and returns to his human form. No one speaks. Everyone stares at Luis as the wind stabs at the wall of tension. Both Matt and Hal put their hands back on the butts of their guns. As do a couple of Koko's men, their weapons no longer pointed at the ground.

Matt breaks the silence, finishing the introductions. "And this is Silver."

Koko gasps as her eyes settle on me. "You're the one." She steps closer, but offers no explanation to her cryptic comment.

"Come, come. This way." With her smile back in place, Koko walks a few yards up the highway. We all stare after her, wondering if we have a choice in the matter. "Please."

Hal and Matt begin a procession and we take a turn to the left and follow a snow-covered lane into the trees. After a couple of miles, we arrive on the main street of a small village. People bustle back and forth, in and out of shops and houses, pushing wheelbarrows of goods, clearing snow drifts from the road. Some stand guard, brandishing weapons. Children run in the street, cheeks pink and buttoned up against the winter chill. People. Children. Alive.

I turn in a slow circle, trying to count heads, losing count as people mill in and out of buildings. "How...where...where did you all come from?"

"An emergency broadcast was sent out instructing people to convene here. More people arrive every day, but the rate of new arrivals is slowing. You're the biggest group of people we've seen in a long time," Koko replies.

"How many?" Hal asks.

"There are two hundred of us so far, all immune."

"Immune to the disease?" I ask.

Koko nods. "Everyone here has been bitten by an infected animal, but we all survived."

"We've travelled from Central City. We haven't seen a single soul, until now that we've have almost crossed the entire country." Matt tucks his hands in the pockets of his jacket.

"Damn," she mutters. "I was hoping you were bringing news of other groups. You're on the edge of Nevada now, and I doubt there are many survivors to the west. That's where the disease began."

A young boy bounds up to Koko and wraps his arms around her legs. Pale behind his chilled, pink cheeks, he wears the skinny frame of prepubescence and a trimmed, school-boy haircut. His blue eyes are startling, like Matt's, but there is a wariness pooling in them, as though he's seen too much, as though some trauma lives under the surface. Like all of us, really.

"This is Adam." Koko runs a gloved hand over the boy's head.

"He's so cute." Lyla says. We haven't seen children for weeks.

Koko slings an arm around his shoulders. "Adam's an orphan. Well, most of the children here are. But Adam is a bit different. He happened into the camp one day and no one knows where he came from."

Adam wriggles out of her grip and runs in circles around her, laughing, furtively glancing at each one of us.

Koko leans close and lowers her voice, her breath pluming between us. "We don't know what happened to him, but it was obviously traumatic. He doesn't talk much and he has nightmares, but he's a special boy. Like you, Silver." She smiles.

What on earth does that mean?

"Beware of the devil, Silver." Adam stands in front of me, his wary blue eyes holding my own, and then runs off to a group of children playing farther down the street.

I stare after him, wondering what he can do.

"What does that mean?" Paige says in my ear.

I splay my hands. "I have no idea. But I don't like it one bit."

Beware of the devil.

The strange warning echoes in my thoughts and becomes my companion for the duration of the day. Despite the benign appearance of this small group of survivors and their functioning town, the sense of foreboding I've been carrying intensifies. Does the boy know something or is he playing childish games?

A couple of residents bring us mugs of steaming coffee and tea while Koko shows us around the town. They've gathered produce and food from all the supermarkets within a fifty-mile radius, which explains the empty gas station. They siphoned off gasoline and stored grain from neighboring farmlands. The food and supplies are rationed, but there is plenty to go around, for the moment. I'm impressed by Koko's foresight. She has a plan for the future and intends to plant and harvest crops in the neighboring fields. She has sequestered the surviving livestock for milk, eggs, and meat. Koko is building a new world from the ashes of the old. Hopefully Francesca, back in Central City, is making the same plans.

After the tour of the village, Koko takes us to the town's one functioning diner, which serves dinner to the entire population each day. My mouth waters uncontrollably as the bowl of beef stew and the chunk of fresh bread is set down before me. The team eat in silence, wolfing down the meal.

Koko sits at a table with Matt, Hal, Paige, Jacob and me. Einstein woofs quietly at my feet. I throw him a piece of beef from the stew, even though he's already devoured his own doggie meal. Over the pleasing scent of the food, I catch whiffs of grease and coffee, both of them welcoming.

When Jacob gulps too big a mouthful of the stew, Paige wipes the gravy from his chin. He grins sheepishly, then carries on shoveling the food into his mouth.

Across the room a burst of raucous laughter erupts from the table where Erica, Sean, Lyla, Kyle and Sawyer sit. Kyle is the first to finish his meal and he manages to nab a second bowl, despite Sean protesting how much bigger he is than Kyle. Luis, Mason and Carter form another group in one of the red-leather upholstered booths, drinking mugs of chilled beer, baskets of French fries between them.

"Most of the houses and apartments have been taken over," Koko says. "But there is a guesthouse at the end of

Main Street that's empty. If you double up on rooms there should be enough space for you all."

The thought of a real bed and warm blankets almost makes my eyelids droop and my head fall to the table right then and there. But there is more I need to know.

"Tell me about the boy." I wipe the last of the stew from my bowl with a piece of bread. "Adam. Am I correct in assuming he has an ability?"

Koko rests her hands on the table. "Yes. He has the ability to see the future."

I blanch. "The future?"

Hal emits a low whistle and Matt's mouth falls open.

"That would have come in handy when I was facing competition in the dojo," Jacob says with a wink. "Knowing if I was going to win or not."

"We could use a power like that," Paige says thoughtfully.

I rub my temples. "I can't think of a worse power to have." I turn my attention to Koko. "He can see the future? Are you sure?"

No nanite exists for that. I've never heard of such a modification. I don't even think it's possible. It was difficult for my parents to identify the gene sequence that contained the power for telekinesis, but a psychic power? That's something else entirely. That goes well beyond genetics. Perhaps this seemingly supernatural power is the result of the union of altereds?

Koko takes a small tube of hand cream from her pocket

and rubs it over her cracked knuckles. "It's not always accurate. He can see the many possible pathways. The future changes depending on the choices each person makes, so he can only see possible futures, not definitive ones."

"That's not an ability you can modify," I say.

Matt pushes his finished bowl away. "Where did his ability come from?"

"No one knows. He strolled in here one day a couple of weeks ago, alone. He didn't speak for two days, and he still refuses to tell us where he comes from or how he acquired his ability. We knew he was special when he warned one of the other children about the well. It's in one of the back alleys behind Main Street, old, disused. It had been covered up with a rotten board and dirt. One of the children was walking on top of it when the board crumbled and she fell in. She managed to hold onto the edge until help could arrive. No one knew she was there. Across town, I was working in one of the fields. Adam came running to fetch me and he led me to the well and the trapped girl. The night before he'd warned me and the girl to 'beware of water,' but I'd dismissed the comment as part of his odd behavior."

"What do you think he meant when he told me to 'beware of the devil?'" I ask, feeling the hairs on the back of my neck rise.

Koko tenses, but doesn't avoid my eyes. She looks at each of us, unflinchingly, before returning her unyielding gaze to me. "I don't know, Silver, I was hoping you would tell me. You're the one with the special abilities." She emphasizes the last two words.

A woman collects our dishes. Before she carts them away, she lights a single candle in a red vase in the middle of the table. I cradle the vase in my hands, making the flame grow bigger and smaller.

"So, you know about me?" I return Koko's steely gaze with, I hope, a matched confidence.

"Of course. There isn't a survivor of the resistance that doesn't know who you are and what your part in it was, Silver. How special you really are." She pats my hand with maternal pride. The touch makes me ache for my parents. "When you hear the lone wolf howling, when sky comes crashing through." She speaks a couple lines of my freedom song. I didn't realize it had travelled this far west.

I guess living and working within the presidential compound lent an ignorance to the notoriety I gathered in the outside world. I feel a brief moment of pride, as though I'm a famous pop star adored by millions, before I'm reminded of the seriousness of our situation.

"What about the rest of us?" Hal laughs. He takes the vase out of my hands when the flame leaps a foot high. "We were there too."

"Of course, you too." Koko turns her warm smile to Hal. "The whole team is here." She lets those words hang in the air, perhaps waiting for an explanation. Then she lowers her voice. "I was hoping you were alive. That you hadn't succumbed to the disease."

"What do you know?" I ask.

"That it's still a threat." Koko presses her hands against the chipped tabletop. "I don't know much about the disease or where it came from, but I share a room with Adam, and what he utters in his sleep terrifies me."

Einstein woofs urgently as a woman approaches our table, cutting off the exchange of information. She is wrapped in the fluffiest and most expensive looking fur coat I've ever seen. I think it's real. Her long blonde hair tumbles from beneath a matching fur hat, and she walks toward us in heels that make my ankles ache.

"Ah. This is Carmen." Koko gestures to the new arrival. "Carmen arrived two weeks ago, she's been helping with the animals, our resident veterinarian. She's very good with them."

Carmen shrugs shyly and takes a sip from a flask. Einstein growls softly, shoulders hunched, hackles raised.

"Maybe not all animals," she laughs, as she takes my offered hand.

The pain is intense. A stabbing sensation in the center of my forehead, a burning on my palms. My vision turns red and blurry.

"Are you okay, Silver?" Paige asks.

Einstein continues to growl. Koko frowns. Matt shuffles closer to me.

Nodding, I gulp water from a glass. The pain recedes as suddenly as it arrived. As I drink, I look at Carmen out of the corner of my eye. She watches me and the group, waiting to see if I'm okay. The pain I just experienced is familiar and only occurs at a specific time. Carmen possesses an ability and I have now acquired it. I have no idea what it is, but I know she's been keeping it a secret.

Carmen flashes a look at Einstein. He whimpers and hides his tail between his legs. She fixes a smile on her face, but I catch the flash of anger in her eyes. There is something very wrong here.

"Well, it was nice to meet you all." Carmen steps away from our table, one hand held in a half wave, the other pocketing the flask.

Koko slides out from the table. "Let me show you to the guesthouse."

Matt pokes my hand. "You okay?"

I nod, then check my fingers. No lightning. "Yeah. Yeah, I'm okay."

Koko leaves us at the guesthouse with wishes of a good night's sleep. "And we have a doctor here too, Paige, he can give you a look over tomorrow." She winks as she departs.

Paige's hands fly to her belly, protective. Then I notice the bulge. She is showing, already. She can't be more a few weeks along. Even I know that's too early to be showing.

CHAPTER TWELVE

STANDING in a bedroom of the guest house, I become aware of the itchiness on my palms, as though I've had an outbreak of eczema. I bring my hands to my face. The black lightning jumps from my fingers onto my palm, spreading out in concentric circles, building in heat and intensity. Other, smaller sparks flicker between my nails. The whispering starts in the back of my mind.

Use it.

You know you want to.

There is so much power.

Einstein whines and backs into a corner of the room. I hold my hands away from my body, inspecting them. The lighting is black, sparking with a depth that's hard to clarify. It is restricted to my fingers and hands, but I know it wants to reach out and touch something, destroy something. The sparks mingle, growing bigger, tingling my skin. It's a vaguely pleasant feeling. I turn my hands over and watch as the tiny bolts scurry to the back of my hands. I make a fist, and feel the tingling inside my clamped hand, watch it dance across my skin. Without warning, it winks out, and all the sparks extinguish.

My hands shake. "What the hell is going on?"

Einstein whimpers and disappears into the bathroom. The itchy sensation subsides but I'm left feeling as though evil has touched me. Slowly, I catch my breath. I try to shrug off the tainted feeling, but it settles in the back of my neck like a burrowing tick.

Voices in a neighboring room draw my attention. Paige. The doctor's visit. Grabbing my gloves, I leave my room and push the door open to Paige's room.

"Everything looks good." The doctor, a tall, lanky man with salt-and-pepper hair, hangs a stethoscope around his neck. "The fetal heartbeat is strong and from all indications I'd say you are about sixteen weeks along." He smiles, picks up his medical bag and leaves the room.

Paige lays on the bed, her dark hair flowing over her shoulders, her hands cradling the small bulge of her stomach, her emerald eyes clear and determined.

Frowning, I step into the room and sit down beside my best friend. "Sixteen weeks?"

"Jacob and I have always been a bit different, so I guess it's not a surprise this baby is going to be different too." She strokes her stomach.

"But Paige, neither of you possessed any modifications

when this baby was conceived seven weeks ago, at the most."

Did I alter the fetus? Back in my lab in Central City, when I gave the team their abilities, did I somehow alter the baby's genetics when I modified Paige's?

"It's not your fault, Silver." Paige places a hand over mine, reading my thoughts. I quickly remove it from my friend's grasp, fearful the lightning will return. "I knew the moment this baby was conceived that it was going to be different. You know everything there is to know about science, genetics." Paige settles her emerald gaze on me. "But you know nothing about the miracle of life."

My father always spoke of a God-factor. There were elements, side-effects, to the genetic modifications he and my mother could never explain. They claimed it was as though the Hand of God had an influence in each modification and nanite pill issued. Maybe there is something left over in Paige and Jacob's DNA that remains unaffected by the cure, that is unseen by the human eye, unexamined in science, and has passed to this baby invitro. There is no other explanation.

"Paige, are you not worried about the rate of growth? About what the baby's ability might be? What if it hurts you from inside?"

"No." There is no fear in her beautiful eyes, only love for the child that grows within her.

"How are you actually feeling?" I rub my temples, wishing for clarity.

"Much better. The doctor says another day of rest and I'll be back to my fighting self. The nausea has passed and I don't feel so exhausted. It's typical when you reach the second trimester to regain your energy levels. Plus, I actually feel better when I use my abilities. I feel ready to go on, Silver, I won't let the team down." She tucks her hair behind her ears and a single green feather floats between us. I grab it from the air and run my gloved fingers along its stem.

"I'm not so worried about the team. *I* need you. You're my best friend. I don't think I could face...whatever it is we're going to face, without you." I smile and throw my arms around her, hoping, that when the time comes, she can help me figure out the lightning.

"How is your new power?"

Putting the feather on the bed between us, I remove my gloves and cradle them in my lap. "I'm still figuring it out."

"You know, it was really impressive what you did to Bear," Paige says. I blush. "I don't say that to inflate your ego. But to tell you, you didn't know you had that power in you then, and you were still able to master it when you needed to. You'll be able to do so again."

"I hope you're right."

I leave Paige to explore the town. Einstein keeps pace with me along Main Street until we near the end of the road and stop outside a music shop. I try the door handle. Open. A recorded chime of piano chords welcomes my arrival. Einstein sneezes. A thin layer of dust covers the pianos and stools, more swirls of motes dance lazily in the air. No one has been in this store for a while, probably since the outbreak began.

Taking off my gloves, I thumb through the sheet music, admiring the wealth of choice. I approach the section of guitars and pluck one gently from its stand, then back up and find a stool to sit on. The only light in the room comes from the sun shining through the window at the front of the shop. Here, in the back, shadows fall over me and the musty smell of things old and untouched hit my nose. Closing my eyes, I take a measuring breath and let my fingers play. Hesitantly at first, tuning the strings, learning the strength of the steel wires beneath my fingertips. Then more decisively, playing my favorite songs, tunes that make me happy.

My throat thickens. I didn't realize how much I missed my guitar, how much happiness the instrument brought me. My thoughts turn to my mother, of all she must be enduring under Earl's watch. An anger consumes me that drowns out all other emotions; fear, grief, the burden of responsibility, and a steely resolve surges through me. I will master my dark power and I will make Earl pay for his sins.

The piano chimes sound again and Einstein chuffs. My heart races for a couple of seconds before I see Adam. He eyes me nervously and tiptoes toward me. When he reaches Einstein, who is sat at my feet, he drops to one knee and ruffles his fur. Einstein is immediately accepting and rolls onto his back, wanting his belly rubbed.

Keeping my distance, I watch Adam's smile spread as Einstein licks his face. After a few minutes, Adam rises. He looks at his worn sneakers and then raises his gaze to meet mine. I can't read his expression.

"Don't go in the water, Silver. Don't go near the water." He turns and flees from the shop, the piano chords chiming again.

What the...?

If he's talking about the well, I know about that, I won't be investigating that alley any time soon.

I throw down the guitar and run out of the shop. This time I'm determined he gives me more information. No more of these ominous cryptic warnings.

Looking up and down the street, I spot him. He slows to a walk and is nearing the end of the street. I catch up to him and reach out to grab his arm. At the last second, I pull back from making contact. Adam can see the future. He can see all possible futures. That is not an ability I want to possess, and if I touch him, it will be mine.

I let him walk away, toward the plaza where the other children play with melting snowballs. I don't want to know my future. I don't want to know if our quest will fail or succeed, or which members of my team, my friends, I might lose along the way. How could I, with that inerasable knowledge, ever be able to send my friends to their potential deaths? It would be an impossible situation.

"Woof." Einstein barks. *Strange kid.*

"Indeed," I mutter, rolling the velvet skin of his ear around my forefinger.

Lifting my face to the strengthening sun, I unzip my

jacket. The days are lengthening, the sun rising higher in the sky each day, beginning to thaw winter's grip. Snow drifts melt and the promise of spring hangs in the air.

Strange kid. Hold on a sec. I didn't say that.

"Einstein." I bend down on one knee and take his furry face in my hands, stare into his soulful brown eyes. "What did you say about the kid?"

"Woof." *He is a strange kid.*

"I can hear your thoughts!" I throw my arms around his neck. "So that's what Carmen's ability is, she can communicate with animals."

Einstein growls. *I don't like her.*

Standing, I watch the people milling about the street. On the opposite sidewalk is Carmen herself. She still wears her fur coat and matching hat, but she's swapped the heels for a more sensible pair of fur-lined snow boots. She takes a sip of water from a plastic bottle.

She smells bad.

I cross the street with Einstein trailing reluctantly behind me, using my body as a shield.

"Carmen." I wave in greeting as I draw level with her.

"Oh, good morning, Silver. I'm just off to tend to the animals. We have a cow that's in labor." She attempts to walk on.

I catch the sleeve of her coat. She pivots on her foot and faces me, a flash of annoyance travelling across her face.

"I know about your ability," I say. "I know you can communicate with animals." I wait.

Her face crumples and her gaze drops to her snow-crusted boots. "Oh, Silver." She looks right and left, then over her shoulder. "Please don't tell anyone."

"Why not? It's a wonderful ability to have."

Carmen squints against the sun and raises a hand to shield her eyes. "I never passed my vet exams. I'm not the real deal. I'm a fake. I was never any good at the science stuff, but I love animals. I took the nanite pill so I could excel in veterinary medicine. If you tell people, they'll know I'm just a waste of space who could never amount to anything."

"Carmen, I hardly think that matters anymore. Look around you. There are hardly any people left in the country. I don't think anyone's going to care whether you passed an exam or not. Koko says you're good with the animals. If that's good enough for her, whether it's because of your ability or not, then it should be good enough for everyone."

Her eyes pool with tears. "Please don't tell, Silver. I still couldn't bear the shame. My family…We came from…I just…I can't quite seem to shake it."

"Okay, okay." I hold my hands up.

"I really need to…" Carmen indicates the direction of the barn.

I gesture to her to continue on her way. "Of course."

I watch her walk away, all high shoulders and raised chin.

"Carmen," I call after her. She turns, bracing for whatever I might say. "How did you manage to keep the ability?

Since the cure is in the water, *all* water, why haven't you lost it?"

Carmen shrugs and plasters a smile on her face. "Someone once showed me how to purify my water supply. I just purify the water before I drink it." She turns on her heel and marches down the road, thwarting any attempt at further discussion.

There are only three people in the country I know who can purify the water supply and I am one of them. As is my father. Taking the cure out of the water is a complicated process. It's not just a question of boiling away the bacteria that contains the cure.

Carmen knows Earl.

"Woof." *Can we go now?*

"What did she say to you, yesterday, in the diner, that made you so scared?" I ask Einstein.

She said that if I continued to bark at her or cause her any problems she would string me up like a pig and drain me of all my blood.

CHAPTER THIRTEEN

I HAVE to reach Matt and Hal. I have to warn them about Carmen. Running back down the street with Einstein on my heels, I'm momentarily derailed when I stumble into Jacob and Adam in the middle of the street. Jacob is teaching him Tai Chi, right there in the middle of everything. Adam has his eyes half closed against the sun, trance-like, focused on the task at hand. They seem so still, so at peace amongst the flurry of surrounding activity. I feel a pang of envy as I wish I could soothe my own anxieties so easily.

With my boots slushing in the melting snow, I continue down the street. I find the real estate office next to the diner. Koko has taken it over and turned it into her office. Three heads, poured over maps and plans and in deep discussion, swivel in my direction when I throw open the door.

Matt rises. "What is it?"

I bend over, panting, catching my breath, unable to talk. "It's Carmen," I gasp. "I think she's in league with Earl."

Koko's hand flies to her mouth. Matt gestures for me to join them at the table. Hal closes the door gently behind me. I relay the conversation I had with her, how I acquired her ability and the threat she issued to Einstein.

Hal grabs the rest of the team from the diner next door, cutting their lunch break short.

"I don't know what she has planned, *if* she has anything planned," I say to my team when everyone is present, all except Paige who is still resting at the guesthouse. "She might just be here as a spy and is reporting back to Earl. But the one thing that scares me," I pause, looking my friends in the eyes, "is that he has anticipated our every move. Earl seems to know where we are going to be before we do." I let that sink in. It's what I've suspected throughout the entire journey, becoming clear when I saw how uniformly the bridge was destroyed.

Sawyer has brought a basket of fries with him. He sticks one in the air as one might hold up a hand in class. "But he might have planted other altereds with other groups of survivors, covering all bases."

"True," Matt says. "But I wonder how many groups of survivors there are? I wonder if there *are* any more?"

"And," I add, "he had to know that Koko and these survivors were here. It's almost as if he engineered there to be a survivor population."

Erica sits on one of the desks, her ankles crossed, her

back ramrod straight. "He's not God, he can't control everything. He's not all seeing." Her wings flutter out and turn an acid green.

"Exactly. He's just an egotistical scientist with an inflated opinion of himself and a few tricks up his sleeve," Sean says, reaching out a finger to touch one of Erica's wings. The green deepens to a spruce pine.

"Yeah, but," Kyle says, swinging his legs from where he is propped on a desk next to Erica. "He can't kill off all the unadjusteds or he and his altereds will go insane. And then what would be the point of the virus?"

"Excellent point, Kyle," Matt says. Kyle blushes and his feet blur.

"Unless he's figured out the insanity problem," I say, not liking the thought.

"We have no idea what Earl is capable of." Hal stands at the front, addressing the group. He presses his palms together. "During the resistance he was President Bear's right-hand man. Now, God knows what modifications he may have given himself. We have no idea what power he really has."

"If Silver's right," Matt says, "and he's somehow been able to anticipate our every move, was able to engineer the destruction of the bridge, then he has more power than we thought."

The sense of foreboding cuts through the overcrowded, suddenly silent room.

"Okay, let's not get ahead of ourselves." Hal paces a

small line at the front. "So far, all we know is Carmen can communicate with animals." He begins ticking off points on his fingers. "Whether she has any other abilities or whether there is more to the communication ability, we don't know. So, we need to keep tabs on her, subtly, without alerting her that we know she's in league with Earl. And there is the possibility that she's innocent. Maybe she did know Earl, maybe he did show her how to purify the cure, but maybe she escaped the mountains, maybe she didn't want to be with the altereds. We just don't know."

"We need to be cautious," Matt says. "We need to follow her, track her moves, and see if she communicates with anyone."

"Any volunteers?" Hal asks.

"What about Paige?" Mason says. The rolled sleeves of his black fleece reveal a plethora of tattoos on his brown arms. Numbers. Soldier identity numbers of fallen comrades. Dozens of them. He was a soldier before the resistance. Then switched sides when his unadjusted wife was killed. "Could she give Carmen a few subtle suggestions with this new mind control of hers?"

"It only seems to work on animals," Jacob replies. "And she's still resting."

"I'll go." Erica's wings turn a putrid blue and she ties her lavender hair into a ponytail.

"Aw, dude, you get to have all the fun," Kyle whines, much to the amusement of the bulks. "Wish I could shrink, I could be like a speedy elf thing…" he trails off when the laughter gets harder.

When the laughter dies down, I turn to Erica. "You can't take your bow and arrow. That would be too aggressive."

"I can if I go as Tinkerbell. I'll shrink down, my bow and arrow with me, and Carmen will never notice I'm there." Already she is doll size. She stands on a desk, wings fluttering.

"Good idea," Hal says. "Sawyer? Kyle? I want you nearby. I want you to be Erica's back up. If anything goes down, Kyle you can use your speed to run back here and let us know, and Sawyer, you can use your telekinesis and pyrokinesis to control Carmen, but only as a last resort. I'd rather not give anything away if we can help it."

"Yes!" Kyle pumps a fist into the air. "Some action!"

"I'll go too," Sean says. "In case they need a little muscle." He flexes his biceps in Erica's direction.

"No turning bulk yet," Hal says, as Erica rolls her eyes.

"And keep your weapons with you." Matt checks the status of his own gun holstered on his hip. "We've all become a little lax since arriving here, but it seems we need to be vigilant once again."

There are nods and mutters from the group. Erica, Sawyer and Kyle leave for the farm where Carmen is working. As Erica flies out the door she shrinks to the size of a hummingbird, barely noticeable.

"Carter and Mason." Hal points at the two bulks. "I need you two to drive a supply truck. Koko has informed us of a motorcycle shop a few miles down the interstate. I want you guys to take the truck to the shop and fill it with the motorcycles. That's how we'll be continuing our journey to the mountains."

Carter and Mason rise and leave the room.

"Silver and Matt, Koko would like a separate meeting with you. There are some survivors here Koko feels will be valuable to our mission if they choose to join, and if we choose to have them. The rest of you can help set up the plaza for this evening's entertainment."

"Entertainment?" I ask.

Hal nods. "There's a little light-hearted fun every Saturday night."

We shuffle to our feet to carry out our individual instructions.

"And don't forget your weapons," Hal calls after us. Luis grabs his gun and puts down the trash can he was holding. I haven't seen him puke for days.

Matt, Koko and I enter the diner and sit down in one of the red-upholstered booths. As drinks are placed in front of us, Koko massages her temples.

"If you're worried about Carmen, we'll figure it out. It's what we do," I say.

"It's not that," Koko says. "Well, maybe a bit. But more Adam. He had a nightmare last night. Several in fact. Well, the same one several times."

"Nightmare? Or something else?" I ask.

"I'm pretty sure this was just a nightmare. Something

about birds lost in the woods. He was trying to save them and they either flew away, too fast for him to catch, or they just disappeared into thin air. Then they attacked him, clawing him every time he tried to approach one. Each time he woke up screaming. Needless to say, both of us are a little tired today." Koko smiles apologetically.

Matt fiddles with a water glass, turning it round and round. "That doesn't sound too ominous. Considering."

A slight girl approaches the booth, not much older than me, stepping over Einstein to reach us. She has dark, cropped hair, pearly skin like she's never seen the sun and a smattering of freckles across the bridge of her nose. She stands by the edge of the table, one hand on the corner, looking at her feet.

"This is Delta." Koko introduces our new companion. "Please sit, Delta."

Delta slides into the booth beside Koko and looks at Matt and me under a severely cut fringe. She wears an over-sized sweatshirt and hides her hands in its sleeves.

"Delta was one of the first survivors to arrive here," Koko says. "But the interesting thing about Delta is that she has an ability."

Delta shrinks further into the bench. A blush rises up her neck.

"Inherited?" I ask.

Delta nods. "My parents were one of the first to have their DNA modified. Before the nanites were produced. And then I came along."

"What's the ability?" Matt asks.

"Delta can change any liquid into its gas or solid form and back again," Koko says. "Show them what you can do Delta."

"Pick up your glass, please," Delta says.

I do as instructed. She waves her hand in my direction. The glass in my hand turns heavy. I lose my grip on the wet glass and almost drop it onto the Formica tabletop. The liquid inside turns solid. Instead of a bubbling root beer I hold a solid mass of dark brown...*something.*

"Root beer in its solid form," Delta says. Her hands stay outside the confines of her sweatshirt and she picks at chipped, pink nail polish on her fingers.

"Delta would like to join you on your mission. And with her ability, she might come in handy." Koko pats Delta's hand.

She looks at Matt and me. "I haven't used it in battle before. My range isn't far. I have to be quite close to objects, and I have to be able to see them, but I think it could be useful."

"Definitely," I say, thinking of all the possibilities. If I had her power when I faced Bear, I could have frozen him from the inside out.

Matt leans over the table, studying her. "Are you sure? It's quite dangerous. We can't guarantee anyone's safety."

"I'm sure," Delta replies, sweeping her fringe out of her eyes. Her voice hardens. "My parents had abilities, they were one of the first. They thought they were doing something good. They were killed by altereds. I want the opportunity to avenge their death." Her eyes glisten with unprocessed emotion.

"Hal and I are the team leaders. You good with following instructions?" Matt asks.

Delta splays her hands on the table. "I'll do whatever is needed."

"Okay then. Welcome to the team," Matt says.

"There's just one thing left to do." I reach for her hand.

The pain begins in the center of my palms. A prickling sensation that very quickly turns to a burning. I'm almost sure my palms are on fire. Then a dull ache grows at the nape of my neck. It steals my breath, making me grab at my neck with my free hand. Within a few minutes it's over and I've acquired Delta's ability.

I smile. "Now there's two of us."

"There are five more," Koko says. "Five more people that want to join your mission. Men. Big men."

"We could use all the help we can get," Matt says, draining the last of his coke. "But I don't want to leave you here without guards."

"We've got people to spare. And I don't think there's anything I could do to make them stay," Koko says. "Silver, I wonder if you might be able to give them the bulk modification, or something."

"I have some spare nanite pills that are invisible to the cure. It will make them stronger, faster, able to see in the dark. That's as much as I can do, I don't have the equipment with me to alter their individual genetic codes to a bulk."

Koko squares her shoulders. "I guess that will do, thank you, Silver."

I snap my head toward a commotion on the other side of the room

"Adam!" Paige shouts.

The boy lays on his back on the black and white check floor, convulsing.

CHAPTER FOURTEEN

MATT, Koko, Delta and I rush across the diner. Jacob inserts a wooden spoon into the boy's mouth. Paige kneels beside Adam, attempting to cradle his shaking head in her arms. Adam's eyes roll back in his head. He moans softly. Einstein licks his face, until Matt pushes him away.

"What's wrong with him?" Matt asks.

"I don't know." Koko crouches by the boy. "This has never happened before."

I'm tempted to lay a hand on the boy, to ease his suffering. But then I will acquire his ability. I will see what he sees.

Squatting next to him, I hesitate, willing the fit to end so I won't have to intervene. I hold my hands poised, waiting to be sure of the right decision. I may wish for the healing glow, but it might be something else that appears. The convulsion eases, then subsides. I sigh with relief. Adam moans again.

"It's too late. They're already here," he whispers, before his head lolls to one side and he appears to fall asleep.

Matt and I look at each other.

"Who's here?" I mouth.

Einstein stands by the door, hackles raised, barking. But his thoughts are too fast to follow. Agitated, his claws slip on the tiled floor. I catch something about birds in his scattered thoughts, reminding me of Adam's dream.

Matt fingers the automatic pistol in his holster, brings out the weapon and lets it dangle by his side. Koko follows his actions with her own gun.

Screams sound from outside. Loud and panicked. Several people all at once. Screams of pure terror. Adam mutters. Einstein barks. The rest of us rush toward the door. The screams continue. Some are cut off abruptly, some manage a garbled *"nooo..."* before fading to nothing.

"That's coming from the plaza," Koko says, flicking the safety switch off.

"Jacob, stay here, with Adam," Matt says.

The rest of us dart out the door and run down the street to the plaza. Paige, Delta, Koko, Matt and I all stop at the same moment, on the edge of the plaza, not quite believing what we are seeing, not sure of the action to take. People run in the courtyard, in all directions, slipping on the slush, panic contorting their features. They dash into the streets, eyes wide with terror, clothes smeared with blood, hands covering their faces.

Scanning the wild gathering, I can't see the threat. Lyla stands to my left, her back to the wall, pressing herself as far as she can into the building, her shoulders hunched to protect her neck. I count five bodies in the square. Limbs, heads, dismembered. Puddles of blood streak across the stone courtyard. Entrails coil in messy piles. I look for my team, hoping desperately that none of them have been killed. The screams continue, but I still can't see the threat.

Something big passes by my left side. A fetid breath washes over me. Feathers brush my cheek and a cacophonous squawking sets my teeth ringing. A startling pain gouges my shoulder and I scream. Knives? Claws? Teeth?

Falling to a knee, I grip my shoulder in one hand, my knife in the other. An unnerving caw blasts next to my ear. Part animal and part something else. Koko, Paige and Matt train their guns, scanning the immediate area, but there is nothing to shoot. I can't see anything. Until...wait...what is that?

An eagle? But it's so much more than that. Bigger. More powerful and partially invisible. The animal flies into the square and turns its head back to look at me. It fades from view, the shining, dark eyes the only part of it visible, until it moves. Then, as it stalks its next helpless victim – a teen-aged boy running directly toward the huge avian creature - it merges with the wall it flies next to, adopting the rusty brick color, borrowing the bonded effect of the bricks until I can barely make it out. Camouflaged. Invisible. And I thought hellhounds were the worst creation I ever saw. This is something else entirely. Hell...*birds*. They have to be Earl's.

The eagle shimmers into visibility, as though the effort to sustain its invisible camouflage is too much. With its massive talons, it plucks the terrified boy off his feet and tears him into strips with a wickedly pointed beak before any of us have a chance to act. Delta screams. Matt and Koko fire their weapons and I ready myself for its next move. Paige stares at the animal, attempting to appease it with her new mind-control. But the hellbird squares itself to our position, thrusts its chest out and opens its sharp beak. Paige grips her double-barreled shotgun with white-knuckle ferocity.

I transform to bulk. Paige levels Tallulah, her shotgun. Her finger rests on the trigger. The hellbird advances. It caws, a screeching sound that assaults my eardrums. Blood drips from its beak and talons. Before Paige can squeeze the trigger she and Lyla are yanked into the air.

"Hey!" Matt calls, grabbing for their feet.

Flying out of his grasp, Lyla and Paige tumble head over feet in the air. They remain a few feet above our heads and come to a rest inside a strange blue bubble. It floats above the bloody scene in the plaza. The hellbird caws again and stretches out its talons. It hunches, preparing to pounce.

Lyla claws at the confines of the bubble. It wobbles and morphs, but does not allow her to leave. Unperturbed, Paige sits in the bottom of the bubble, raising her gun once again. Lyla crouches at her shoulder.

About to attack, the bird screeches. But it isn't the one we can see who makes the attack. An invisible force leaps toward us. Screeching fills my ears. I slash with my knife, but can't see the hellbird.

The bubble wobbles and Lyla rolls in the bottom of it. Paige squeezes off a shot, but it goes wide. When the hellbird reaches the bubble, it bucks and falls to the ground. What is that bubble made of?

"What the...? Matt mutters.

Carmen appears on the other side of the plaza. She marches toward us, her fur coat flapping wildly. At least three hellbirds circle her head. With their beaks wide and their talons slicing at anyone who wanders close, she laughs. A manic cackle like an evil witch from a children's story. Erica flies behind her, an arrow in her bow and growing back to human-size with each passing second. She releases the arrow. It finds purchase in Carmen's right shoulder, cutting off her laugh.

Kyle and Sawyer run up the path behind them.

"Invisible hellbirds!" Kyle screams, running at full pelt. It's the last thing he ever says.

One of the birds swoops onto him. Its talons scratch at his neck, slicing a cut so deeply that he is decapitated. He didn't even have time to scream. I stare in shock and horror as the body of one of my best friends topples to the ground.

Sawyer turns his fiery eyes on the murdering hellbird

and lets loose a fireball. The fireball engulfs the bird and burns it to ash in mere seconds. Sawyer marches on, his face streaked with mud, his eyes determined. When another bird swoops to the attack he throws it in the air with his mind, hurls it a hundred yards away and engulfs it in another fiery inferno. He makes progress, but there are so many.

Matt fires a couple shots into the plaza, then stops as people weave before him. At least twenty hellbirds fly and swoop in the small square, isolating victims, killing without mercy. Luis and Hal turn bulk, their impenetrable skin protecting them from tearing beaks and ripping claws. They take position behind a broken fountain, taking shots at the birds.

Another screech. It's the hellbird a short distance away. Finished with the teenage boy, it readies itself to pounce. A ribbon of entrails hangs from its mouth. I grip the wound at my shoulder. The blood flows freely. Woozy, the ground teeters. Struggling to my feet, I immediately sink back to my knees.

Eyes fixed on Matt, the bird lunges. Matt fires several rounds from his gun, but the hellbird knocks him to the ground with one powerful talon.

"No!" On buckling legs, I run at the hellbird, slashing with my knife.

Paige levels her shotgun at the bird and fires. The bullet passes through the membrane of the blue bubble. The hellbird falls out of the sky and lands on top of Matt. Both are still, quiet, unmoving.

No, Matt, not you. I cannot lose you. I will not lose you.

Another scream sounds on the other side of the plaza as Sean, who has not turned bulk, is sliced in two by the biggest hellbird I've seen yet. His cowboy hat is blown across the plaza and lands gently in the broken fountain, its fabric darkening from the stagnant water.

"No!" Erica screams, releasing three arrows, only one finding its target in the suddenly invisible animal.

Remaining in my bulk form, I search for my pyrokinesis ability. Using two abilities at the same time will drain me faster, but I can't let any more of my friends die. I throw a couple of fireballs, scoring a hit as I catch a hellbird on its wing, scorching its feathers. It squawks briefly before I cut the sound off with a fireball to the face. I gag on the smell of roasting flesh and bile swims up my throat.

A dizzy spell gives way to a feeling of hysteria. I can't see the damn birds. I have no idea how many there are or how fast my abilities will drain.

Matt is on the ground, covered by a dead bird. Not moving. My chest squeezes painfully as I long to reach for him, but there is too much danger. I throw fireball after fireball, but engulf nothing but air, scorch nothing but the ground, ignite nothing but dry crates of wood. I can't see the damn birds. The townspeople are attacked and killed, one by one.

Bleeding and on my knees, the winter wind whips my hair into my face. Delta cowers behind me, waving her hands, freezing the birds from the insides out. But her range isn't far and she has to be able to see them for it to work.

Paige and Lyla are in the blue bubble ten feet above me. *Matt*. Matt unmoving. I choke on a sudden sob as I realize I might have lost him forever. Sawyer and Erica battle in the plaza, firing arrows and throwing fireballs. Koko shoots at anything that moves and accidently grazes a child's arm. Tears sting my eyes. Desperation blinds me.

"What do we do?" Delta whispers in my ear.

Raising my hands to the sunless sky, I plead and beg and wish for a miracle. It takes a moment for me to register the itchy sensation on the palm of my hands and the tingling in my fingers.

"No!" I scream, as I look at the thickening bolts of electricity that spark between my fingers. What possible use can this evil darkness bring? Despair threatens to swallow me. Perhaps oblivion is better, then I won't have to witness the death of all those I hold dear.

Abruptly, silence descends upon the plaza. There is a second, the briefest of moments, when everything and everyone is still. Like I've managed to press pause on the entire world. For that instant I can see quite clearly. I see where each bird is, each injured person, every dismembered limb, each child cowering in fear, every falling leaf, Sean's hat resting in the bottom of the fountain, discolored from blood and mud and water. The pulsating blue of Paige's bubble. The blood trickling slowly from my own wound. I'm aware of each person's breath, those who suck in fearful, ragged breaths, and others panting with exertion and others still holding their breath, waiting for the terrible ordeal to pass. With inexplicable instinct, I raise my palms toward the sky once again. The black lightning streaks from my fingers, shooting off in all directions. It skirts around the people, narrowly missing exposed flesh, as if knowing they are not my target, and zooms toward the birds. Simultaneously, each hellbird explodes. As quick as a flash of lightning, the hellbirds cease to exist. There is no shower of blood and guts like when I killed the wolf in the drug store. Here, in the plaza, the birds simply evaporate into the tiniest of particles and cease to exist. The battle is over.

"Nooooo." Noises creep into my awareness. Pinned to the ground, Carmen yells and reaches for the arrow in her shoulder. Groans of relief and pain sweep through the bloody plaza. Hunched over with wild eyes, a young girl screams uncontrollably until Koko cradles her in her arms.

With a face streaked with dirt, Sawyer walks toward me, along with Hal and Luis, who retches uncontrollably. Erica crouches on her knees beside the torso half of Sean's lifeless body.

I stare at my palms. The black sparks prickle my fingertips. I have done this. I killed the hellbirds. With my black lightning. Unlike the healing ability which comes from a place of love and kindness, this new ability comes from a place of rage and anguish. This is not a power I elicited willingly, it's one that came of its own accord, when it felt it was needed. As the immediate terror of the ordeal leaches from the people in the plaza, a new terror envelops me. I am not in control of this ability. I am a puppet committed to moving with each string that is tugged.

Paige's bubble floats to the ground and then evaporates, releasing her and Lyla.

"What was that about?" Sawyer asks her, as he draws level with us.

Paige pats her stomach. "The baby's way of protecting me."

"Quickly, Silver, Matt needs your help." Koko draws my attention to the hellbird covering Matt's lifeless body.

I kneel beside Matt. Lyla crouches at his other side, blonde curls obscuring her face and tears. Sawyer hoists the bird off Matt with his mind and throws it away from the plaza. It lands with a dull thud and then erupts in a burst of flames.

I put my fingers on Matt's neck. A pulse. And he's breathing. Three deep wounds, claw marks, rip his torso open from his right shoulder to his left hip. I can see the bone of a rib. Lyla sobs. His pulse is weak and thready. With a wound like that, there is only one thing that can heal him. But my palms are still itching with the dark power.

CHAPTER FIFTEEN

I LOOK AT MY PALMS. My hands shake. How can I heal him now? What if I lay my hands on him and the lightning comes back, killing him? Hanging my head, my thoughts whir and panic churns in my stomach.

"Do something," Lyla shouts, her blue eyes accusing.

"Silver." Paige crouches beside me. "He's going to die if you don't help him."

I shake my head. "If I kill him, I'll never live with myself."

"Will you be able to live with yourself if you don't try?" Paige says. Her wings float above us, shielding us from the slaughter of the plaza. "None of us know what happened. How you killed all those *creatures*, but we know it was you." My friends nod and murmur encouragement. "And it was a good thing. We would probably all be dead if it wasn't for what you just did."

I take a steadying breath and will my hands to stop shaking. Tentatively, I place my hands on Matt's body. He groans. I squeeze my eyes shut and push the blackness away, wishing for the healing light instead.

An eruption of itchiness crawls across my palms, followed by another moan from Matt. Taking another breath, I push all the anger and grief away, thinking of Matt, of how much I love him. The healing warmth tingles in my fingertips. If I open my eyes, I know my hands will be glowing in a golden luminescence. Matt coughs. Strong arms surround me. I chance a look.

Matt smiles at me, covered in blood and muck, but perfectly healed. "You took your time."

"I'm so sorry," I whisper, afraid my voice will crack. "I'm so sorry." This time to Lyla. She squeezes my arm.

"Silver, there are others." Koko motions for me to follow her.

Matt checks out his body, marveling at the torn clothes and all the blood. He glances at Delta. "Still want to come?"

Both her thin eyebrows rise. "More than ever."

Koko leads me around the plaza, showing me each injured victim. I only have enough energy left to heal the life-threatening injuries, the rest will have to wait until tomorrow.

Steeling my breath, I approach Kyle's head, which has rolled a good twenty yards away from his body. His features are intact. His eyes wide with his last warning. Picking up his head, I carry it to his body and place it near his torn neck. Tendons and ligaments tumble out of the stump. Hopeless. But I have to try. I stroke the hair out of his face, but the healing light will not come. My abilities are depleted.

Kyle. Sweet Kyle. Silent tears run down my face and land on his cheeks.

Sean. And others of Koko's group. We have lost twenty souls in the attack and some of them are children.

Earl Landry, you will pay for this.

"Can you heal yourself?" Matt asks, gesturing to my wounded shoulder. At least the bleeding has stopped.

"Not right now," I say, as exhaustion tugs at my eyelids. But the sadness in my heart dwarfs all other feeling.

"Let me." Koko wraps a bandage around my shoulder. "That should do for now. I'll get the doc to come look at it later."

My team gather around me. Koko's survivors drift in from the fields and streets where they were at work, unaware of the attack. Quiet, Erica sits on the ground by Sean's body. Carmen groans, pinned on the ground by six of Erica's arrows.

I shuffle to Erica, take her hands, and encourage her to rise to her feet. Her lavender ponytail is disheveled, her face streaked with dirt, her eyes swollen with tears. "Is there nothing you can do?"

I bite down on a wobbling lip. "I've already tried."

Her shoulders drop and she averts her face.

"Let's get out of here," I say.

Matt and Hal haul Carmen to her feet.

"Ow, watch it!" She cradles her shoulder, the one with an arrow still poking out.

"You should be thankful that wasn't a venom-tipped arrow," Erica hisses in her direction.

Hal leads Carmen in the direction of Koko's office.

"I'm coming too." Erica holds her bow in one hand and a clump of arrows in the other. Her wings are a dark brown, a color I've never seen before. Losing the man she was in love with during the first mission was bad enough, but now Sean. Just when she started to fall for him.

"Everyone, keep your powers turned on, at all times." Hal instructs before he disappears into the office with Erica and Carmen.

"I never thought I'd say this," Matt says, his gaze sweeping over the group. "But right now, I'm wishing I opted for a physical ability."

Koko calls a brief meeting in the townhall to explain what happened to those who were away in the fields. After, most people head to the diner to drown their sorrows or numb their pain with whatever method is available. Some of the men return to the plaza and begin burying the dead. They dig a pit, then gather the bodies and body parts strewn across the plaza. It is a mass grave. I can do nothing but stand and watch as Kyle and Sean are placed in the dismal hole. It's not what I pictured for their final resting place.

Choking on a sob, my hands tremble and the sorrow threatens to drown me. Images of Joe's death tumble through my mind. Then Kyle and Sean. A vicious cycle of bloody images that cause a scream to build in my throat. Hal finds me and isn't afraid to show his own tears. My whole team stare at each other with glistening eyes.

"Kyle…" Sawyer croaks, then turns away.

Unable to speak, I walk away.

Matt, Koko and I enter the diner to find Jacob and Adam still sitting in a booth. Conversations stop when we enter. People stare at us, not trying to hide their wary inspection. If Koko's people didn't know who I was before, or what I can do, they do now. After a few, long seconds, conversations start again, but they are conducted in muted whispers punctuated with sideways glances.

"I'm so sorry, Silver, it's all my fault." Adam slumps in his chair and refuses to meet my eyes as I slide into the booth.

"It's not your fault, Adam, it's Earl's and Carmen's," Matt says.

"But I didn't understand the dream." He works his fingers into a scurrying frenzy. "I never understand the dreams!" Adam covers his face with his hands.

I want to reach for him, to reassure him, but I can't.

"You couldn't have known." Jacob throws an arm around him instead. "We're just going to work on the inter-pretations."

Adam makes a loud, strangled noise behind his hands.

"Breathe, Adam, like I taught you," Jacob says.

Adam lowers his hands and takes deep, steadying breaths.

"I'm sorry, Silver," he whispers again.

"It's okay, Adam." But it really isn't. Not that any of it is his fault. But the whole situation is far from okay.

Diana. Joe. Addison. Kyle. Sean. It can't be normal to lose so many friends.

After a few minutes of numbed silence, the shock dissipates, and my thoughts clarify. "Can you tell me anymore about the warnings you've given me? Why do I need to beware of the water? Is it to do with the well that little girl fell in?"

Someone puts a rock song on the jukebox and starts dancing in the middle of the floor. Stumbling all over the place, the guy is obviously drunk. Maybe it's better that way. The cheerful music produces a headache in my temples. I'm not sure I'll ever feel cheerful again.

"No, no it's not that." Adam frowns, then rubs his forehead hard. "I don't know what it is."

Jacob massages the back of Adam's neck. "Focus, Adam, deep breaths, let your mind wander back to the dream, try and piece it together."

Adam lifts his head, closes his eyes and resumes the breathing exercise. I wait for a few dragged out minutes, thinking he might have fallen asleep, when he snaps his eyes open. His pupils are wide and worried.

"It's not just you, Silver, it's everyone. Everyone that goes to the mountains has to beware of the water. The big water. There's something in it." Adam scrunches his face in effort.

"Well, that's something," Koko says, patting his hand.

"Big water?" I ask. "Like an ocean? We're not going anywhere near the ocean."

Adam shrugs. "I can't tell you any more than that."

The discordant rock song comes to an end and the muted conversations weave around the room again. The drunk man stutters to a halt, then slams out the door, throwing the bell off its hook.

"Mono Lake," Matt whispers. "That's near where we think Earl is hiding out. That's the only body of water we'll come across."

I turn to Matt. "Well, how about we just don't go that way?"

Matt purses his lips. "The detour would take us weeks."

So, we'll be walking right into a trap. Maybe. Adam sees possible futures, not definitive ones. We've just lost Kyle and Sean. How can we knowingly walk into a trap?

"Thank you, Adam." I try on a smile, but it doesn't take. "Now, can you tell me more about the devil?"

"You know. Like. *The Devil*." Adam takes a sip of soda from a glass on the table.

"*The* Devil?"

He rubs his fingers up and down the glass, clearing the condensation. "I saw a red devil with horns, pointed ears and a horrible tail. *The Devil*."

The Devil. Like in every bad comic book or horror movie.

I scan the diner. People huddle in whispered conversations, but I don't miss their furtive looks in my direction.

"Why is everyone looking at me?" I ask.

Koko leans over the table, her dark eyes fierce and serious. "It's because of your power, Silver. No one has seen anything like it."

"But I don't even know what it is. It just happens. I can't control it. One minute the hellbirds were there and the next they were gone." I lay my hands flat on the table, examining them, trying to understand the mystery of the black lightning.

Matt's lips curl in sympathy and he blows a long sigh into his growing fringe.

"It's the destroyer ability." Koko shifts in her seat and touches my palm with a gentle fingertip, tracing the lines. "I've seen it once before."

Lurching away from the table, I press my back into the booth. "The *destroyer* ability? What is that?"

Koko lowers her voice. "All healers possess it."

"They do?" Joan, the lady I gained my healing ability from, never told me that.

"Koko takes my hand again, touching it gently, reassuringly. "You can heal, and you can also take away life."

Matt blanches. "Fuck me."

I look at him. "You were right. Back in Central City. It's

the yang to my healing ability. You were right. What a nightmare."

"It *is* a dangerous ability. But it can be managed," Koko says.

"How?" I push out the single word.

Holding my gaze, she curls my palm around her fingers. "I don't have an easy answer to that. It's different for everyone and it has to come from inside."

My palms grow itchy as a flicker of fear tightens my chest. "But I don't know how to use it. It just happens."

Matt laces his fingers through my free hand, extinguishing the itch. "We know, Silver. We'll figure it out."

Koko's face brims with sympathy. "It comes from the dark part of you. Everyone has darkness in their soul, and that's what you tapped into when you used the ability." I gulp. "The power can be intoxicating. It has no limits. I've seen it destroy a very good healer."

I glance at Matt and his face fills with warmth. "There's nothing but light in your soul. You know that." He kisses my cheek.

That's not true.

Matt is wrong. There is great darkness in my soul. There always has been. Wanting President Bear dead. Now wanting Earl to pay for taking my mother. This is personal. Vengeance calls to me in my dreams and spills into my waking thoughts. It's the only emotion that manages to dwarf my anxiety and fear.

My thoughts spin and I try to hang on to logic. "That sounds more mystical than a genetic ability."

"That depends on your interpretation. There are more things in heaven and earth than in your genetics, Silver." Koko flashes me a tight smile.

I recognize the Shakespeare quote, but it does nothing to help me now. Unless, perhaps, to forewarn me of how far gone Earl really is. If he ruined the bridge and somehow knew we were coming here, then that has nothing to do with genetics. Other things are at play here and I need to start thinking outside the box. And if I'm going to fight outside the box, I need abilities that exist outside that box.

It's useless to fight against this new power. It is deeply entrenched in my core and exorcising it would be impossible. Anger rumbles in my stomach. I think of everything I've been through, the people I've lost and the ordeals I still must face. It's not fair, but then no one ever claims life is. "How do I control it?"

Koko's lips purse. "I don't know." She pulls her hand away. "It's different for everyone, so I think you need to learn for yourself. My advice would be to practice harnessing the power and letting it go so you can learn to resist the temptation it brings."

Her words ring true. Each time the lightning manifests I feel a darkness building inside me. That I'm capable of such power and destruction scares me. But I have to learn to control it. I've already hurt Lyla. I almost took out both her and Matt. I refuse to take those kinds of risks again.

Although Matt's fingers are still laced through mine, I sense tension in his grip. He keeps his gaze on Koko. I examine his profile, but I can't read his face.

A truck reversing snaps my attention away from my thoughts. Carter and Mason park the vehicle and unload the motorcycles on the street. Hal emerges from Koko's office. They weren't here during the massacre. A devastated grimace forms on Mason's lips and Carter drops his gaze to his feet.

My thoughts focus, and my eyes narrow. "I think it's time I visited Carmen." A tingling flashes across my palms. The darkness. The power. The destruction.

No. I don't need the dark power now. I follow Jacob's advice and take some steadying breaths, then put my gloves on, just in case. With each breath the tingling fades, inch by inch.

I enter Koko's office to find Carmen tied to a chair with her wrists cuffed behind her back and her legs tied. Her shoulder has been bandaged, but blood leaks through it, staining the fabric. A swelling bruise blooms over her right eye and a thin ribbon of blood drips from a fresh cut on her temple. I smell sweat and fear.

I look at Hal and Erica. "What's going on in here?"

Hal runs a hand over the nape of his neck. Erica flutters around the room at half her human size.

"Carmen isn't feeling particularly talkative," Hal replies.

Torture. I'm not even sure I care. Removing my gloves,

I pick up a pair of pliers from a group of tools lined up on a desk. "What have we learned so far?"

Glaring at the pliers, Carmen spits on the floor. "I'm not telling you anything, *bitch*."

Hal lifts a hand and Carmen falls quiet.

"Not much that we don't already know," Hal says. "She's verified the hellbirds are Earl's creation; that she brought them here to kill us. She's confirmed Earl has the ability to see us, to see where we are and knows we're coming—"

"How?" I ask, glaring at this traitor. This person who caused the deaths of so many. I want her to hurt, to make her bleed, for her to feel the same pain I do.

Carmen's eyes narrow. "Wouldn't you like to know."

I'm tempted to slap the smug smile off her face. Squeezing the pliers, I step closer. "I don't need these to hurt you, to make you talk. It will be easier if you tell me what I want to know." Lightning streaks along the length of my hands and the pliers, jumping out at her.

Carmen flinches. "Okay, okay! Just, don't zap me with that freaky power!"

"Could have used you before," Erica mutters.

I put the pliers back on the table, but don't do anything to make the lightning bolts retreat.

Carmen eyes me carefully. "He's changed. Earl. He's spent the last few months experimenting on himself. He can…see things. Things that used to be impossible to see."

"Like the future?" Hal asks.

"Kind of," Carmen says, rolling her injured shoulder. "It's more like he can see what's going on in the world, wherever he wants to look, whoever he wants to look at."

How the hell can we beat something like that? If he knows about all of us, our powers, then he will be prepared. He will anticipate every move we make.

"Where is he? What abilities does he have? How many?" I shoot questions at her.

Carmen clamps down, refuses to say anything more. I take a step closer, raising my electric hands. She cowers and averts her head. But I don't have it in me to kill her in cold blood. Not like this. That's not who I want to be.

I spend another hour peppering her with questions, threatening her. Hal makes use of the pliers, but she stays strong. She tells us small things, but not his location, and nothing of his abilities, which are the two most important pieces we need. How can she defend a man like Earl? What does he have over her?

Erica looks at my still sparking hands, her brow lines flickering with thought. "It doesn't look like there is anything more she can tell us. Perhaps she's outgrown her usefulness." Her wings flutter a muddy brown and the ice in her violet eyes freezes the room.

Carmen's eyes widen and a string of expletives and pleas pour from her bleeding mouth. In one fluid motion, Erica removes Hal's gun from his hip, levels it at Carmen's head, and fires.

CHAPTER SIXTEEN

CARMEN'S FACE registers an instant of shock before the back of her head blows out, splattering on the wall and floor behind her. Her eyes fade to a cloudy film and her face sags.

"Erica!" Hal yells. But she's already flown out the door.

Shoving the door open, I run after her. "Erica! Stop! *Stop.*"

Erica, at her normal size, turns and lands gently on the ground. The brown wings fold into her back. "I'm sorry, Silver. I couldn't take her smug self-righteousness anymore. The moment Sean died, she lost her right to live." Something in her jaw clicks and her eyes flash dangerously.

I dare a step closer to her. "I'm so sorry about Sean. I didn't know you two were—"

"We weren't. Not yet anyway. I was just beginning to think of him that way. He has a way of getting under your skin you know." Erica's voice cracks. She looks at her feet, taking a moment to compose herself. "I've lost two now, Silver. Two loves that I held very dear. Three if you count Jess...I can't imagine there will be an opportunity for another. I can't imagine I'd want one."

"It's not your fault," I say. I remember a conversation we had a long time ago, when Joe and I were flirting around each other. She loved him, but didn't feel she deserved love. Her best friend died when Erica pressured her to take a nanite and her girlfriend at the time never forgave her. Erica still carries the guilt. She only took up archery to remember her dead friend.

"You haven't done anything wrong," I say.

She throws her hands in the air. "I do everything wrong!"

"That's not true." I risk another step toward her. "You've done so much."

She raises her face to the frosty air and sighs, her breath pluming. "I used to think I'd made amends. Now I'm not sure if anything I do will ever be enough."

"Oh, Erica." I touch her wing. "You've done more than enough. Maybe it's time to forgive yourself."

She shakes her head. "When I think of who I used to be...And then Joe." She swipes at her cheeks. "I don't know, Silver. I wish I could forgive myself. But I don't know how."

What would I do if I met Diana's parents now? I cycle through the memories, avoiding the one of her death. Matt and Diana and I had been inseparable, until her parents forced pill after pill on her. Much like Erica had done to her friend.

I try to imagine what I would say to them, but I don't think I have anything left. It doesn't matter anymore. Diana is dead and nothing can bring her back. I used to think I would kill them, given half the chance, but I'm so tired of death. The whole point of the cure was to give everyone a second chance, even those who'd made extreme errors of judgement, like Diana's parents, like Erica. We can't move forward if people are still stuck in the past.

"The world is so very gray, Erica. Maybe your wings should be that color."

A reluctant smile skirts her lips.

"I don't think there's much I can say that will take away your pain. That's something only you can work through. But know this, I value you. We haven't always been friends, but Erica?" I hold her gaze. "I love you very much. And I can't imagine this fight without you."

"Thanks, Silver." Her eyes glisten and her wings fold away. "I hope you take your own advice." She gestures to my hands.

I hold them up, encased in thick gloves. "Yeah, well, I'm all about doing as I say, not as I do."

She sniffs, and her folded wings change to a more pleasing orange. "Please excuse me for a while to get my head screwed on straight."

I nod. "Erica? Please don't shoot any more hostages."

She juts her chin in agreement, pivots gracefully on the balls of her feet and walks away.

Weary, I go to the guesthouse. After taking a hot shower and scrubbing the grime and dirt and blood from my body, I clean and bandage my shoulder wound. Looking at my hands, I'm tempted to bathe them in bleach, any attempt at purifying the destructive power they contain. And now everyone knows about it. Everyone will be watching me, waiting for me to slip up.

Wrapping myself in one of the guesthouse's fluffy white bathrobes, I bury my nose in the fresh smelling fabric. I haven't smelled anything so clean in weeks. I stifle a sob as thoughts of home and what life used to be like overwhelm me. Is my father okay?

Einstein nuzzles his head into my hand. I lean against the bathroom door and close my eyes, forcing myself to relax. It's a mistake. Anxiety creeps up on me. A familiar sensation tightens my chest. My limbs tremble, my knees buckle and I drop to the floor, pulling the robe tighter around me. The room tilts at an unnatural angle as I struggle to breathe. The bed sheets shine with such intense whiteness that I am forced to turn away. Lights are too bright and I close my eyes against the visual overload.

Curling into a ball, I wrap my arms around my knees while pain throbs at my temples. My chest burns, as though I've drunk acid. I gasp, trying to drag in a breath. Maybe this time my heart will give out. Maybe this time I'll die and fade into oblivion. There's almost something tempting about a permanent blackness. Then I won't have to fight anymore, I won't have to feel anymore. I can rest.

I can give it all up, let it go, not care anymore.

Holding on to the pendant at my neck, I wish for it all to go away, I wish for Matt, and I wish to be someone else. Someone stronger.

Einstein barks softly and drops something by my side. It's a brown paper bag. Bringing it to my mouth, I cover my mouth and nose. Trying to slow my breaths, I suck in great, shaky lungfuls of air, remembering to breathe as deeply and slowly as I can, like my father taught me. The panic attack consumes me and all I can do now is ride it out.

Einstein nestles close to me. I grab his fur, a small measure of comfort. Eventually my breathing returns to normal, my limbs stop shaking, and my vision clears. In the aftermath of the attack, I'm left with a searing headache and a feeling of utter hopelessness. Weariness settles over me, numbing every muscle in my being into an avoidant passivity, depleting me of the energy to raise myself off the floor.

The door opens and Matt walks in. The concern on his face almost breaks me. Rushing to my side, he kneels next to me.

"Panic attack?"

I nod and feel the shame of my inherent weakness. "Bad one." I want to hide, I want to run away from it all. I can't go through this again. I can't watch more friends die in what seems like a futile battle. Especially when Earl can anticipate our every move.

Matt wraps his arms around me and strokes my hair, waiting me out. Waiting for the tears to run dry and for me to gain control over the fear. I have to. "Shh, it's okay now."

"It's never going to be okay, Matt," I croak. "I miss my father. I want my mother. I can't lose her."

Matt hugs me tighter. "I know. I know."

My hands fist into tight balls. "I feel so desperate. We were supposed to carry the element of surprise. How do we, a small group of moralistic survivors, ever stand a chance against Earl and an army of altereds? Good doesn't always win, this isn't some underdog movie, this is real life. Now Earl knows we're coming. Carmen confirmed that. He's blocked our every more; the virus, the bridge and now hell-birds. What will be next? I'm so tired of death. I'm just so tired. I don't think I can do it anymore."

Silence lingers between us and I wonder if Matt is lost for words.

"I'm scared too," he whispers.

I pull away from him. The tightness around his eyes reveals the depth of his fear. The Caribbean blue of his irises deepens to a frightened sapphire color. "I'm terrified I won't see my parents and Megan again. I'm afraid I won't be able to keep Lyla safe."

"You are?" I hold his cheeks.

"I'm not as good at talking about my feelings as you." He blows his fringe away. "I hate voicing my fears, it feels as though—"

"They might come true?"

He grimaces. "Yeah."

I raise a hand to smooth his unruly hair. He catches it and kisses my palm. "It's just, I got through the last mission and I needed you to heal me. And I needed you to heal me again today. Thank God you could." Another kiss. "Now I don't feel so lucky."

"You're supposed to talk me out of my fear," I say.

Matt tilts his head. "I think we need to help each other here. There's no point denying fear. That would be dangerous. Fear will help us act cautiously."

I poke his shoulder. "Or freeze us into indecision."

He chuckles. "The temptation to run the other way is strong."

"But Earl will find us, no matter where we go."

"Exactly. We don't have a choice." Matt ruffles Einstein's ears. "There was always going to be a battle with Earl, it's just a question of where. He has your mother for a reason; bait. He's not going to leave us alone to get on with rebuilding our lives. He wants to finish what he started with the virus. He wants to finish us."

"Okay, so we fight," I say, as my stomach flips. "But what about my destroyer ability? I have no idea how to control it. There's something wrong with it, something evil. It wants…to be used…no, that's not right, it wants more of me."

Matt kisses my temple. "We'll practice. The team are going to give a funeral in the morning and then start preparing for the onward journey. You and I, we're going to get to the bottom of this ability."

I pull away. "I think I should do it alone. I almost killed you last time, Matt. I can't take that risk again."

"No, Silver, you didn't. You saved my life and many others. That's what you have to remember. You overcame your fears and saved us all. You are one of the strongest people I know. And I'm not just talking about when you turn bulk." He smiles at me.

I wipe away frustrated tears, refusing to laugh at his joke. "I'm not strong, Matt. I'm so flawed. I can't even rid myself of panic attacks. How *strong* is that?"

"I think it's one of the strongest things about you." He holds my chin in his hand and makes me look at him. "You have panic attacks because you *care,* Silver. You care about people, about the fate of our world. You are moral and just and your mind and body fight against the horror that you must live through to help us all. And you do help us all." Matt places a finger against my lips, quashing my protests. "With ceaseless determination, because of the abilities you possess. And how you discovered your powers, I can't begin to imagine what that must have felt like. But you came to accept them with an attitude and grace to rival the queen of England. And you won't stop until you've done everything in your power to change the world. I've seen you overcome a panic attack. I know how awful they are for you, and yet you go on. In my book, that's the epitome of strength." The admiration in his tone fills me with pride.

Is it true? Yes. Yes, it is. I need to stop being so damn hard on myself.

"And if you can deal with the panic attacks, I know you can learn to control this new ability."

I lean my head against his shoulder and together we watch the sunlight fade to night. "Thanks, Matt."

"I love you, Silver." Matt kisses the top of my head, then my ear, then my neck. He pulls the robe from my unwounded shoulder and kisses the smooth skin there. Feeling a hunger that only he can sate, I turn to him and let the robe fall from my body. His hands reach for me, caressing, warming my cool skin with his gentle fingertips.

Einstein heads to the bathroom and nudges the door closed.

Matt chuckles. "I guess he's giving us some privacy."

We've had no time to ourselves since the mission began and now, I crave the feel of his skin against mine. Thoughts of the mission are banished from my mind as I concentrate on Matt and the way his body makes me feel.

Afterwards, we lie on the bed together, limbs entwined, catching our breath. Thoughts of what we have yet to face circle back to my mind. Of course they do. I can't get rid of them, so I dive in deeper, trying to anticipate Earl's next move. But it could be anything. Anything at all.

CHAPTER SEVENTEEN

THE FIRST HALF of the day is spent marking our memories of those we lost in the plaza massacre. There are no words to portray the depth of our love in losing Kyle and Sean. I choke every time I think about Kyle. I've known him for years and I always think of him as a younger brother. We were Claus' top students and trained regularly together. But never against each other. He was always too fast for me before I discovered my own abilities.

Hal does a good job in speaking, remembering their strengths and even manages a joke or two. You can't not smile when you think of Sean. Erica claims his hat and it never leaves her head. The shape of it compliments her elfin features and I'm glad to see that part of him will stay with us.

After the funeral, Matt and I walk down the street, past the fields and into a small copse of pine trees.

"Are you ready?" He asks.

I nod, tense with dread. Suddenly a rabbit scampers across our path. Matt and I look at it. It pauses and stares at us. Matt looks at me.

"No," I whisper. "Run away, little rabbit."

The rabbit scampers into the trees.

"Let's start with a tree. That's what your power targeted the last time I was with you," Matt says.

Placing my hand on the nearest pine, I pull out the memories of the hellbird attack, the death of Kyle and Sean. The rage and grief rise quickly, burning my chest, causing me to choke out a sob. My fingers tingle with electricity.

Matt claps. "That's it!"

I glance at the tree. The lightning shoots up and down its trunk, all the way to its loftiest branches, singeing leaves and turning the air acrid. The tree and nine of its neighbors begin to sway. Huge cracking sounds echo around the small copse. As pine needles shower us, small animals run for cover. Electricity sparks out of me in all directions, tunneling to the ground and whizzing into the sky. Without warning, the ten trees fall to the ground with consecutive thuds.

"That's it!" Matt claps again.

I frown. "I was going for just the one tree."

The darkness inside is bigger than me. It's an awesome power, like trying to harness a tidal wave.

"Well, let's try something small then." Matt plucks a wildflower from the ground and hands it to me.

I cradle the delicate white flower in one palm, fingering the velveteen petals. Caressed by my lightning bolts, the flower and stem turn black. The flower turns to ash, disintegrating, and blows away.

"That's what happened to the hellbirds," Matt says. "And President Bear's heart." He hands me more flowers, leaves, insects.

Each time I manage to control the ability, releasing just enough power to desiccate the desired object. But I feel the tidal wave threatening. It wants to escape the fragile damn that is my mind, my morality, my sense of fairness. It wants to smash it all to pieces and cause mass destruction. I shudder at the imagery that unwelcomingly claws through my mind, what could be if I give into it.

"I knew you could do it." Matt smiles, unaware of what I'm really capable of.

The rabbit reappears on the path. I look at it, wondering. It returns my stare, perhaps sensing my inner conflict.

Matt inches to my side. "Silver?"

I stare at the rabbit. It would be so satisfying to watch the light in its eyes go out, forever. To know that I can do it with one flick of my sparking fingers.

"Silver, no." Matt dares to place a hand on my shoulder and turns me away from the rabbit. His piercing blue eyes stare into my own and he holds my chin firmly in his hand. "No, Silver."

The darkness leaves me as suddenly as it arrived and I'm left feeling like a shell of my former self, exhausted with the strain of controlling a beast that knows no bounds.

"I...I..." I attempt to justify the incident with the rabbit.

"It's okay, Silver. You did well."

"But it would be so easy, to—"

"I know," Matt whispers and kisses my nose. "That's why I'm here."

"I want to try something else," I say, leaning against the trunk of a tree. "I want to see if I can go back and forth between the destroyer power and the healing ability."

Without another word, Matt takes my knife and slices his palm. He holds it out to me. His trust in me makes tears prickle.

I wrap my hands around his bleeding one. My love for him swells in my chest, threatening to burst out of me. I love him more than I can quantify. The healing glow surges to my fingertips and heals his cut faster than any injury I've been presented with. At the same time, my shoulder is also healed, and the tight ache I've had for the last twenty-four hours disappears.

Matt smiles, then hands me a large stick. As the healing glow fades away, the black sparks return. The stick disintegrates. The whispers in my head start to yell, but I ignore them, making them listen to my will.

I spend the next few hours testing all my abilities, bringing them to the surface one by one. I fly as a bulk, I heal with butterfly wings, I jump high and throw a fireball into the melting snow. Between physical abilities, I go back to the destroyer power and healing light. Matt slices his palm ten times, deeper each time. Every time I manage to heal it.

A confidence that I haven't felt since the caves seeps into me. It fills me up when I make a successful transition, when the black lightning performs exactly how I want it to, and each time I heal Matt. I practice all the abilities, their movements coming back to me like muscle memory, and I relish the power and strength that I exhibit. I am formidable. I can beat Earl. He has no idea what's coming.

"Okay," I say. "I think I'm beginning to understand how this destroyer ability works."

The dark whispers are still there, wanting me to do more, but I know how to evoke the power and how to push it away. Now it's just a question of not giving in to it. I've always been a determined person, and I'm sure, despite what Koko said happened to her healer friend, I can get the better of this darkness.

)(((((()(((((((((

THE FOLLOWING morning my team rise early and approach the motorcycles secured by Carter and Mason. It is decided that Adam will come with us in the hope his visions can offer more solid information. He rides with Jacob. Delta straddles the saddle behind one of our newest recruits; one of Koko's sentries, and Sawyer climbs onto Lyla's bike. Hal found a small side car to attach to my motorbike, so

Einstein can travel along. Now that I can communicate with him, there's no way I'll leave him behind.

"Good luck." Koko folds me into her thick parka. She shakes hands with each member of the team and offers heartfelt encouragements.

"Hmmm," Matt mutters, as he glances in his sister's direction.

I follow his gaze to where Lyla has her arms wrapped tightly around Sawyer's waist. Her hair whips in the wind and she wears a mischievous grin on her face.

"Hmmm?" I question.

Matt's eyes narrow. "I'll be keeping an eye on that."

I roll my eyes. "They're just riding a bike together!"

"We'll see." Matt guns his engine and takes off to join Hal at the front of the procession.

Nausea flutters through my stomach as I turn my bike toward the road. It will only take us two days to reach the mountains, to reach Earl. Then we'll have our final reckoning.

I glance over my shoulder as we leave. Koko remains in the morning chill, her arms crossed over her chest. She offers me the slightest of nods and the barest of smiles. But somehow, her small motions give me confidence. I know she has faith in me.

Travelling west on the highway, the road is clear. We are nearing the origin of the virus where people didn't think to flee, where they were caught by surprise and remained in their homes, waiting to recover from what they thought was a normal flu bug. The road belongs to us and we make good progress. I grit my teeth, realizing that I hoped for an obstacle to slow us down and delay the inevitable.

As the sun descends that evening, brilliant hues of deep oranges and reds light the sky, but rather than take pleasure in the rare, natural beauty, the sky seems to me to be full of omen and portent, the red hues a warning of blood yet to be shed. Hal gestures for us to turn off the highway. We make camp on the edge of a forest. A full moon casts an unearthly glow on the ground, causing shadows to dance and people to jump. There is little chatter as we cook our dinner over a campfire. While we set up camp, Adam paces with an uneasy frown on his face, muttering to himself.

"Adam, take it easy. Let's remember the breathing." Jacob lays a hand on his shoulder and takes him through a relaxation exercise.

Adam's tension puts me on edge. "Have you seen something new?"

"No." Adam shakes his head. "But I feel something coming. Something in the water."

"But we're not going *in* the lake," I say.

Adam shrugs.

After we settle in for the night, Hal and Mason take first watch and pace a perimeter around the campsite. Matt and I set up another watch by the campfire. As the flames crackle and the pleasing scent of burning wood fills my nose, I stare into the distance. Bats fly from the neighboring trees looking for prey. I hear the occasional howl of a wolf. The wind rustles the leaves at our feet and the temperature drops to near freezing. Matt and I sit with our backs against each other and Einstein drapes himself across Matt's feet. The dog's thoughts are centered on food, and I fish out a few tidbits for him from my backpack.

"What do you think is in the water?" I whisper, leaning closer to the fire, trying to warm my freezing hands.

Matt rests his head back on mine. "I don't know. I can imagine any number of things. I hope it's nothing like what's in my imagination."

I rub my hands together to push warmth into my fingertips. "I wish we could all crawl into Paige's protective blue bubble."

"Me too." Matt's head falls to my shoulder and he gazes at the stars. "She has no control over it though. I suspect the baby senses when she's afraid, when she releases some stress hormone, and reacts accordingly."

The constancy of the stars and moon is reassuring. Looking up into the night sky, I can almost believe the world is normal. The moon and stars continue their role as beacons during the hours of darkness and the sun continues to rise each morning. Even here, on the earth, on the ground, rivers continue to flow and trees continue to grow toward light. It's the people who've vanished. The rest of the world stands quietly existing, waiting for the next chapter in its evolution.

"I'm worried, about the baby," I say.

Matt kisses my cheek. "Paige looks much better, I think she's through the worst of it."

"It's not just that. It's growing too quickly. There's no precedent for this situation. We have no idea what that baby is doing to her. What other abilities might it possess? Abilities that might hurt her, kill her, albeit unintentionally." I press my fingertips against his. His hands are as cold as mine.

"But what else can she do?" Matt turns to face me.

"Maybe she should have an abortion," I whisper. "Before it's too late. For all we know she might be ready to give birth in a week, but to what? Maybe she should get rid of it before she can't."

Matt's voice pitches. "You really think there's something evil inside the baby?"

"I'm not sure." I run my fingers across the ground, looking for acorns to rub. "Nothing starts out as evil. Look at my lightning ability. And look how powerful the baby is already. Can you imagine what it will be like when it's two? When it has a tantrum and manifests other abilities. I have a feeling this baby is going to be extremely powerful."

"But, Silver, if it were us, I could never destroy it. It would be part *you*. I could never destroy something we made, something that was half *you*." On his knees, he grips my hands, almost as if he's begging.

I pull my hands out of his grip and run my fingers across his stubbly cheek. "Matt, we won't ever be having children." I stare at his kind face. "I could never bring a child into this world. It's full of death and sadness."

His eyes glisten. "But we have to have hope, Silver, we have to have hope for a better world."

A noise breaks into our conversation. The unmistakable sound of a zipper on a tent flap. Paige pokes her head out of one of the nearby tents.

"Silver?" She hisses.

"Yes?"

"Remember those nanite pills you gave us? Back in Central City? The ones that give us strength and increased our reflexes and made our hearing better?"

"Yes?" I cringe, knowing what's coming. I'd forgotten about them. The new temporary nanites last for over a month. Shame heats my cheeks.

"I know you care, but seriously, it's *my* body, *my* baby, and *my* decision. I will not kowtow to pressure. This baby is going to be born, so get on board. I'm going to need you." Paige disappears back inside the tent and re-zips the flap.

"Crap," I mutter.

"Don't worry." Matt takes my hand again. "You're just concerned. She'll understand. We'll talk to her in the morning."

Erica and Mason take the second watch by the fire and Matt leads me to our tent. My boots crunch over the frozen ground and the heavy sense of anticipation fills our small tent.

"Silver?" Matt whispers before we fall asleep. "I can't

imagine not having children. I mean, not now, we're too young, but in the future, it's something I want."

I snap my eyes closed and feign sleep. I don't reply. I can't. Matt would be disappointed by my response.

"Good night, Silver," he whispers after a few minutes.

I stare at the roof of the tent for hours, listening to the whispered conversations of those on watch, hearing the nighttime animals hunt in the forest, worrying about our onward journey. I try not to think about Matt's last words before he fell asleep, but my thoughts keep circling around to them; babies, children and the future, mine and Matt's future together.

It's impossible to think beyond the imminent battle with Earl, to imagine a world where people are happy, *safe*. Will it be possible for children to run carefree in the woods again? The image of a little boy pops into my head, with Matt's Caribbean blue eyes and sandy blond hair, running through a field with a dog, a retriever like Einstein, laughing and filled with innocence. Is it possible? Do I even want it?

As the thoughts swirl, I feel myself becoming increasing distressed by the decisions I'll have to make, by the pressure Matt has unwittingly poured on my shoulders. Clenching my hands, I will the tension to leave my body. Instead, a familiar itchiness erupts on my palms. Einstein whines quietly where he lays at my feet. The electric sparks illuminate the small tent, becoming stronger, wanting to be released. I force my brain to think happier thoughts. I will myself to relax. If Adam can do it, so can I.

With exhaustion attacking my limbs, it takes over an hour for me to feel in control of my emotions again. The small sparks of lightning remain on my fingers, growing and shrinking, depending on the thought that enters my head, before I'm able to vanquish it completely. I may be able to call on it at will, but it's much harder to push away.

CHAPTER EIGHTEEN

REACHING FOR MY CANTEEN, I find it frozen solid. The temperature dropped below freezing during the night.

"Delta," I call, when I spot her across the other side of the camp. "Would you mind?" I hold the canteen toward her.

Delta brushes the canteen with a finger. "There you go."

The canteen turns slack, all the frozen stiffness leaches away. Shaking it, newly thawed water sloshes inside.

"Thanks." Taking a swig, I blink my swollen eyes. My cheeks are chapped and puffy. Sleep eluded me last night and the water burns icily as it slides down my throat.

Packing up my gear, I bundle everything into my backpack. Paige and I approach our motorcycles at the same time. I lay a hand on her arm. "Paige, about last night."

She shrugs off my touch. "Don't worry about it. Difficult times. Difficult decisions. We all think differently." Her tone is neutral but her body paints a different picture, all hard angles and stiffness. I'm supposed to be her best friend, to support her unwaveringly in all matters, with no judgement. I've let her down.

As we straddle our bikes, the proverbial light bulb goes off in my head. Paige would never abandon her own child. I should have realized. I remember the story she told me about her parents abandoning her through their own greed and vanity. That's why she joined the resistance, to fight against the lust for power. She would never harm or abandon a child, any child, especially her own, even if it is still a fetus, even if it is potentially harmful for her to carry on with this pregnancy. She'd die for the life inside her, die to protect it, die for the opportunity to love it.

Sighing, I gun the engine. I've made such a mess of things. I don't want to go into the eve of our reckoning with Earl with my best friend and I at odds.

Matt bounds up beside me and plants a kiss on my cheek, a big smile lighting his face. His presence only reminds me of the little boy in my late-night thoughts, our son. My hands itch and I clench them hard against the handlebars.

Today we'll reach the edge of Mono Lake, a stone's throw from Earl's rumored hideout. With Einstein in the sidecar, I shoot off after Matt, hoping the destroyer ability will remain as tingling and not manifest into something more powerful. Frustration becomes a permanent collar.

It's a long, uneventful day on the road. The cold seeps

into my bones and the smell of diesel drowns out everything else. The constant drone of the engines causes a headache to form across my forehead. I listen to Einstein's excited thoughts as he spots wildlife from the sidecar.

As it grows dark, we arrive at the edge of Mono Lake. Considering this is the only body of water between us and Earl, it has to be the area Adam warned me about. A drum roll goes off in my head, the beat building to a crescendo to symbolize our final leg of the journey, and my hand floats to my knife.

Hal directs us off the road. The land is barren and rocky and grass struggles to grow from the granite ground. None of us wants to camp near the lake, but we're all too exhausted to carry on. And if we continue along the road, we'll end up fighting Earl tonight. We settle in an area with the lake in view so we can keep an eye on it. Adam hides in a tent and won't come out, mumbling about the water.

Sawyer approaches Hal and me as we stack logs for a fire. "Is this really the best area to set up camp?"

"We've had this discussion," Hal snaps.

"It's here, or we take the fight to Earl now. There's nowhere else between here and the mountain," I say, scanning the distant peaks. There is only ice and snow. I feel eyes on me from behind the craggy niches.

Sawyer glances at the calm lake with a twisted grimace on his face and a hand that won't stop raking through his curls. "Right. Okay. Whatever."

Carrying a few more logs, Matt joins us. "We can't

avoid things just because a ten-year-old kid had a vague dream." He positions two more logs on the towering stack. "It's not like anyone is going for a swim anytime soon."

"Yeah, but we don't know what the threat is, what might come out of there," Sawyer mutters, as he turns to help Lyla with her tent.

"We'll be careful," Hal says. "We'll have extra sentries on watch per shift."

Matt digs into his backpack and removes some of his homemade explosives. "I'm going to lay a trip wire around the camp and connect it to a few of my grenades."

"Silver." Hal gestures toward the bundle of sticks and logs on the ground. "Would you mind?"

I throw a mental fireball at the pile and the wood ignites in a *whoosh*, sparks flying into the air, the flames instantly warming my cold hands.

We manage to coax Adam to the fire for dinner, which he gobbles down, licking his fingers to the knuckles. He doesn't go back in a tent, but paces a nervous circle around the fire. His eyes never leave the dark lake and he mumbles under his breath. Paige finally makes him sit down and take a shot of whiskey. She sits behind him, throws her arms around him and rocks him like a baby. Maybe it's practice.

Adam softens into her body, his eyes drooping. Paige lays a sleeping bag over him and lets him curl up on her lap.

Paige will make a wonderful mother, she has a natural instinct. Who am I to question that?

"I'm sorry," I mouth, when she looks in my direction.

She nods, a hint of a smile at the corners of her mouth, and I'm unsure whether I am forgiven.

In bulk form, Hal crouches beside me. "Silver, we need you to do a recon of the lake." Even though he squats, his body towers above me, casting a dark shadow over the fire. "Maybe you could do a fly around with your wings. I'd ask Paige, but you know…"

"Sure, Hal." I kick the stiffness out of my legs.

Einstein whines at my feet and tugs at my trousers. *Don't go in the water.*

I ruffle the fur at his neck. "Don't worry, I have no intention of going in that freezing lake."

My shoulder blades ripple as my blue wings rise over my head. I raise them high and allow the cold thermals to lift me. I soar upwards, gaining altitude, surveying the mammoth body of water. With enhanced eyesight, I spot every flickering shadow, every wind-rustled shrub. Einstein trots around the campsite below, his snout raised skyward, howling. His thoughts are unclear from this distance.

I fly around the perimeter of the lake, taking in every detail of the scrub, rocky land; the three islands that stand in the middle, the calcium carbonate spires rising out of the water like marching trolls, the rippleless water that yearns for a child to skip a stone across its glassy surface. The Sierras rise tall on the far side of the lake, most still covered in winter's white blanket. Somewhere out there is Earl. Somewhere in those mountains we will have our final reckoning.

For now, I can't discern any threat.

Returning to the campsite, the fire stretches impossibly high and flames shaped like fairies, bulks, elves and other altereds float in the dark sky above our heads. By the amused look on Sawyer's face I'd say he is no longer worried about the lake and is enjoying creating the evening's entertainment. Marshmallows are stuck on sticks and hung in the flames.

Matt hands one to me sandwiched between two graham crackers. "Compliments of Koko."

"Thanks," I mumble, as I give in to the sugar rush and fold my wings into my back.

Adam sleeps in Paige and Jacob's tent. Einstein presses himself against me as though trying to escape the darkness at his back. He is too preoccupied to lick the crumbs from my fingers. Matt stares across the fire at Lyla, where she is nestled against Sawyer's side, hanging on his every word, her eyes sparkling. A fireball shaped like a heart appears in the sky. I giggle. Lyla's blush is obvious, even in the dark.

Matt frowns and his legs tense, as if about to stand up.

"What's up?" I ask.

He flicks a finger toward the new couple.

I give him my best sardonic smirk. "Are they not allowed to fall for each other?"

"It's *Lyla*!" He hisses at me.

"And?"

"She's my sister!"

"I repeat. *And*?"

Matt rests back on his elbows. "It's weird."

Hal, Mason and Carter take the first watch while the rest of us attempt to sleep. They sing the freedom song softly, but with force.

"Young, like a new star shining
Bold, like a lone wolf stalking
Lost, like a child wandering
Scared, like the whole world's falling
But I am free. And I won't back down."

Einstein whimpers in his sleep and soon I dream too. I'm transported to a world of snow and rock, of mountains protruding like the teeth of a yawping monster, and into a sky filled with storm clouds and thunder. I know, without a doubt, this is Earl's hideout. Without warning, altereds charge out of an opening in the mountain. Some carry weapons; guns, knives, and swords. Others possess abilities of strength and power so extreme that a weapon is unnecessary. My team are taken by surprise. The occasional strike of lightening illuminates images of undefinable menace and terror and I'm momentarily stunned to inaction. But they are not alone. They bring animals. Animals with such deformities and genetic enhancements that their original species is impossible to determine. And then they attack.

With a haphazard aim, Sawyer throws desperate fire-balls in every direction, trying to delay the moment when the altered army will reach us. Paige's protective bubble carries her high into the air, away from harm, but also too far for her shotgun's range or her wings to be of any use.

Jacob falls to his knees with a single blow to the back of his neck. He lays still, in the snow, his chest refusing to rise with life's breaths. Carter and Mason battle what can only be described as a dragon. Their hair and clothes catch fire and they roll in the snow, trying to put the flames out. A sword skewers Delta's torso and Matt receives a mace to the head. One of Erica's arrows, by the whimsical control of an altered, boomerangs back to her and pierces her left eye, lodging in her brain and killing her instantly.

One by one my friends drop dead in a pool of wet, bloody snow. The carnage is quick and total. All the time I stand there, transfixed, unable to move, unable to raise the sparking lightning on my fingers, unable to act. I'm paralyzed by some inexplicable power that roots me to the spot, unable to even twitch a finger, until it's all over, until it's too late. The invisible hold releases me, and with Einstein on my heels, I dash toward the opening in the mountain. I sneak deeper into the mountain, following the winding passageways, hearing human pleas for help from somewhere deep. At last, I come to a room. It contains a small table and bed, a chair. Tied to the chair is a headless body, having been sliced through at the neck. On the floor, the head, having rolled away from the body, leaves a bloody trail of gore. It is my mother's head. Her white, clouded eyes are unseeing, her mouth distorted into a grimace of fear and pain. I open my mouth and scream.

I wake in the tent, still screaming, thrashing at my sleeping bag, still seeing my mother's lifeless, broken body, to find Adam crouched beside me, his palm on my head, trying to soothe me. I scream again. Backing away from him, loud, wretched protests spill out from somewhere inside me. It wasn't just a dream. Adam touched me.

I now have the power to see the future, or any possible futures.

The dream is a vision, one possible outcome of our onward journey and battle with Earl. Death to everyone.

Matt pins my arms until I stop screaming, then wraps his arms around me as a rush of words came out, trying to tell him what I saw. Adam backs into a corner, his eyes wide and his bottom lip trembling, not understanding what's happening. He doesn't know. No one told him of my ability to acquire other powers through the slightest of touches.

"I was just trying to...you were having a nightmare..." Adam looks at the floor.

"What did you see? What did you see?" Matt asks, the stress in his pupils obvious.

Paige, Jacob and Hal run into the tent. The rest of the team hover outside.

"Death. Everyone dead," I whisper, almost too afraid to voice the vision aloud.

I turn my head into Matt's chest and try to ignore the bloody images that surface. Clinging to his shirt, I physically will the vision unseen. If only.

"You've seen the vision." Surprise lifts Adam's narrow eyebrows.

"Yes," I mumble.

"It's not the only possible outcome." He reaches for me.

I slink back, still wary of his touch. "Please, God, I pray that it's not, or we might as well turn around now and take our chances back in Central City."

No wonder Adam is so affected. To live with these horrific, bloody images day after day is enough to make anyone lose touch with reality, to want to retreat to an inner, more peaceful world. But he stays focused, accepts Jacob's training and forces himself to examine his gruesome visions so he can help. He's one hell of a kid.

"There's something in the water," Adam says.

Weariness tugs at my limbs. "Yes, you keep saying that."

"You don't understand. It's coming. It's coming *now*." Adam glances around the tent as though looking for a weapon or a place to hide.

Matt, Jacob, Paige, Adam and I scramble out of the tent. We are met by the rest of the team. Hal throws me a questioning look. Matt gives him a quick explanation of what happened. Hal pales and tenses his armored limbs.

Adam stumbles toward the shore. "The water."

Although it's dark, our enhanced genetics allow us to see as though it is day. I crane my neck to peer into shadows, but there is nothing to see. No ripple of water, no glinting eyes in the dark, no vicious growls from the craggy rocks. We stand, as a group, turning in circles, trying to anticipate the moment. My chest balloons with expectation.

Lyla shrugs out of her jacket. "I'll go check it out."

She undresses quickly until she stands in her underwear. She splashes into the water, gills appearing along her rib cage, before anyone can stop her. Sawyer grabs for her arms as she passes, but she easily dodges him.

"Lyla, no!" Matt shouts.

"Don't go in the water," Adam whispers. He inches backward, away from the water, away from everyone.

Lyla dashes through the shallows and dives under the icy surface. The rest of us approach the shoreline, the disturbed water lapping at our boots.

"I'll go after her," I say, starting to remove my own clothes.

"No!" Matt shouts, even though he stands beside me. "We can't risk both of you." His face tightens as he stares at the spot where Lyla disappeared.

The rest of us wait. Adam whimpers. Einstein barks, trotting back and forth between Matt and me, his thoughts frenetic and unreadable.

"I guess it's not coming *now*, now," Hal says.

Carter digs a boot into the dirty sand. "Or the vision is wrong."

Light appears on the horizon as we stand together in silence. Shadows dance into existence and the water calms. A faint dripping noise comes from somewhere beyond the lake's edge, somewhere out there in the dark, murky water.

"No!" Erica trains an arrow on the water.

A few yards from the place Lyla disappeared the water changes color. A hint of purple spreads out concentrically, quickly turning to a darker pink, then a crimson red. Blood.

"Lyla!" Matt yells, charging toward the spot. "Lyla!"

CHAPTER NINETEEN

A STRANGLED NOISE comes from Matt's throat as he follows the spreading red patch of water. He clutches my hand, digging his nails into my palm.

The dripping noise intensifies, like the insistent plop of rain on an empty oil drum. First a single flow, then others join in, making an odd kind of hollow music. The music turns cacophonous as the lake begins to ripple, spraying us with a fine dusting of water. Louder and louder, faster and faster, until I feel like I'm standing at the bottom of a raging waterfall. Waves lap the shoreline. I hold my palms high, readying myself for battle.

The group releases guns and tightens grips on weapons. Erica nocks three arrows on her bow. Levelling her shotgun, Paige sprouts her green wings and flies above the churning water. The bulks adopt hunter stances and aim at the burbling lake.

"Lyla!" Matt continues to shout for his sister.

The red area bubbles. The entire lake bubbles and foams, like something gargantuan is about to emerge from its depths. Hackles raised, Einstein barks ferociously.

"Get ready!" Hal yells.

Sawyer throws a fireball. The water hisses and spits and swallows it without complaining.

"Easy," Hal tells him. Then to the rest of us, "Hold the line!"

We aren't in a line, more of a haphazard grouping, but with Hal's instructions we spread out and a flood of confidence sweeps through me. The memories swirl back to me; killing President Bear and the adrenaline of battle. My fingers tingle. I am ready.

The water parts. Shapes materialize. Slowly. Agonizingly slowly. We hold the line and we wait.

As the shapes grow, we take a collective step back. The shapes become humanoid and spray water as they rise from the churning lake. A notch of relief releases in my coiled muscles. Humans I can kill.

The entire lake becomes alive with burgeoning forms. Countless. People. But not quite. Reminiscent of the terracotta armies of China, they are clothed in impenetrable armor. But these warriors are not made of terracotta. They are transparent, made from the water of the lake itself. As they rise, the level of the lake drops. They emerge, absorbing the water, increasing their bulk and menace.

The first line of warriors reaches the edge of the lake.

Unsure what to expect, we scuttle backward. The warriors hesitate at the shoreline, as if uncertain whether their watery bodies won't sink through the earth once they plant a foot on firm ground.

But the hesitation is brief and the first step on land does not send the army plummeting through the porous rocks. Instead, as the sun pops into the sky, they reach for weapons at their sides; bow and arrows, knives, spears, swords. It is time to fight.

Erica releases three arrows, scoring direct hits, felling three of the warriors. But they are immediately replaced as more forms march out of the water. There are hundreds of them, walking toward us atop the water like some kind of freaky Jesus act. They are slow, but determined, and Erica's arrows do nothing but put a pause in their step.

Sawyer throws fireballs but receives nothing more than hisses and steaming warriors for his efforts. Everyone with a gun fires. Each warrior hit explodes in a spray of white water and sinks into the earth. They are made of water. They are easy to kill. But there are so many and now their weapons are flying at us.

Paige's bubble floats above the commotion. She levels her shotgun and takes aim, vanquishing one watery warrior after another. The bulks and Koko's five men destroy the front line of warriors as they march toward us. But they are soon replaced with more. An endless amount. While they can die and others will take their place, we will eventually tire.

Matt throws his hand-made grenades into the fray, destroying dozens of the water warriors at a time. One of the warriors steps on Matt's tripwire and the entire perimeter of the camp explodes, destroying a few of the tents and drenching us all in water and ash and burning embers. My ears pop and sound becomes muted as I struggle to hear. I open my mouth wide, swallowing hard as I try to get my ears working again. Hal shouts at me, but I can't hear what he's saying.

Jacob takes Adam to safety. Delta hovers at my side, poking at her own ears. Einstein barks, dodging arrows and spears. Sawyer turns to his telekinesis, throwing one warrior after another, smashing them on rocks and the ground.

The earth turns soggy beneath our feet. So far, Lyla is the only casualty. But I don't know how long we can keep up the fight. The army is infinite, our ammunition and strength are not.

I'm ready to turn bulk and decimate warrior after warrior with one strong fist or a flick of my knife when I sense a different power vying for dominant position. As the headless image of my mother appears in my mind, the destroyer power itches on my fingers. The lightning has risen, and with it, images of my loss and fury. The power flows into my chest and winds its way to every muscle of my body, willing me to release it. I grit my teeth against the urge I know could end us all. If I'm going to use it, on this large a scale, it will take an inordinate amount of control. Control I'm not sure I possess.

I practiced with Matt. I can do this.

With the lightning dancing across my fingers, I step toward the water, raising my hands at the closest warrior. Suddenly, my head spasms in pain. Clutching my head with my hands, I rub at the painful throbbing, wondering if I've burst an eardrum. The splashing of the warriors and the report of gunfire echoes around me, muted, but I can't see anything. I'm blind.

Completely and utterly blind. A white sheet of nothing consumes my vision. I drop to my knees, still clutching my head, the agony almost too much to bear. Somewhere nearby Adam cries out. Whatever is happening to me, is happening to him too. A vision.

"Silver!" Matt calls.

"They keep coming!" Hal shouts.

"We can't hold them off forever!" Carter's voice sounds distant along the shoreline somewhere.

"There's more over here!" Luis calls in his Spanish accent.

Splashing and roaring. The *thwack* of Erica's arrows. The cry of Adam's pain. Paige's booming shotgun. Einstein barking. Delta yelling warnings. And then I hear nothing at all. My vision and hearing collapse in on itself.

In my mind's eye, I see The Devil. The real Devil as depicted in so many mythical books and movies. A creature with red reptilian skin, a swishing pointed tail, horns atop his head, grinning, laughing maniacally. Adam's warning was not a metaphor. I'm now witnessing the same vision.

And what I see is indeed The Devil, real, in the flesh, the sun shining at his back casting his huge frame in formidable shadows, standing atop a mountain of human bodies.

Sounds rush back at me, but my vision remains blurred.

"Delta," I gasp, sensing her nearby. "Freeze the lake. Freeze the warriors." They are the last words I manage before I pass out.

XXXXXX

WHEN I CAME TO, I can see again and the brutal sounds of the battle are gone. Matt crouches over me.

"Is it over?" I rub my sore eyes.

"Not quite," Matt says.

Looking at the lake, the warriors stand strong. But Delta must have heard my plea because each warrior is frozen solid, as well as the lake itself.

"It was a great idea," Delta says, tucking her hands into her sleeves. "I didn't know my power was quite so big, until I tried."

I push myself into a sitting position. "You did good."

The sparkling crystals of the frozen warriors are beautiful in the morning sun. I attempt to count them, but there are too many.

"What do we do with them now?" I ask.

"We destroy them," Hal says. "We don't know how long they'll remain like that. And they might follow us."

Standing up, I join my team. Together, we wind our way

through the frozen statues. Matt throws grenades. Sawyer shatters the warriors with his mind. Erica releases more arrows, retrieving them when she runs out, refilling her quill and starting the process all over again. The bulks and Koko's men walk on the frozen lake, slicing through each warrior with knives and swords, until they fall to the icy ground in a tinkling noise akin to breaking glass. Jacob with his karate chops and Paige with her shotgun destroy a fair number of warriors themselves.

The lightning disappeared from my fingers when the vision arrived. With the warriors unable to attack, it's just a question of time before we destroy them all. But there are thousands and it would be so much quicker if I released my power.

Before I have a chance to change my mind, I sprint to the middle of the lake using my superspeed. Standing among the icy warrior sculptures, I briefly admire their crystalline beauty caught by the sun's rays. My breath frosts.

Raising my palms, I allow the lightning to come to me. It isn't long before the tingling crawls over my palms and fingers, impatient, eager for blood. The power builds inside my body, pulling at my self-control, willing me to let go.

I raise my hands higher and focus on the frozen warrior immediately before me. Without warning, its head explodes in a shower of ice, raining down on top of me, cutting my skin with its sharp, icy blades. I increase the power and the body follows suit. Then two more explode, ten more, a hundred more. It isn't long before every warrior standing frozen on the lake becomes a pile of icy shards. The satisfaction warms my insides.

The power wants more and I strain against the yearning to wreak more damage. I breathe slowly and picture all the goodness in my life. Finally, the black lightning retreats from my fingertips and leaves me alone.

I walk back to the campsite to meet my friends. They stare at me with gaping mouths and wide eyes. I'm unsure of their expressions, is it awe or fear?

"That's a whole other level of power," Hal says, offering me his knuckles. The gesture reminds me of Kyle.

"Thanks… I think." I return the fist bump.

They drop their weapons on the ground. Some sit by the dwindling fire to warm their hands. Matt stares hollowly at the frozen lake. We lost one of Koko's men and Lyla. She never returned.

I want to go to him, I want to fold my arms around him and tell him everything is going to be okay. But that's not true. I know loss. It will never be okay.

Earl has a long list of atrocities to answer for, many deaths notched against him. He will pay. I will make him. I will avenge Lyla's death and everyone else who died for the cause.

Unexpectedly, I fall to one knee, suddenly no longer able to support my own weight. Using the destroyer ability took all my energy, controlling it even more. The world goes dark for a second time.

)O(O(O(O(

WHEN I OPEN MY EYES, Hal cradles my head and Paige helps me sip from a canteen. The rest of the team, all except Matt and Sawyer, bustle about, packing up the gear that wasn't blown up in the explosion, getting ready for the final day of our journey. By the end of the day we will reach the mountains and Earl.

Matt sits apart, near the water's edge, close to the spot Lyla dove into the water, where the red patch of ice is a permanent reminder of her fate. The lake is still frozen. Hal thought it best to contain anything else that might be lurking under the murky surface. Sawyer refuses to pack his tent and instead sits silently by the shrinking campfire, staring into nothing, his usual, lopsided smile is nowhere to be found.

When the group have almost finished packing, Matt shouts, pointing to a distant figure walking toward us. The figure stumbles to one knee, then rights itself. It gets closer and the sun shines on her blonde hair.

Lyla.

Drenched and bleeding, she hobbles toward us.

CHAPTER TWENTY

SAWYER LEAPS TO HIS FEET. His jaw is tense, but there's hope in his eyes. "Lyla!"

He and Matt take off at the same time, running toward Lyla as she limps closer.

Lyla! Lyla! Einstein woofs at me and my spirits lift.

Matt and Sawyer reach her at the same time, almost barreling into her. She collapses into Matt's arms. He picks her up and carries her to the fire. Her dripping wet, blonde curls are flattened and darkened by the water and her skin is covered in goose bumps.

Sawyer wraps her in his winter parka. "Thank God you're alive."

Her eyes flicker as blood leaks from her side.

"Silver!" Matt calls. "We need you!"

I dash to her side, my healing glow already warming my fingers. I kneel beside her and place my hands on a large ragged wound that takes up most of her side. Although I'm exhausted from using my black lightning, the healing light comes to me easily, perhaps as unwilling as I am to give up.

Her side heals, and so does the burn on her shin, as well as her singed hair, which grows back to the length she had it before I burned it.

"Thank you, Silver." She looks at me, her blue eyes no longer hold a grudge. Shivering, she turns her head and the light of the campfire exaggerates the anxiety in her pupils. They dart left and right, widen and narrow, as if unable to focus on one thing. Maybe she shouldn't have come. She's so young. But then, we all are. Sticking together and going through what we have made us who we are.

"It's the least I can do," I say, truthfully. She wraps her arms around me and gives me an unexpected hug.

"I owe you an apology," she says. "A proper one."

I clear my throat. "What for?"

"Trying to out your power. Putting so much pressure on you to let me come. Not that I'd change anything, and I'm glad I'm here, but—"

"It's not what you thought it would be?" I finish for her.

She nods and her gaze drops.

"You've kicked some good altered butt. You've proven your worth," I say. "No apology necessary." I smile to let her know I'm sincere. In truth, she has exceeded my expectations.

Hal throws more wood on the fire and brings it back to life.

"Can you tell us what happened?" Matt asks, when we're all settled around the fire.

Lyla's teeth smash together and she holds her hands closer to the flames. "Shark, or something like a shark."

Sawyer hands Lyla her clothes and I help her dress. With a towel, she dabs at her hair, then sits sandwiched between Sawyer and her brother. Sawyer holds her hand, rubbing it fiercely to keep her warm. Einstein lays at her feet, not willing to leave her for a moment. The fire's shadows flicker across her face. As she tells her story, her expression turns haunted, a feeling I know will never leave her.

"It had teeth inside its mouth and teeth outside and its jaws were practically double-jointed. After I dove into the water I couldn't see much for a while. Then shadows came at me, fast. The shark was on me so quick I barely had time to react. I thought I was going to be swallowed whole." Lyla shudders and rubs her hands up and down her arms. "I grabbed onto its dorsal fin and we spun around and around in the water. I was trying to get to my knife. Finally, I grabbed it and stabbed it right through one of its eyes." Lyla pulls Sawyer's arm around her shoulder.

"That's my girl," Sawyer says. The flames leap and spark, higher than any natural fire.

"Then I saw five more shapes coming for me. I dragged myself out of the water and everything froze. The sharks were stuck in the ice." Lyla pulls her parka tighter.

"We're glad you're back with us." Hal digs at the hard

ground with the heel of his boot. "We saw the giant pool of blood and thought it was too late."

Matt massages the back of her neck. "It's all over now, you're safe now."

Glancing at the lake, Hal reties the strings on his pack. "And the sooner we get out of here the better."

Before we leave, I return to the water's edge while the rest of the team pack up the remaining gear and put the fire out. Hal joins me. He hands me a vial of clear liquid. Using Delta's ability to melt a small section of the lake, I uncork the vial and pour it in.

"Think it will work?" Hal asks.

"The cure? Of course it will work. If this is the lake Earl has purified, he's in for a nasty surprise."

"If anything goes wrong in the mountains..." Hal looks at the horizon and the towering rock structures that seem as impenetrable as his own bulk body.

"Any remaining altereds will get a nasty shock."

We return to the others. With the winter sun low in the sky, we mount our bikes for the last leg of our journey. We'll reach the Sierras before it turns dark. Their craggy outlines rise in the distance, the peaks covered in snow, the mountain range as old as time itself. It waits, unaffected by our cause.

After we ride through the smaller foothills of the Sierras we park our bikes a couple of miles away from Earl's suspected mountain and take refuge behind some large boulders. We are hidden from anyone who might be peering at us from the mountain, but we have a good outlook of the towering behemoths from our hiding place. The winter wind whips around us and makes everyone pull their coats tighter. Einstein chuffs at the snow and eats large mouthfuls.

"First of all." Hal faces our huddled group, his bulk muscles strong, his face serious. "We don't know exactly where this bunker is. It was used during the water war fifty years ago and then abandoned." He sticks a finger on the map.

"A map. A real map. That's old school," Sawyer comments, to the laughs of everyone in the team.

"This bunker's been here for over fifty years," Matt says. He affords his sister a worried glance. He won't stop wanting to protect her and I hope he's not too distracted. "It was supposed to be a secret base and haven for military personnel which is why we're not sure of its exact location. Even Francesca didn't know."

Hal removes a pair of binoculars from his pack. "We'll have to stay here and case things out for a while, see if there is any movement."

Hal and Matt kneel, elbows resting on a boulder giving an outlook to the mountain range. Periodically, they pass the pair of binoculars back and forth between them. The facing peaks remain breathlessly still. The rest of us sit huddled behind them. Lyla scrapes her knife against a granite rock, sharpening the blade, a new ferocity shining in her steely gaze.

Luis and Carter play a game of 'rock, paper, scissors,'

while Mason munches on a handful of crackers. My heart aches for Kyle and Sean. They should be here, kicking altered ass.

Erica, still wearing Sean's hat, and Delta curl themselves into a niche in the rocks, keeping out of the frigid wind as Delta heats water for coffee. Paige and Jacob tend to Adam, giving him a cup of water and taking him through more relaxation exercises.

"Is there anything you can tell us, Einstein?" I whisper to the dog as he sinks into my side.

His ears prick up and he woofs quietly. He can only smell the air and the cold and traces of squirrels. Out of acorns, I pick up a handful of pebbles and circle them in my hand. I've always found the motion calming. As we sit, my butt turns numb with cold but I feel my strength returning. I'm almost back at full power. Expectant, my fingers tingle. Oddly, the anxiety has left me. Anticipation is always worse. Now that the battle is imminent, I just want it to begin. I am finally ready for this fight.

The altereds in the mountain are the last of their kind, the worst of their kind; they'll never go quietly. Sparks dance on my fingers, but I will the power away. It's not time yet. This destroyer ability is becoming more controllable, but it's thirst for destruction is getting stronger.

"*Silver...*"

A voice whispers from my left. There is no one sitting on my left, and it seemed to come from farther away than within the confines of the group. Beside me, Einstein is asleep. His doggy voice usually fills my mind with warmth and lightness. This voice is dark and cold.

"Silver..."

This time the voice comes from my right. Sawyer and Lyla talk quietly beside me. Erica and Carter have wandered off a few yards and are looking over the top of another boulder. Adam sits with his knees bent, arms around them and chin resting in the cup of his knees, rocking gently forward and backwards to an internal rhythm. Everyone else is either silent or blowing on their hands. No one glances at me, no one has called my name.

"Silver..."

The voice is all around. I rise to my feet.

"Silver...Silver...Silver..."

Surrounded, I'm cut off from the group by the mysterious whisper. The voice, although still quiet, has become hard-edged and menacing. I detect a threat between the soft, luring tones. Turning in a circle, I scan the boulder for the source. I see nothing, not even an animal that might be communicating with me telepathically. Earl. It has to be him. I know it in the pit of my stomach. And he's waiting for me.

"Silver..."

The sun dips away for the night and the snow shines with luminescence under the moon's reflective light. I catch Matt's eye.

He's watching me with a cocked eyebrow. "Everything okay?"

"Did you hear that? Someone calling my name?"

"No." Matt surveys the members of our group. No one is gesturing for my attention.

"Silver..."

I spin around. "There. Did you hear it then?"

Matt shakes his head. Hal turns, cocks his head, and gives Matt a worrying look. My muscles tense. Earl knows I'm here. A successful ambush is now unlikely. The images of my horrific premonition tumble through my mind. I shake my head clear. That is an outcome I refuse to let happen.

Hal kneels on one knee and addresses the group. "We'll give it an hour. Let darkness settle in, then we'll make our move."

A flutter of anticipation curls through me. The moment we've been building toward is almost here. My mother, within that snow-covered rock, so close. My hands fist with the thirst for vengeance.

"Adam, Lyla," Hal addresses them. "You have no offensive or defensive abilities, so when we make our move, you are to remain here, with Einstein."

They both nod and I don't miss the relief that swims through Lyla's eyes.

Hal pets the dog. "Einstein, if there are any problems here, you come and get Silver."

"Woof." *Yes.*

"The rest of us will take these." Hal digs into a pocket of his pack and removes a small medicine bottle. He pops the lid and hands out invisibility pills Dad made back in Central City. They are effective for about three hours. "Once they take effect, we'll make our approach to the mountain." He points to the nearest peak where he believes the bunker to be housed. Everyone follows his finger, taking in the deep powdery snow, the smears of black rock struggling for an appearance, the frozen vegetation stretching for the last rays of the sun. But where is the opening? Where will we find access to Earl's lair?

Hal catches each of our eyes. "Powers on. Bulk up. Switch on. Whatever it is you do, now is the time."

The bulks turn bulk. Sawyer transfers a small flame across his fingertips. Erica's wings unfold and she shrinks to half her normal size. I stay human, for now. Transitioning is nearly instantaneous for me and I don't yet know which abilities I'll be forced to call upon. I need to retain my strength for as long as possible.

It isn't long before Hal's head disappears, shortly followed by his body and lastly, his boots. Watching each of my team members disappear, I realize we can no longer call ourselves unadjusted. We are altereds, in the purest sense of the word. Altered not just by genetics, but by experience and war. We may have taken nanite pills and modified our genetics, but our reasons are altruistic; for the greater good, for the survival of humanity. And we don't stand a chance against the *other* altereds if we don't level the playing field. We'll have to come up with a new name for ourselves.

An invisible hand ruffles Einstein's ears and then grabs my hand.

"I love you," Matt whispers in my ear.

I squeeze my eyes tight. "Don't say that. Not like that."

He exhales against my cheek.

"Be safe," he says to Lyla. "Look after each other."

Nodding, Lyla throws an arm around Adam and huddles into the shadows with Einstein.

Bumping against each other, we climb over the boulder and approach the valley. Pausing to look up at the foreboding mountain, the temperature plummets and snowflakes whirl in the frosty air. My breath plumes as I exhale, the only visible part of me. It's beautiful and ghostly and creepy all at the same time. We spread out in a rough line, a few yards apart. Hal calls for a halt to perform some last-minute checks. There are a few clicking noises while people check guns are loaded and safeties switched off.

"All clear! Carry on," Hal calls.

Matt is somewhere to my right, Paige to my left. Although I can't see either of them, their boots make impressions in the falling snow and I hear the squeak of each footfall as it compresses the frozen ground. Together, we approach the enemy bank. The incline rises swiftly and I lean my hands on my thighs to aid the climb. After only a few steps up the rising bank of the mountain, my black combat boots suddenly appear. The invisibility pill should have lasted much longer.

I stop. Scanning the area, I see some of my fellow team

members farther up the hill. All completely visible. Those on the same level as me show only parts of their body.

The snow falls thickly, the flakes large and clumpy, reducing visibility dramatically. Blinking to clear the snow from my eyelashes, something shimmers in front of me, directly at the point where my boot becomes visible. A subtle blue shimmer. I pull my boot back and it disappears again. Then I step forward and it reappears. Repeating the action twice more confirms my suspicion; the mountain is cloaked in some sort of invisibility revealing veil. Have Earl's powers become so impressive that he can alter the physics of our earth? I shudder at what might lay in wait within the mountain. Our approach will not be stealthy. Our attack will be reliant on speed and the abilities we possess.

A boom echoes around the mountain. Like that of a heavy metal door forcefully reaching the end of its track. Every member of my team stands stock still, listening, waiting for whatever is to come next. A small rock tumbles from a nearby ledge and lands at the tip of my boot. There is a moment of pure silence, the muffled veil of falling snow reducing all sound, seeming to create a protective barrier between us and the altereds. But it is an illusion. Halfway up the mountain, where the gradient turns steep and perilous, a gaping hole appears.

CHAPTER TWENTY-ONE

FAR BEHIND ME, Einstein barks. For an elongated moment, it's all I can hear. He calls my name, again and again and again.

Hal unholsters his gun and points it skywards. "Weapons! Charge!"

Together, we run up the slope of the mountain, hoping to reach the wide black hole before it closes again, or something comes out of it. Accelerating to close the distance, I keep my eyes on the opening. Something within its depths shifts.

A flurry of manic activity and ear-splitting noise spurts out of the hole. Black comes out of black. A medley of flapping wings, rushing wind and shrieks of glee or terror – I can't

tell which - streak toward us, endless. With my hands over my ears, I stand transfixed, unable to move my limbs or tear my eyes from the creatures pouring out of the mountain.

As angry as a volcanic eruption, unimaginable beasts screech and fly and snap and bite and yelp and howl and nip and growl. Beasts from another world, from an unimaginable hell, as evil as the mountain is indifferent.

Gunfire bursts around us. Banks of snow shift and tumble toward us. The wind howls and the icy snow stings my cheeks. With freezing hands, I grip my knife and ready myself to fight.

Someone yells. "It stings!"

The creatures flying toward me are black, small, about the size of my hand. At first, I assume they are bats, then I see the curled tail held prone with a large stinger vacillating on the end. Scorpions. *Flying* scorpions. I'm sure the stings in their tails are modified and fatal.

"Let's go!" Matt yells over the howling wind.

Weapons ready, we charge up the mountain. A scorpion lands on the face of one of Koko's men. Screaming, his body arches in a backwards 'C'. His face dissolves, the skin eroding under an acidic venom until there is nothing left but bone. All in a matter of a few seconds. As he falls to the ground his finger depresses the trigger of his automatic weapon, sending a wild arc of bullets shooting into the sky. Bullets we can't afford to waste. Most of the bullets go wide, some of them find targets within the scorpions and they thump to the ground, dead. At least they are killable.

In a perpetual, violent rush, the scorpions continue to

pour out of the hole in the mountain. Their sheer volume obliterates the moon and stars. Matt throws his grenades into the sky, killing dozens with each blast. Sawyer uses his telekinesis to deter their advancement and change their path whenever they fly too close to a member of the team. Despite the snow and the venomous swarm, Sawyer and I lock eyes. Together we send fireballs chasing after them, burning them. The smell of charred flesh fills the air and scorpion body parts rain around us, restricting visibility to all but a few feet.

One scorpion makes a bee line for Carter but merely bounces off his armored skin. Turning bulk, I charge up the mountain. With Matt's grenades exploding, Paige's shotgun booming and Sawyer's fireballs whizzing above our heads, the bulks: Carter, Hal, Luis, Mason and I run through the hailstorm of scorpions, trying to reach the entrance to the bunker. We only cover a hundred yards when new monstrosities appear.

Spiders.

Not just spiders. Tarantulas. As high as my waist. Hairy and solid, they run toward us making an odd shrieking noise that grates on every nerve I possess. Their eight eyes are large and black, settling on targets to attack.

Running with my knife, I leap toward the closest eight-legged atrocity. It rears on its back four legs, its eyes boring into me, its beak twitching, ready to bite. I scurry under its body and thrust my knife into its abdomen. The hairs covering its abdomen shoot out like deadly daggers but bounce off my bulk skin. A shower of yellow guts and blood pour from the slit, while the stench of ammonia assaults my nose. I roll out from under the spider as its forelegs crash down in a death dance. I spin away, the snow on the mountain washing off the acrid spider guts.

A scream from my right. Turning my head, I spot another tarantula spit a projectile of silky thread. The thread lands on Luis and wraps around his body, immobilizing him and toppling him to the ground. Even though Luis' bulk skin will most likely protect him from whatever poison that webbing contains, he is trapped and unable to move.

The spider scuttles closer to him. One hesitant hairy leg probes Luis' head. Luis screams. As I run toward him, an arrow lands in one of the spider's eight eyes, eliciting a primal wail of anguish, a sound that I didn't know bugs were capable of making. It scuttles backward before rolling onto its back, dead. I nod at Erica in thanks. Her bow is still raised and she releases several more arrows into the oncoming swarm of deadly tarantulas. I run to Luis' side and attack the thick thread with my knife. Once free he turns and fires his gun into the army of approaching spiders. So many of them. Still flooding out of the mountain.

A brief, backwards glance reveals Sawyer's fireballs dancing like macabre fireworks in the dark sky, causing the air to fill with the scent of burned flesh. The gun powder from Matt's endless grenades turn the falling snow a murky gray and produce a veil of smoke that hangs over us and the creatures. Scanning the area for anyone that needs help, I spot Paige with her shotgun, shielding Jacob from a spider attack. The bulks make headway through the minefield of Earl's creatures, machine guns slicing through air and animal as they progress up the mountain. But the progress is slow. And the creatures keep pouring out of the hole. We are being overwhelmed. There are too many of them.

Deciding to call on the destroyer ability, I revert to my human self. Fingers twitching, I hesitate. With my friends fighting among the enemy, will the power be able to distinguish between the two? I'm not sure. But the longer I hesitate the more overwhelmed we become.

My attention snaps toward the source of a mighty shriek from one group of spiders. The scorpions surrounding the bunker entrance disperse in a panicked flurry, creating a gap in the sky. Something emerges from the hole. Something big. Something ancient. A creature so primal that the spiders and scorpions flee in terror. A beast so black it's darker than the night sky. It leaps into the air and beats enormous wings, swirling the snow into violent flurries. As it flies over the top of my head, its noxious breath, like the bowels of hell itself, envelop me. I sense scales and leathery skin. It seems an eon before the creature passes by, all sound sucked away in its wake. It flies toward the small group of bulks and Koko's three remaining men. That's when I get a clearer picture. It's a dragon.

An honest-to-goodness two-headed, scaly-skinned, wing-flapping, fire-breathing dragon. And it comes out firing. Tendrils of white-hot flame erupt from both its teeth-lined mouths. The flames engulf the group of bulks and Koko's men. The bulks survive, hair burned off their scalps but otherwise intact thanks to their flame-retardant skin. Koko's men do not meet as positive an outcome. All three are immersed in flames. They throw themselves on the snow-covered ground, hoping to douse the flames consuming their bodies. The damage is too extensive, the fire too hot. All three scream in the final moments of their agonizing deaths. Hal raises a pistol at one, putting him out of his misery and then turns his attention back to the dragon as a second fiery missile seeks the bulks.

The dragon provides a small respite from the scorpion and spider attack. The smaller creatures momentarily flee over the other side of the mountain, seeking a haven from the fire-breathing beast. But there is no respite for me or my team. More shapes emerge from the hole in the mountain, but this time they are human, and I know the altereds have come out for a reckoning.

"Delta," I shout, as I spot her running from a spider.

Delta turns and raises her hands toward the spider. It freezes. A thick, thready projectile emerging from its body, stretching a couple of feet into the air, motionless. The eyes take on a glazed appearance. The brown hair covering its body lightens, as though frosted. Suddenly it crumples, its legs giving way, breaking apart from its body.

Dodging a breath of flame, I march toward her. "Can you do that to the dragon?"

Nodding, she takes off toward the top of the mountain where the dragon circles us.

"Sawyer, Matt, Paige, Jacob!" I yell, gesturing for them to join me.

Paige pulls Jacob away from the oncoming attack of a spider, the blue bubble surrounding her but not quite encapsulating Jacob. Sawyer throws fireballs at the altereds, backing up with every step as they advance. Matt is down on one knee, grenades depleted, gun raised. An altered, one with a human head and the body of a snake, slithers toward him. Before he can fire, the altered sinks long fangs into his shoulder. Matt yelps. I run toward him and throw the snake person away from him with my mind. I lift Matt with bulk strength and join the rest of the group.

The bulks shield Delta as she tries to get close to the dragon further up the mountain. They dodge fiery tendrils and send arcs of machine-gun fire toward the impossible creature. The dragon is unaffected. Perhaps its skin is as impenetrable as the bulks.

With my friends huddled close, I throw a fire ball at the approaching altereds. An individual with icy eyes and horns that shoot projectiles bursts into flames. Despite the snow and the cold, the ground catches fire. The sudden heat flushes my face and singes the ends of my hair. I hear nothing but the crackle and spit of fire.

"You need to get to that hole in the mountain," Matt shouts over the fire. His face is filthy and his eyes glint with desperation.

The opening is unguarded. No more creatures emerge from the dark entrance. For the moment, we seem to have the advantage, at least over the genetically-engineered creatures anyway.

"But, Matt..." I gesture to the group of altereds advancing toward us. My black power will be needed.

I see one man with three-foot, pointed horns on his head. A woman who is completely blue and freezes everything in her path, the flames dying – almost in reverence - beneath her feet. One man flashes in and out of visibility, much like the hellbirds we encountered in Koko's town. Another teleports in the blink of an eye from one section of the advancing group to another. One man has a shark's head protruding from his belly, complete with snapping teeth. An unnatural light radiates from a young girl covered in a thick white fur. With each strobe of light, a toxic cloud puffs out of the end of every hair. Another woman's translucent skin reveals bones and organs and blood vessels within. I wouldn't have believed the medley of monstrous modifications if I weren't seeing them with my own eyes. They are a frightening mixture of power and gore.

Without warning, Matt convulses and drops to the ground. His eyes roll into the back of his head. The altered. The snake person. Its bite must have been poisonous.

I kneel by Matt's side and put my hands on his wound. For reasons I don't have time to contemplate, amidst the surrounding battle and the advancing altereds, the healing power comes easily. Of course it does, it's Matt, and I'll never hesitate again when it comes to healing him. The warmth flows from my fingertips into Matt's shoulder. Within seconds he's getting to his feet.

"Thanks. Again," he whispers, pressing his cheek close to mine. The warmth of his skin renews my energy.

Looking into his warm blue eyes, I feel a surge of hope. We can still win this.

A rouge fireball flying past my ear slams me back to reality. The noise of the battle surrounds me once again; fireballs, arrows, bullets, knives, fangs, and projectiles of poisonous venom swirl around me in a whirlwind of destruction.

The altereds are only yards away. One of them with six-inch spikes covering his back and arms, locks his gaze on me. Recognition flashes through his pupils, then urine runs down his leg. He stops, turns and runs away. A couple more follow suit.

"Damn." With displaced feathers floating around her head, Paige reloads her shotgun. Her floating blue bubble takes her almost out of range. Her eyes follow the movements of the teleporting woman.

"You have to go! Now!" Matt pushes me toward the mountain. "We can handle the rest."

I'm coming with you. Einstein appears at my side.

"Lyla? Adam? Are they okay?"

Yes.

I grab Einstein, and with my flea ability, leap over the altereds and fiery mountain. Landing directly at the entrance to the bunker, I peer inside the dark hole. Nothing. I can't see anything.

The battle has drained me, but I still have power left. I turn back toward my friends for one final look. The bulks continue to battle the dragon. The creature reaches out one long, sharp talon and plucks Luis from the ground as if he's made of nothing more substantial than the snow he stands on, and carries him high into the sky. It takes the dragon only seconds to reach a height where he appears to parallel the moon. My hand flies to my mouth as I realize what it's doing.

The dragon opens its claw and lets Luis fall. His bulk skin may be impenetrable to fire, but his bones are not made of steel. They will break, all of them. I wince as he lands on the ground, and I can't close off my ears from the sickening thud as he impacts on rock, just like William when he fell from the bridge.

When I dare to look again, Erica has shrunk to humming-bird size and loads a venom-tipped arrow onto her bow. Delta gets close to the abominable creature and manages to freeze it from the inside out. It crashes to earth, landing heavily, and showering the bulks and Erica with snow and ice. Erica releases a volley of arrows. Each one makes its mark.

I look for Matt. He levels his gun at the altereds and takes rapid shots. The teleporting woman engages Jacob in a fight. He dances around her, but she is faster. She deals him a blow to the back of his neck. Jacob crumbles to the frozen ground. It's the scene from my vision. It's playing out just as I saw it.

"Mother, no!" Paige screams, her wings beating furiously within her bubble.

Finger-like tendrils emerge from Paige's blue bubble. The teleporting altered faces Paige and smiles a wicked smile. The blue tendrils grab the woman just as she winks out of visibility. The tendrils wrap around the invisible person, tighter and tighter.

Paige raises her gun and takes aim. "Screw you, Mom!" With tears streaming down her cheeks, she pulls the trigger and shoots her mother in the head.

I spot a man with a sword running at Delta, another with a mace edging close to Matt. Erica nocks another arrow. Will this be the one that boomerangs back to her and lodges in her eye?

Ready to run to Jacob with a healing hand, I catch Matt's look. *'It's too late, you need to go now'* is the message in his eyes. He fires on the man holding the mace, killing him. Maybe this won't play out like my vision after all. Anger rises from my stomach, hot and hard. Earl is responsible for the death of another friend. It's time to make him pay.

It's all the motivation I need. Squaring my shoulders, I turn my back on my friends, on Matt, and take a step into the mountain.

CHAPTER TWENTY-TWO

BLINDED BY DARKNESS, I creep along the dark tunnel. There is only a vast, black emptiness. Sensing the tunnel is long, I feel cold, damp, carved out limestone under my fingertips, reminding me of my time in the cave. I keep one hand on the wall and the other in front of me, in case I need to call on the black lightning.

"Silver! Silver! Wait for me." Hal charges into the tunnel. "I'm coming with you."

I can just make out his shape in the gloom. "The dragon?"

"Dead. That power of Delta's is awesome." I hear the grin in his voice. "I think we've finally turned the tables on the altereds. The battle is slowing down." He scans the tunnel. "Jeez, it's dark in here."

"I can't see *anything*," I say. Hal rests a hand on my shoulder. "Even with the night-vision nanites."

"I think that's the point. Earl's anticipated we might have abilities and he's cloaked the tunnel."

Einstein woofs. *Follow me.*

Hal and I both grab the fur of Einstein's neck and allow him to lead us blindly down the tunnel. He can't see any better than us, but his canine senses steer him well along the path. I smell oil. And the musty scent of mildew growing on the walls.

As we inch along, the noises of the battle outside fade until I hear nothing but our breathing. Too loud in the muffled darkness. For the first time since the battle started, fear coils in my stomach. Dizziness threatens. With nothing to focus my eyes on, my balance is off.

There's nothing here.

Thirty minutes pass when I feel a shift in the space around us. A weak light from somewhere above allows me to make out Hal and Einstein and the lip of the shadowy tunnel.

Hal glances from side to side, then steps into a cavernous chamber. "It must be an old hangar."

The vast space is worse than the tunnel. "Where do we go now?"

Across. There's another tunnel across.

Stepping out of the tunnel, out of the safety of darkness, Hal and I follow Einstein across the empty hangar. The smell of metal and dust makes me sneeze. Halfway across, the loud noise of a clunking machine startles us and sends Hal and I into each other's arms. We stand, entangled, holding our breath until the noise settles and nothing else happens.

After another few feet I trip over something. A metal object goes clanging off to my left. The sound lasts for a full minute before whatever it was finds a resting spot, issues a metallic revolving noise, like a hubcap spinning on tarmac, and settles on the ground with a final creaky protest.

"Crap," I mutter.

"If Earl didn't know we were here before, he does now," Hal says, taking my hand and urging me forward.

Woof. Woof. Einstein's thoughts come fast and garbled.

He is afraid, but of what? Dancing in circles around us, his claws tap on the concrete floor. A fearful whimper whines from deep in his throat.

"Shhh!" I whisper to the dog.

It's coming. It's coming.

"It's coming," I repeat Einstein's words.

"What's coming?" Hal asks.

A shape looms out of the opposite tunnel. An impossibly large shape. Bulk sized. Hal's grip tightens on my hand. As we stand there, waiting, watching and wondering, booming footsteps march toward us.

With his hackles raised, Einstein barks. The footsteps stop and two feet emerge at the rim of the tunnel. The feet wear black army combat boots. Boots from before, from another time. Familiar.

"I think it's just a bulk," Hal whispers, taking in the towering but inert shadow.

I frown. "This is Earl we're talking about. It won't be *just* an anything."

Einstein continues to bark, dancing in circles, but he sticks close to us. *Stay back. Stay back. Stay back.*

As the shadow steps out of the tunnel, I pull out my knife. Light spills over the towering shape. I gasp. My knife clatters to the ground. But I don't care. The vision standing before me is too impossibly wonderful to believe.

Hal edges forward. "Joe?"

The head of the bulk twenty feet away swivels toward us.

"Joe!" I call, running toward him. Alive. Joe alive. It's impossible, but I don't care. He's here. Now. Alive. I want to touch him, smell him, wrap myself into those strong arms.

"Silver?" Joe questions, his booming voice filling me with joy. "Is that you?"

Tears run down my cheeks as I nod, reaching for him.

"Silver!" Hal shouts, keeping his distance.

As I pull close, Joe's chocolate eyes rest on mine. I remember our kiss, in the meadow. I remember my friend.

I smile. Joe frowns. I stop a couple feet short of him, suddenly uncertain.

"That's not Joe, Silver," Hal says.

I turn back to him. "Of course it's Joe."

An unbelievable force knocks the back of my head. I crumple to the ground and spin across the smooth concrete until I hit the wall, my elbow making an odd popping sound, but the new pain is dwarfed by the blow to my head.

Einstein runs to my side, licking my face. Seeing nothing but stars, I cradle my throbbing head in my arms.

Hal aims his gun at Joe's throat. "Stay right there, big guy."

Joe smiles. But it isn't the charming grin I remember. This smile is filled with darkness. He takes a step toward Hal.

"Don't make me shoot you," Hal says.

"Joe," I murmur, pushing myself to my knees. I blink rapidly, trying to dispel the flashing stars in my vision. "Joe. It's us. It's Hal. It's me. *Silver*." Unsteady on my feet, I place a hand on the wall for support. Smelling blood, I gently touch the back of my head. My fingers come away red. I call on my healing light and soon the throbbing pain recedes.

Joe's frown deepens. With malevolent determination on his face, he takes one large step toward Hal.

"No!" I skitter between them. "Please, Joe! Please stop!"

With one arm, Joe bats me out of his way. Hal fires. I know he is a good aim, that he sought the weak spot at Joe's neck, but the bullet rebounds as if Joe is made of rubber.

Pulling his own gun from a holster, Joe marches toward Hal.

I leap to my feet again, just as Hal empties his clip at Joe's body. The bullets have no effect.

"Silver!" Panic creeps into Hal's voice. Hal never panics.

"Joe!" I scream, right in his face, bracing myself for another sideswipe. "Joe! It's *me*. Silver!"

Joe nods. "Silver. Yes. Must kill Silver." His voice sounds strange, reconfigured somehow.

"That's not Joe," Hal says.

"I know," I whisper. I see that now. Joe is dead. I watched him die. This is a cruel trick of Earl's.

Looking into Joe's chocolate eyes, I am mesmerized. The image of him has grown hazy in my memory, and now, here, I can recommit his face to my mind.

Hal empties a second clip at Joe, who merely stands there looking a little bemused. Then he stomps forward, grabs Hal around the throat with one powerful fist, and squeezes.

"No! Joe!" I throw myself at his back and pummel him with strong fists.

Hal's eyes bulge. But he can't be strangled. It's impossible for a bulk. Joe obviously possesses more powers than meets the eye. Joe swings Hal around and I tumble off his back. Einstein barks and backs away. Although my black lightning erupts over my fingers, I can't bring myself to use it. Not on Joe.

Joe squeezes. Hal's face turns red. I reach out to Joe with my telekinesis. Something blocks me. I pull at Joe's fingers with bulk strength, but he is strong. And all the time Hal struggles for breath.

"Silver..." Hal chokes above me.

With fisted hands, I push harder with my mind. So hard my temples throb with effort. One of Joe's fingers uncurls from Hal's throat. One. Only one. But it's enough to allow the redness of suffocation to leach out of his cheeks and he sucks in a desperate breath.

With relief, I pause, but too soon. Joe's fingers wrap around Hal's throat once more.

"Sil..." Hal's voice cuts off. Blood pours from his eyes, his nose, his ears as though he is being strangled from the inside.

"No!" With bulk fists, I punch Joe, again and again, but he refuses to let go.

Hal struggles against Joe's grip, both of his hands clenched around Joe's forearms. "Do it, Silver. Do it for all of us. For my son..."

"No!" I aim my lightning at Joe. I don't want to kill him. I have a ridiculous hope that he'll come back to me, that I can conquer Earl's mental grip on him. But in holding on to that stupid belief, I'm losing Hal.

The power erupts from my fingers, tearing a hole through Joe's torso. He gawks as his wounds and releases Hal's throat. They both collapse on the ground.

"Thank God." I crawl to Hal, my healing hands ready. "I promise. I promise, but you have to live."

I kneel next to him. The healing luminescence radiates from my palms. But the healing light can't find entry to Hal's body. It's too late. I'm too late. I crumple on top of him, trying to collect my thoughts, my will, trying to find the courage to go on. I shout at Joe, hitting him with more of my black power, disintegrating his body to nothing. And then I fall onto Hal's chest and weep.

For all I know every one of my friends could be dead out there on the mountain. My mother is probably dead too. Earl will have terminated her when he realized I was so close. I might be the last person standing. And Earl is still to be dealt with. There's no way I can face that on my own.

Standing on shaky legs, I suck in a breath. Then I close Hal's staring eyes. "I'm so sorry."

Einstein growls and renews his staccato barks with vigor. He backs into me, hackles raised again, tail tucked between his legs. A second shape emerges from the lighted tunnel. An impossible shape. I thought my premonitions to be symbolic, but what approaches is every inch what I saw in my dreams.

It is The Devil.

CHAPTER TWENTY-THREE

HELL IS real and Satan now walks the earth.

Without warning, Einstein flies into the air, slams against the ceiling fifty yards above my head and drops back down to the ground. He woofs out one, tiny whimper before he crumples in a heap, legs at awkward angles. With no time to heal him, I avert my face from the dog I love and face The Devil.

It steps out of the tunnel. Ten-feet tall and covered in red-scaled skin, a swishing tail wraps around one muscular calf only to unwind and wrap around the other. On its face, the features are distorted; cheek bones uneven, skull dotted with bony lumps, hair intermittent and sprouting in clumps, skin flaking and peeling revealing oozing sores and pussing infections. But beneath it all is a face I recognize. It is Earl.

"*Silver...Silver...*" That whispering again. Is it coming from Earl?

The tail swishes. Teeth click. Claws scrape against the rough wall, setting my nerves on fire. What has he done to himself? What powers does he now possess? My hope deflates. I don't stand a chance.

I waver, sure I'm about to meet my death. Earl approaches, like a stalking lion, his shape blocking the light from the tunnel and casting his face in shadow. I take a step back, then another. How far can I go? I have to face him at some point, I can't just back my way across the chamber, through the black tunnel and back out onto the mountain. I can't let him get away with all the death; the innocent victims of the virus, my mother, Joe, Kyle, Sean, Hal, and Jacob. I won't let their deaths go unanswered for. I won't let their deaths be futile. They put their lives on the line willingly, heroically. They believed in me.

It's time to face The Devil. Standing still, I grit my teeth and raise my eyes to meet his.

"Where's my mother?" I ask, bracing myself for the answer, picturing a head disconnected from its body.

A high-pitched laugh is my only reply. The sound reverberates around the chamber far longer than it should.

"She's resting comfortably," Earl finally replies, his tombstone eyes glinting coldly. I remember those eyes.

"If you've hurt her—"

With the suddenness of a striking snake, Earl wraps his hand around my throat. It happens so fast, I don't have time to prepare my black power. Squeezing tighter, he cuts off my air. My survival instinct kicks in and I claw at his flaking hand. My face bloats, my eyes bulge, and blood trickles from the corners. I am about to meet the same fate as Hal.

Then a wave of pain washes over my body, stealing my limited breath away. Excruciating. Every cell in my body throbs with a new kind of agony. But there is familiarity in that pain, albeit the worst I've ever felt it. It is the pain of taking on new abilities. As my vision narrows and the world goes dark, I realize I've just acquired every ability Earl possesses. God help me.

I cling to consciousness, but Earl's squeezing hand continues to tighten and limit my air. The chain of my pendant cuts painfully into my skin. Trying to turn bulk, I expand my neck to make him release his grip. It's no use. I can barely suck in a breath and my vision blurs again. Under the effects of oxygen deprivation, my thoughts are muddy, but I sense his grip is not only physical. He is somehow thwarting my attempts to summon my own abilities. A mental cage. The chain of my pendant snaps and the silver quaver falls to the floor with a soft *ting*.

"I'm curious, Silver, most people would have succumbed to my strength by now. And yet here you are, not yet dead." He cocks his head and stares at me as if I'm no more than one of his altered specimens. "An aside if you will." He glances at Hal's lifeless body. "I noticed you eradicated his weak spots. I never intended a bulk to have any weak spots. Was that you or your father? Joe had a bit of a battle there didn't he? Did you like that? Seeing your old friend again? But he was more than that wasn't he?" I wish I could summon enough saliva to spit in his face. Instead, I attempt my best deadly glare. "But you, you're an entirely different enigma. Tell me, how are you resisting me?" He isn't quite ready to finish me off, he needs answers.

Unable to find my voice, I choke out a weak cough.

"So sorry, I didn't realize it was quite so tight." Earl replaces his hand with a mental power and pins me to the wall a few feet off the ground.

Unable to move my arms or hands, legs or feet, I struggle against Earl's leash and only reward myself with a throbbing headache. I can't move. And I can't transition. But there is one power within me I think I can summon. The black lightning. The anger rises inside me, wanting a target, but I'm unable to turn my hands in Earl's direction.

"I'll never tell you anything," I splutter.

"Once upon a time I thought we could all be a happy family," Earl says, marching a small square in front of me. "Margaret, your mother, and I dated first you know? It was all so perfect."

You want to let Silver go unharmed. I push the thought into his mind. I gained Carmen's ability to communicate with animals, and Earl seems more animal than human now. It's worth a try.

Earl turns and giggles. "That's not going to work on me, Silver, but I welcome you to try again." He tightens the mental squeeze around my neck and then I can't breathe at all. But that's okay, I can hold my breath for over half an hour. Panic swims in my stomach as I realize I can only hold my breath that long when I have access to my abilities.

Earl's body suddenly morphs into a hellhound. All apart from the head. It's Earl's head atop a hellhound body. Does he know they are the one monster I can't banish from my nightmares? That I came face-to-face with them, that I killed one, that I lost Joe to one?

"Neat trick, huh?" Earl pauses in his diatribe. Then his body morphs into that of a troll, then a bulk, then something with spikes along his spine akin to a dinosaur and then back into himself. The abilities he possesses are unprecedented, unimaginable and without bounds. He has cut through the shackles of traditional science and leaped into the realm of imagination. But his imagining has become the world's reality.

Rolling back his upper lip, he reveals two-inch fangs. He leaps toward me and clenches his mouth around my leg. I would have cried out if I were able to breathe. Instead, I squeeze my eyes shut and feel the blood drip down my leg. Drip? No, not drip. Pour. He's nicked a vein.

"There is something about the taste of blood." Earl licks his lips. Then he drones on about what might have been and could have been. Deluded. Insane. So much more than I suspected. So different to the man I last set eyes on in my father's lab only a few months ago.

I'm sure the spiders and scorpions and the two-headed dragon are just the tip of his latest developments. For the first time I wonder if there are more monsters to be found within the mountain. Not that I'll survive to meet them.

Racking my oxygen-starved brain for another way to free myself from his grip, I feel a minor shift in Earl's hold on my neck. It's the opening I've been waiting for. Sucking in a few thankful breaths, I concentrate on releasing my hands. I must be careful. I don't want to alert him to the fact that I too possess the power of telekinesis and that I'm slowly working my hands free from his mental leash. One tiny push at a time.

"But your mother didn't want to hear it, so she got what she deserved..." Earl's monologue continues, but his voice pitches and his marching pace increases. He's going to erupt at any moment. My left leg is coated in blood. And what was that about my mother?

With two fingers free, I push a little harder. My right hand nudges out of his grasp. I glance at Earl, afraid he might have noticed the shift in his mental grip. He is still pacing, but his anger is building, his face even redder with rage, steam actually rising from his pores. He is about to explode and I will be the object of his rage.

I circle my hand at the wrist, make a fist with my fingers and then flex again, trying to get the blood flowing, urging the black power to flow into my fingers. The itchiness crawls across my palm in a flash of eagerness, its patience at waiting for release finally rewarded. I rotate my hand toward Earl, take a deep breath.

"...that will be your fate, Sil—"

Earl pivots on his heel and turns to face me. A sense of alarm distorts his features further. His mouth twitches into a tiny 'o' shape and then I hit him with the power. Black lightning streaks from all five fingers on my right hand, zooming around the large room, creating its own thundering noise. An inexplicable wind gusts by, lifting my hair and flapping my clothes.

Earl's leash on me releases and I fall, landing heavily on the floor. The black lightning streaks wink out. Earl stands in front of me, alive. He is bleeding from several cuts, but I spot no mortal wounds. Exhausted, I struggle to my feet. I don't have enough power to defeat him.

"What was that?" He asks, his gaze moving from his dripping cuts to me.

"That was only a taste of what's to come." I raise my hands again and summon the black power. The lightning streaks out again, but Earl raises an arm. He leans into it, as if holding up an invisible forcefield, and remains unharmed.

I grit my teeth and push harder. My hair stands on end. Lightning circles me, streaks out of my hands, and stabs his forcefield. But I feel my energy draining. I won't be able to keep this up much longer. And then he will kill me.

A single shot snaps my attention away. Earl and I both turn to look at the shadowy entrance to the tunnel. Matt stands in the mouth, gun raised, smoke circling the barrel.

"Get away from her!" He yells.

I look at Earl. There is a hole in his shoulder. All the

time he kept his forcefield up, he forgot to use his bulk skin. Gathering the last dregs of my energy, I advance.

With one flick of his wrist, Earl sends Matt spinning across the hangar floor.

I run at Earl, raising both my palms, hitting him with the lightning. With his telekinesis, he lifts me off my feet and my aim veers away. Upside down, I reach for him, pushing my darkness in his direction. I feel a clamp on my brain, as if my skull is being tightened in a vice. Screaming, I fight Earl's hold on me and turn myself right side up.

The wind and thunder stir again. The black lightning flies from my fingers. Darkness ebbs at my vision. With the very last ounce of energy, I throw everything I have at Earl.

Depleted, I collapse on the ground and my lightning winks out. But it is enough.

Earl is on fire. He is surrounded by lightning and his body bucks violently. His eyes roll and his skin smokes, turning black. His hair catches fire and the stench of burning flesh fills the air. No words come out of his gaping mouth. He manages to point one flaming finger at me and I feel a probing in my brain. Then Earl explodes into tiny particles.

I'm left with a pile of delicate ash particles gathering at my feet. As I run a finger through the growing pile, the flecks disintegrate further until there's nothing left but the merest of marks upon the stone floor.

Lying on the ground, exhaustion sweeps over me. Earl is dead. Everyone is safe. I can close my eyes for a minute and rest. Just for a moment. Then I'll check on everyone else.

The deep silence of the hangar soothes me as my eyes flit closed. When I roll onto my side to get more comfortable, a jarring pain shoots up my leg. And then I feel the wetness beneath. My leg. Bleeding. I'm running out of time. With a trembling hand, I reach toward the wound, but the healing light refuses to come. Spent, I pass out.

※※※※※

WHEN I WAKE, it's impossible to tell how much time has passed. It might have been a few minutes or it could have been days. But I'm not alone. Matt is beside me and my leg is bandaged with the sleeve of his shirt.

"You did it. I knew you could do it." Matt winds his arms around me and rocks me in his lap. "I'm sorry I wasn't much help with Earl. I tried, and then he knocked me unconscious. And then I saw Hal's body…" he trails off as his voice cracks.

My throat tightens. "Joe was here too."

Matt frowns. "Joe?"

"Earl did something to him. Brought him back to life and turned him into…some kind of killing machine. I thought…I thought…" I shake my head to clear my thoughts. "It was him who killed Hal."

Matt blanches and pales. His fingers trace a line over my cheek. "I'm so sorry."

The tenderness in his voice threatens to break me. But I don't want to cry. Not now. Maybe not ever.

"Einstein," I say, pointing to an unmoving heap a little way off. Crawling toward him, I detect a faint whimper. Is it possible? I run my hands down his body and note the faint misting of breath at his snout. It *is* possible. He is, unbelievably, alive. I place my hands on Einstein's back and am rewarded with five seconds of the healing glow. But it's enough.

"I didn't think you'd have enough in you," Matt says, stroking his dog.

"Neither did I," I reply. I frown. It should take me at least two hours before I have a single hint of an ability again. Something has changed.

After a few moments Einstein stands and greets me with a sloppy wet kiss. *Well done Silver, well done.*

"Now let's find my mother," I say, stopping briefly to retrieve my pendant and knife from the floor.

CHAPTER TWENTY-FOUR

LIMPING through the vast tunnels in the mountain, throwing open door after door, each time my heart leaping to my mouth, reveals nothing. No one. Where is my mother? Stealing a breath, I turn the handle on yet another door. My heart hammers a few extra beats as I take in the tied-up person, and then slows, my stomach dropping in disappointment as I realize the captive before me is not my mother.

"Help me," the boy whispers. A large mirror flanking one wall is broken and has spilled fragments all over the floor. The boy is tied to a chair in the middle of it all and blood drips down his temple. Did the mirror explode on him? Despite the cuts dotting his cheeks, it's clear how handsome he is.

I hesitate in the threshold. "Who are you?" Einstein whimpers at my side. Matt moves in front of me, protective.

"Eli. I'm Eli. I've been a prisoner here for..." He scans the room wildly. "I don't know...a long time."

I approach the boy cautiously. It's clear he's been the object of torture; his face and torso are bloody and bruised. Dried blood covers his strong jaw. Matt kneels by his side and unties his binds.

"Do you know my mother? Margaret Melody? Have you seen her?"

Eli circles his free wrist. "I've heard her name mentioned. I think she's nearby. I'll help you look. And there are others." His gaze drops to his feet. "Unadjusteds, like us. Kept in a cage in the heart of the mountain."

Earl must have kept unadjusteds so he and his altereds could maintain their grip on reality. It didn't help him though; he clearly went insane. And he must never have figured out why an overdose of genetic modification eventually causes insanity. I smile a weak smile of triumph. Score one point for the home team.

"First my mother," I say, edging toward the door.

This way, I can smell her. Einstein woofs.

Eli stands, tests his limbs, and winces when a movement causes pain.

Einstein leads us past a few more doors into the heart of the mountain. I lean on Matt, my leg aching. But at least it's not bleeding any more. Einstein pauses outside a door, whining and scratching at the handle. Eli shuffles behind us, favoring his right leg.

"Here, let me help," I say, as I gently lay a hand on his

impaired leg. Hesitating briefly, I wonder if any of Earl's powers will be evoked in the place of my healing ability. I sigh in relief as I watch the luminescence glow and sparkle with its unearthly beauty. It crawls along my palm, my fingertips and immerses Eli in its golden light. Then I heal myself. I shouldn't be able to heal either of us. I should be depleted for hours yet. But it's an enigma I don't have time to dwell on right now.

Eli's eyes widen as he tests his leg. "Thanks." Then he feels for the cuts on his face. But they've already disappeared. "How did you—?"

"No time to explain now," I say.

"It's just what she does," Matt says proudly.

I raise my glowing hand to him and heal his superficial cuts and bruises, and all the internal injuries I can't see.

This one. She's in here.

I place my hand on the doorknob, take one steadying breath and push the door open. *Please let me not see her decapitated head on the floor,* I pray remembering my vision.

The door swings open to reveal bright florescent lighting that chases the shadows into the far corners of the room, an empty, disheveled cot and two chairs. Leaning in the corner of the room is a samurai sword. But mercifully, it's clear of blood. My mother sits in one of the chairs, her clothing torn and dirty. She stares ahead, her eyes unseeing, a soft moaning escaping her lips. Thank God I reached her before she met the fate of my vision.

"We found her." Matt squeezes my hand.

My heart soars, then drops as I take in her condition. Her eyes are swollen and coated in sleep, her face puffy and discolored with deep, black bruising. Crying, I kneel before her and gently place my hands either side of her head. I direct her gaze toward my face. But she doesn't see me.

Einstein approaches and rests his friendly face in my mother's lap. Blotting my tears, I lower my head to her lap, sending out a million prayers. I want my mother back. The strong, invincible mother who banishes nightmares' monsters with a single word, who takes away pain with the briefest of hugs, who decimates a fever with one touch of her soft, cool hand to my forehead.

I feel fingers running through my tangled hair. "Silver?" It's little more than a whisper, but it makes my heart soar with hope once again.

I raise my head. "Mom?"

"Margaret?" Matt says at the same time.

"Oh, Silver!" Her eyes focus and she wraps her arms firmly around me while I bury my face in her hair and her maternal smell. "Matt!" She pulls him into our huddle.

I hear Eli shuffle forward into the room.

My mother gasps. Her body tenses as she pulls away from Matt and me. "What's he doing...?" She doesn't finish the sentence. When I lift my head to look at her she has once again slipped into a private mental prison.

"Mom?" I ask. "Mom? What's the matter?" Peering into

her eyes, I grip her shoulders, shaking her gently, not willing to let go of our all too brief reunion.

She refuses to acknowledge me. Instead, she stares at a spot above my head.

"Mom!" I shout, hoping that it's just a question of volume. I reached her once, surely I can do it again.

"They say sometimes a good slap across the face helps." Eli speaks from behind me. "For the shock, or something..."

"Or maybe just give her a minute," Matt says, an edge in his voice.

Crouching in front of my mother, I stare into the silvery-blue eyes I inherited. I raise my hand, then hesitate. She's been through enough. I won't add to her pain.

A vibration pulses in my hand, a new sensation, a new power, hovering, willing itself to be used. But what is it? Will it heal or hurt my mother?

"Mom, please come back to me." I beg. Beside me, Matt stiffens.

Why did she retreat again? It was when Eli entered the room. My skin tingles with unease. Very slowly, I turn to face Eli. Oddly, he is muttering, as if whispering to someone in the room we can't see.

"She recognized you," I say, my hand moving to my knife. He stops muttering and looks at me. "And she was afraid."

Standing tall, I wait. Matt's hand moves to his gun. There's something more to Eli's story and I'm not sure it's going to be good news.

"Please don't, Silver." Eli gestures to the gun and the knife. "I know how good you are with that. And I know about your powers. Please don't hurt me."

Shielding my mother at my back, I step closer. "Who are you?" I demand.

"I'm Earl's son." Eli lowers his hands and his shoulders drop.

Matt gasps.

My grip tightens on my knife. "Earl doesn't have a son. He lived in my apartment building all my life. I would know if he had a son."

The black power stings my fingers, begging to be released. I'm beginning to think that one of the powers I gained from Earl was some kind of increased stamina. Perhaps running out of energy will no longer be a problem for me.

Einstein barks and paces the room. He raises his hackles and then backs himself into a corner.

"My parents weren't married. Earl wasn't exactly father of the year." Eli spreads his hands wide and points to the blood on his t-shirt.

Matt's rubs at his eyes, which are sunken with exhaustion. "He did that to you? To his own son?"

Eli nods and slumps into the only other chair in the room. My mother moans and then begins to rock her body back and forth, back and forth.

"It was your typical one-night stand scenario. My mother was a dancer," Eli explains. By the tone of his voice there's no misunderstanding what kind. "Earl was very generous with his tips one night. One thing led to another." He circles his hand in the air, indicating 'the usual story.' "Anyway, my mom tracked him down when she found out she was pregnant. He didn't want to know about me. For a long time, we made do, just the two of us. Then when I was about five, he came around every so often with birthday presents and promises of being more involved. That never happened." Eli coughs and rakes his fingers through his thick hair. "He started pushing Mom around. When I grew up a little more, I started pushing back. He made threats. We moved, tried to get away from him. It's a classic story really." Eli sighs. His defensive gaze indicates he's never talked about this before.

"I assume you have abilities?" Matt asks.

Eli shakes his head. "No way."

"How did you get here?" I ask, lowering my knife. The black power fades from my hands. Einstein lies down in the corner of the room.

"During the resistance. He killed my mother. I tried to fight back but he had so much power. He forced me to come with him and his army of altereds to the mountain. He's kept me prisoner here ever since." His dark eyes shine at me, willing me to believe him.

The resistance has been over for months. My heart leaps at the thought of the weeks of torture Eli must have experienced.

Matt frowns. "Why? Why did he want to hurt you?"

"Who knows?" Eli shakes his head. "I didn't want to join him and his army of weirdos, so he made me pay for my decision."

"You know he's dead now?" I ask softly. "I killed him." I watch the impact of my words appear in Eli's eyes. First there is shock, then satisfaction, then something else I can't put my finger on.

"I wish I could have done it myself. But I don't have power like him. I don't have any power. I didn't stand a chance." Eli barks out a derisive laugh.

Pity beats in my chest. I may have healed Eli's physical wounds, but the emotional trauma he's suffered will stay with him for some time. I glance at my mother, still rocking.

"This isn't adding up," Matt says, crossing his arms. "Why was Margaret so afraid of you? She retreated as soon as she saw you?"

"I look like him. Earl." Eli grimaces and wrinkles his nose. "Or at least how he used to look when he was my age."

My mother knew Earl at university. She must have thought Eli was him. Somehow, whatever she's recently experienced made her mistake Eli for his father and retreat inward rather than deal with the fear of facing whatever further torment he might inflict.

"That makes sense," I say to Matt. Suspicion lines his face, but he doesn't ask any more questions. I point at Eli's bloody T-shirt. "Clearly he's not on Earl's side."

Matt nods but keeps a watchful eye on Eli.

Turning toward my mother, I kneel in front of her again. I place my hands on either side of her head, hoping the healing power will come, that it will work. The golden light radiates from my fingertips and shrouds my mother from head to toe in its glimmering power. I allow myself a moment of hope when her bruises and cuts disappear. The light extinguishes.

I look into my mother's eyes, but I'm met with the blank stare of someone unreachable, someone who has experienced too much, someone who can no longer cope with the outside world. For a moment, I'm jealous of the cocoon my mother has concocted for herself, how cozy and safe it must be there, how easy it is to curl up on the floor and ignore all that's happened. But it's all over now. Earl is dead and the reign of the altereds has ended. Whatever I'm going to find on the outside of the mountain has already happened.

Einstein rises from his corner of the room and licks the back of my hand. I push myself to my feet, steel myself against a perplexity of emotions, and ready myself to carry on. I must go outside again and deal with the aftermath of the battle.

CHAPTER TWENTY-FIVE

PROGRESS through the passageways of the mountain is slow. Eli leads the way in what he thinks is the general direction of the imprisoned unadjusteds. Einstein sniffs the floor, trying to pick up a scent, whimpering quietly when he doesn't like what he smells. My mother is capable of a fast shuffle. I hold one arm and Matt holds the other, encouraging her forward.

We make it into the heart of the mountain to find a bank of elevators. Eli ushers us into one of the cabs. "All the way to the bottom." He punches the 'B' button for basement.

The elevator cab lurches. My mother stumbles into me. My stomach seems to lose its position in the center of my body and takes up residence in my throat. We reach the end of the ride with an abrupt stop which sends us all tumbling into each other. The doors open to darkness.

Stepping from the cab, I wait for my eyes to adjust to

the gloom. Eli and Einstein venture forward into a dark passageway. Matt loads his gun. My mother commences her shuffling with a gentle tug. Mournful cries reach us. Moans, whimpers, whispers and screams float to me on some unbidden wave of terror.

"This way." Eli walks stiffly further into the tunnel. "I've been down here before."

"I don't like the feel of this," Matt says.

I peck is cheek. "Earl is dead. There can't be anything worse than him."

The gloom never abates. The screams and cries rise in volume as we walk. I catch a faint whiff of urine and the stronger scent of damp limestone. Eli pauses outside a large, metal door.

"In here." He taps the door with a fingernail, the small noise grating my exhausted nerves.

An electronic keypad glows by the side of the door. I don't know the combination. I focus on the locking mechanisms, imagining them releasing. After a few seconds I hear a faint click and the doors part, sliding smoothly along their tracks.

Matt raises an eyebrow at me. "I thought you'd have nothing left, after Earl."

I shrug. "Must be running on adrenaline." I don't feel like speaking about my inner suspicions, not now. I've only recently learned how to control my destroyer ability, and the thought that there is now more inside me to discover fills me with trepidation. I refuse to think about it.

The cries cut off abruptly. The doors slam into their finishing position at the end of their metal tracks. I stare into a large chamber. Dozens of eyes stare back at me. There are people, mostly scantily clad, or in clothing of such disrepair that the remaining scraps hang from their bony frames. They are dirty and malnourished, many with the unemotive eyes of those who've given up on life. Like my mother.

One young girl, clad in a sun dress of indeterminate color, approaches me and tugs on my sleeve. "Are you here to save us?" Her pupils are wide with tentative hope.

"Yes." It's all I can manage around the lump in my throat.

Others stumble forward, hands before them, reaching out. They come slowly at first, cautious, not believing help has arrived. I'm not sure I can classify myself as 'help' exactly. I'm not an army of blankets and food and retribution, but I can free them from their cage. They come faster, running on scraps of energy. Each one stretches to touch me as they pass.

"Thank you."

"God Bless you."

The thankful platitudes are uttered with such awe, arms caress me with such love and reverence, that I find myself unable to move. The unexpected adoration freezes the words in my mouth. Matt pats shoulders and shakes hands while others wait to meet me.

"Silver, you are an angel."

"We knew you would come, Silver."

How do they know my name?

Triumph fills my veins and a joyous sense of achievement pours into my soul. I paid so much to be here, but every moment is worth it. The fear, the panic attacks, even the deaths of my friends. It was all to defeat Earl and free these innocent souls so we can rebuild our lives and begin to dream, again.

The little girl opens her mouth and sings, in a voice so angelic and pure it brings tears to my eyes.

> *"Just close your eyes and breathe in deep,*
> *Look to the new sun's sky.*
> *Because our voice is freedom,*
> *And they will hear us cry."*

Matt grabs my hand and we stand there, listening together. The girl's eyes glisten as she finishes the chorus of the resistance song. Others join in, increasing their volume and stirring passion in my soul.

As the torrent of human souls slows to a dribble and the group gathers by the elevator doors, I notice the tunnel we arrived from continues further into the mountain. Unable to see where it leads, I squint. Sounds reach my ears, but I can't tell if they're real. I'm about to dismiss the faint noises and turn my back on the tunnel when I stumble under an unknown force. There's something else down that passageway and it isn't as harmless as the prisoners.

"Eli." I motion for him to join me. "Is there a place we

can take them? A place where they can get food and clothing?"

"I know where the cafeteria is. I think I can find my way there," he replies.

"Good, can you take them? There's something else I need to do first." My gaze wanders to the unventured end of the tunnel.

He places a hand on my shoulder. "Of course."

Matt looks at me. "What's going on?"

"I'm not sure yet," I reply.

Eli ushers the freed prisoners into elevators.

"Okay, Einstein. I might need you." I ruffle his fur.

There are bad things down there. Are you sure you want to go there?

"We'll be okay," I say, with more confidence than I feel. Einstein chuffs quietly. He doesn't believe a word of it.

"What did he say?" Matt asks.

I look into the blue eyes I love. "That there might be something else down there. But I have to go. I have to see. And I can't leave my mother either."

Matt nods, kisses my cheek. "So we go together."

With my mother between us, we creep along the passage, the slow ambulation of the condemned to a slaughterhouse, suddenly afraid of what lies ahead. The unadjusteds might be saved and the battle on the outside of the mountain might be over, but I'm sure there are more dangers to face.

This section of the tunnel swirls darker than Earl's heart.

When we arrive at another heavy metal door, I sense we've reached the bowels of the mountain. There are things around me I can't see. Einstein whimpers. Heavy emotions weave in and out of the gloom as a new level of weariness accosts my limbs. I'm tempted to sleep where I stand. But I know what I'm feeling is not mere exhaustion. There's something here affecting me, affecting the air, affecting everything. This is the epicenter of Earl's perverse experiments. It's as though his intentions have become a physical entity. A thing filled with evil and death and wanton destruction. It's here, biding its time, waiting to make its presence known.

I gaze at the steel door, debating whether I want to open it or not. Einstein whimpers again and paws at the metal. My mother stays quiet, and Matt looks left and right.

"Okay, Okay," I whisper.

The locking mechanism springs open and the door slides open. It isn't until I hear the boom of the door locking into its open stance that I realize my eyes are closed. I open them quickly, fearing an ambush. But there is nothing except the expectant hush hanging in the air around me. I inch forward.

"I don't like this, Silver," Matt says. "Maybe we need back up."

I show him the black lightning dancing delicately across my fingers. "I'm all the backup we need."

A dim red light spills out of the threshold. I smile momentarily as it conjures up thoughts of my father's lab back in Central City, the many hours I spent there, impatiently, under the same red light he claimed helped him and his colleagues to think, waiting for him to finish work for the day.

We have arrived at the center of Earl's world. This is his lab. This is where he created his monstrosities.

Noises come from inside. The scared keening of caged, dispirited animals. A scurrying sound like a hamster running its wheel. The clicking of nails on metal.

"Silver...Silver..."

I look at Einstein, but it's not his voice.

"Did you hear that?" I ask Matt. "It was the same voice that was calling me on the outside of the mountain."

He purses his lips and shakes his head. "All I can hear is a whole bunch of angry genetically modified animals inside that lab."

I take a hesitant step and cross the threshold. The dim, red light bathes us in a bloody glow, an omen that seems to mark me for imminent misfortune. Telling myself the worst is over, I shrug off the portent and sudden goose bumps that decorate my skin. Another few steps and we're among the cages and clamorous noises in the lab.

"Holy hell." Matt whistles as he helps me guide my mother around the room.

The room is bigger than any lab I've seen. Warehouse size with ominous echoes to match. Cages, some empty, some housing unfortunate chimeras of science, line the walls, benches, and tables. The hissing and whispering and clawing and clicking noises grow until it reaches such a cacophonous din, I can no longer distinguish one noise from another.

"Silver...Silver..."

I look at Matt, but he still hasn't heard anything.

Where is it coming from?

I look in a cage. Two eyes glare at me from a midnight black body. The size and shape of a house cat. But that's where the resemblance ends. The animal hunches its back and coughs violently. A hairball the size of a golf ball emerges from its mouth and rolls into its water bowl with a soft *dink*. The hairball starts to shake and sizzle. A flash explodes in front of my eyes, momentarily blinding me. When my eyes readjust, the strange ball has disappeared. A flash bomb. An organic flash bomb.

Matt sits my mother in a chair. "I don't think we should stay here much longer."

"Just a second."

I move along the aisle. There are jars of heads with unseeing eyes. Not human heads, but those of dogs, wolves, other canine animals. I jump when the unseeing eyes of a hellhound locks gazes with me. Something behind me growls. A claw with sharp talons almost digs into my shoulder. A hellbird. A live one. Einstein barks, retreating. The cage rattles with its efforts to escape. The hellbird pushes its body against the cage, lacerating its skin with the effort until its feathers are matted in blood, a vicious fury in its eyes.

"Silver...Silver..."

Raising my hands, I retreat. I wince as the black power

erupts from my palms and decimates the hellbird to a pile of fur and ash strewn across the bottom of the cage. Pausing, I allow myself a moment of reprieve before I face the next nightmarish creature.

"What was that?" Matt calls from across the room. The click of his safety goes off.

"I'm okay!" I call back.

As I walk the aisles of cages I witness one impossibility after the next; a butterfly the size of a small car, a large stinger protruding from its abdomen; a sabre-tooth tiger brought back from extinction; a three-headed snake spitting an acid poison; a seemingly friendly rabbit that reveals fangs as long as my hand. There are no more hellhounds, bats or spiders, but the list of genetic monsters is long.

"There's nothing we can do for these creatures," I mutter to Einstein. It's clear most of them are in pain or experiencing extreme mental distress having been caged for their entire existence. They are too dangerous to be released.

"Silver...Silver..." The voice pleads, as though it can sense its imminent death. *"Wait...please..."*

I return to Matt and tell him what I'm going to do. He guides my mother out of the lab and they wait beyond the threshold.

With a remorseful sigh, I raise my palms. It's over in seconds. The creatures reduced to piles of ash and bone fragments. The lab is quiet once again. The whispering stops.

As my footsteps reverberate in the now silent lab, I feel

the echoes of the creatures in the air; the release I've given them. But the evidence of evil still lines the walls, is evident in the tools that sit on the worktops. The mountain is a witness to the worst atrocities that people, altereds, are capable of. It's become tainted and now feels like a house of evil, perhaps even a gateway to Hell itself.

I meet Matt and my mother in the hall. As Einstein leads us back along the passageway, a dull throbbing pounds at the base of my skull and my eyes roll up. I recognize the signs of a coming vision.

Reaching a hand to Matt's chest, I collapse against him. He guides me to the floor and then the world turns dark. Except I am now dreaming. Of the future, and all the possible paths.

A cornfield growing in a strong sun, disease darkening its leafy stalks. Golden wheat frames the corn, also withering and dying. I turn in a circle. I am alone in this farmland. A shadow passes over the sun and a crow caws from a nearby tree. The only tree to offer shade in the vicinity. I shield my eyes to look at the sky. A huge flock of birds flies in a circle above my head. Ants scamper across my feet and a snake slithers through the corn.

I hear hissing and scuttling and skittering and I grit my teeth. The birds swoop closer. A black horse neighs from a nearby field. The snake produces friends. All black, all menacing. The ants grow and sting my exposed flesh. The animals gather together, an army, targeting me. There are scorpions and tarantulas. Black panthers and mountain lions. Midnight stallions and scuttling centipedes. The sky clouds over and I am thrust into darkness. Behind all the animals is another force. Something I can't see, something big, something strong. And I am alone. There is nothing I can do.

I wake with a gasp.

"There's more," I say. "We're not done."

Matt smooths the damp hair away from my face. "You just took out Earl. Of course you're done."

I sit up and Einstein curls into my side. "You don't understand. My visions are of the future."

Matt holds my cheeks in his hands. "One possible future. And you do still dream. And you're exhausted."

I accept his hand and get to my feet. "Why won't you believe me?"

A thin smile flickers across his lips. "It's not that I don't believe you, but I don't have space to think about anything more right now. We've just fought the battle of our lives. We've done enough."

I hug him, and let the vision drain away. He is right. We have done enough. I am exhausted and my anxiety has been known to produce strange dreams. That's all it is.

We make our way to the elevators and to the cafeteria where Eli took the survivors. That's where I find the rest of my friends.

"Matt! Silver!" Lyla runs to us. Dirty and covered in blood, but mercifully in one piece. "Silver!" She reaches us and throws her arms around both of us, then hugs my mother. "The altereds are dead, most of them anyway, and those who are left have fled. But they won't last long without a pure drinking source. It's over. Finally." She inspects us for injuries.

Scanning the cafeteria, I see most of my team still alive, still intact, helping the survivors to food and clothing and the pain meds I took from the pharmacy. I catch a glance from Eli across the other side of the room and he raises a hand in a small wave. Matt and I ease my mother into a chair and help her sip water.

"Thank goodness," I say. I don't have any deeper words.

"I'm assuming Earl is dead," Lyla says.

I nod. "He's a pile of ash."

Lyla grins and her blonde curls bounce, regaining their youthful confidence. But her blue eyes are still haunted. They probably always will be.

"I seem to have acquired his powers though."

"Like Bear?" Matt grips my shoulders. "Wow."

"Big wow," I say.

"Do you know what they are?" Matt asks, handing me a glass of water.

I shake my head. "He was so…so…so *evil*. So many abilities…" My chin dips and tears prick my eyes. I don't want any more abilities. Especially ones I don't know how to find or control.

"We'll figure it out." Matt strokes my hair. "I'll help you."

"Me too," Lyla says. "You figured out your black lightning. You can figure out anything else."

"I don't want to end up like him. He was a monster. Red, scaly, huge, and that was just the physical stuff." I'm terrified of losing my mind and turning into some insane power-crazy *thing*. "He looked just like The Devil."

"You won't." Matt holds both my shoulders and stoops to look into my eyes. "Silver. You won't. You've always been able to turn your abilities on and off. You haven't acquired Earl's powers like he experienced them, you've only obtained them through your chameleon ability." He hugs me.

He's right. Maybe it won't be so bad. Maybe there's something useful in there amidst the strength and the power and the offensive abilities. Maybe there's something that will help me heal my mother.

We stand there for a while, holding each other, wiping blood and grime from each other's faces with a damp cloth. My team clean themselves up, talk, laugh, cry, and recount our experiences of the battle. Slow smiles sweep across the prisoners' faces as they adjust to their freedom.

"What do we do about my mother?" I ask softly. I glance at her rocking body. "She needs...help. Help I can't give her."

"We'll make her better." Matt wraps me tighter and rests his chin on top of my head. There isn't anything else to say.

It's just Matt and me, standing together, alone amidst the aftermath of a battle. The sounds of clinking silverware, the whimpers of people hurt and in pain, the laughter of those discovered and released, the whispered conversations of relief and hope, even Einstein's playful tugs at Matt's legs, fade to black until it's just Matt and me.

Knowing it won't last, I savor the moment. I put out of my mind the catatonic state of my mother, the death of my good friends Sean, Hal, Kyle, and Jacob, the feeling the mountain is unsafe still, the new vision that niggles at the back of my mind. I visualize each worry as a dark, hovering mass. I put each mass on a big, red bus going straight to hell and let the worries speed away and out of my life until I feel empty and spent and too weary for any further thought. My head finds Matt's shoulder as I let go of it all.

CHAPTER TWENTY-SIX

WADING through the sea of people, I spot Adam and Mason. Adam is unharmed, but Mason wears a T-shirt of blood, probably someone else's. In another corner Lyla and Sawyer huddle together. Sawyer holds his side and accepts a drink from Carter. As I walk toward them, Sawyer gives me his big, lopsided grin and raises his hand for a high-five. A grimace of pain flashes across his face and his arm shakes and sloshes the cup of water all over himself.

"Still can't be trusted with a drink," he says, his smile back in place.

I take a look at the wound on his side; a third-degree burn. I hope he didn't do it to himself.

"I'm afraid to put my hand on it," I say.

"Just get it over with." He clenches his jaw.

Reaching my hand toward the black, glistening wound, I gently place my fingertips on the edge of it.

"Ahhh!" Sawyer cries out and grabs hold of Carter's hand in a vice-clenching grip. Carter barely notices.

I turn on the healing power and after a few seconds Sawyer relaxes. His face sags with relief and color floods his cheeks. At the same time, an unexpected streak of black lightning shoots from my fingers and tears a chunk of plaster out of the far wall.

Carter raises his eyebrows. "Dang, Silver. The battle is over already."

"I didn't…I wasn't trying to…shit," I say, still not quite believing what has just happened. How can I have used two sides of the same power at the same time?

Lyla looks at me. "You've got a lot to process. Earl's powers and stuff. Give yourself a break."

I'm grateful for her understanding. But I'm scared shit-less. I still haven't rested and I'm still flinging powers all over the place.

The lightning fades from my hand. Conversations take up again. I turn back to Sawyer. My hand is still on his side, still healing him. The last of the burn fades under my fingertips.

"Thanks," Sawyer says. "Now I can hug my girl." He reaches for Lyla, pulling her into a slow waltz and plants a big sloppy kiss on her lips.

"Ew, get a room!" Carter calls.

Sawyer's backward glance in Matt's direction doesn't escape my attention.

My thoughts churn, considering the powers I just used.

When using my abilities, my energy is usually depleted in an hour, and that's when I use one at a time. But I've been battling on the mountain, fighting with Joe, killing Earl, healing people here in the cafeteria. I should be maxed out. I shouldn't be able to summon a flicker of healing glow, let alone a second power at the same time. Somehow, I am growing stronger.

I turn to Carter. "Have you seen Paige?"

"Over there." Carter gestures, his voice dropping to a whisper. "I'll come with you."

We walk across the cafeteria and in a quiet corner, find Jacob lying amongst piles of blankets with a pale-faced Paige holding his hand. Erica hovers by them, standing sentry.

I smile. "You're alive!" I say to Jacob. I was so sure that blow to the back of his neck was fatal.

"Erica. You okay?" I hug her. "I saw you fly at that dragon…"

"I'll live." One of her fluttering wings is damaged, burned half off and charred at the edges. They flash in a color I haven't yet seen on her; a very pale, mournful blue.

Paige stands up and embraces me. "Do something, please," she whispers in my ear.

"Don't. You. Dare." Jacob says from the floor. "My legs might not work but my ears still do."

I look at him. "Your legs don't work?"

Paige cries. "He's paralyzed."

Erica wags a finger. "And he's made it perfectly clear he doesn't want to be healed."

I tilt my head at Erica. "What's going on here?"

"Jacob took a blow to the back of his neck, paralyzing him. And he doesn't want to be healed. Nobody should be forced into doing something they don't want to do. Especially when it comes to DNA," she snaps.

I remember the friend she pressured into taking a nanite. The one who died. Is protecting Jacob a notch on her journey to redemption?

I kneel beside Jacob. He attempts to shuffle away from me.

"I won't touch you unless you ask." I hold my hands away from him. "Why don't you want to be healed?"

"This is my penance. This is what I deserve." He averts his head. A muscle twitches in his jaw.

"Why do you say that? Jacob, you've been instrumental in fighting for the resistance, in fighting against the altereds and Earl."

"There is nothing wrong with being healed. It doesn't change who you are, what you've done. You're still you." Paige's voice is gruff and emotional.

"Exactly!" Jacob snaps. "I'm alive, aren't I? Isn't that good enough?" Jacob's voice rises. He turns his attention back to me. "I was an altered. Before the resistance. The worst kind. I was a nanite junkie. You know that. I would have done anything for the next pill. To further my karate abilities. I was heading for the Olympics. I would have done anything to win. *Anything.* I kept taking pill after pill, no matter what effect it had on me, until I could barely walk. It wasn't until my dojo master dropped me that I saw the light. And now the battle with Earl is over, I refuse to take extreme measures to benefit myself ever again." His eyes blaze with determination.

I understand. Claus has a lame leg. Megan, Matt's youngest sister, is in a wheelchair. We all make our choices, and they are to be respected. But something rankles inside. I hate to see the defeat in Jacob's eyes.

"Jacob," Carter says gently. "The mere fact that you arrived in the cave, that you became part of the resistance shows your mentality changed. You don't need to do this to yourself. You've grabbed that second chance with both hands and have done more good than ever imagined. You deserve to be healed. Anyone injured deserves to be healed. Please let Silver heal you."

I touch Carter's arm. "It's his decision."

"No. I'm tired, please go away." Jacob stares at the wall, putting an end to the conversation.

I stare at my friend, admiring the curves of his toned muscles, remembering the speed and agility with which he executed his karate moves, the peace he taught so many on our journey here with his teachings of Tai Chi. I turn to leave.

"Silver." Paige catches up with me. "*Please.*"

I'll do anything for Paige. But I can't do this.

"I'm sorry, Paige. I have to respect what Jacob wants." Tears spill out of her eyes.

Paige circles her hands around her protruding belly. "I don't know how to do this without him," she says softly, glancing at the growing life within her.

"He's still Jacob." I touch her green wing. "It's going to be okay."

In the middle of the night, when everyone is healed, I collapse in a pile of blankets among my friends. Einstein huddles against my side and I hold on to my mother's hand, hoping that she'll come back to me. I brush her hair, whisper to her, and hold her close. Matt talks to her too, telling her everything that's happened since she's been in prison. Sawyer and Lyla, Erica, Adam, Delta, Mason and Carter sit in a loose semi-circle with me. Jacob and Paige are to my right. My mother and Eli sit to my left.

"I found ice cream," Matt says, handing out tubs of Cookie Dough. "There's a ton if it in the freezer. Someone obviously had a sweet tooth." He holds out a tub to Sawyer, just out of reach of his hand, so he has to disentangle himself from Lyla to accept it.

"Gee, thanks Matt," Sawyer says.

"No problem," Matt replies, with a poker straight face.

The sweetness of the cold dessert hits my mouth and makes my jaw ache. It's so good. A thick, happy silence surrounds us as we concentrate on the food.

Later, when most of the freed prisoners fall quiet and

sleep in haphazard groups, I look at each member of the team, each friend, in turn, holding their gaze.

"Thank you all," I say, the emotion I feel barely contained. How would I have accomplished anything without them? They aren't just my friends, they're my family.

"To Hal," Carter whispers, holding aloft a bottle of whiskey he obtained from somewhere in the mountain.

"And to Koko's men," Matt adds.

"To all those that we lost," Sawyer says. "William, Luis, Sean. Kyle." His voice breaks on the last name. "He was my best friend." We all take a swig, passing the bottle around the circle, each with our own thoughts and memories.

"*Silver...Silver...*"

I glance behind me. Nothing but sleeping people on the cafeteria floor. I shake my head. I must be more tired than I thought. Retrieving the quaver from my pocket, I roll it over in my hand, watching reflected light dance upon its metal surface.

"*Silver...Silver...*"

I destroyed everything. There is nothing left within the mountain. I'm tired. I must be hearing things. It must be an echo of the events of the day. All the trauma and death have left an imprint. I refuse to believe there can be a new threat.

"Tomorrow we go home," Matt says.

"To whatever home is," Mason adds.

I lean into Matt's body and contemplate what we'll find in Central City.

"Silver..." The whispering reverberates in my mind.

Straining to hear more clearly, I sit up. The whisper doesn't come again. I lean over to Adam and whisper in his ear. "Have you had any new dreams?"

He shakes his head. "Nothing bad." He smiles. "There's going to be corn. And wheat. And strawberries."

I stare at him, wondering if there's anything more, something he's not telling me. But he looks so happy, so content, so relieved. It must just be me.

From now on my dreams will be light. They will be filled with rainbows and dancing unicorns. Four-tiered cakes and the presence of friends. Balloons and streamers. Baby showers and bringing my mother back to health. Love and friendship. Nothing else. Nothing dark.

"Guys." I wave at my friends. "There's something we need to do before we leave. It needs to burn. The mountain needs to burn."

I refuse to think about the new vision. It isn't possible there can be something more. So the mountain must burn. To eradicate any trace of Earl and his evil scientific experiments, to erase the evidence that his monstrous creatures ever existed, the pain and misery he caused, the torture he performed here, and anything else that might still be hovering in the aftermath of battle. The fire will cleanse and the mountain will be pure once again. We can return home and set about the task of building a life, a society from the ashes of what remains.

THANK YOU!

I hope you enjoyed reading *The Rise of the Altereds*, the second book in *The Unadjusteds* trilogy. If you did, leaving a review is the best possible present for an author!

The next book in the series is *The Reckoning*. It comes out May 2021.

Please sign up to my mailing list to get the latest news, free stories and chapters all set in the world of *The Unadjusteds*.

www.TheUnadjusteds.com

Alternatively, if you'd like to learn more about my other books, *The Shadow Keepers & The Mermaid Chronicles - Secrets of the Deep*, please sign up to:

www.MarisaNoelle.com

You will receive the first three chapters of The Shadow Keepers FREE!!!

ACKNOWLEDGMENTS

Books cannot come into existence without a tremendous amount of support from other people. It really does take a team. With that in mind, there are a few people I'd like to mention and thank for the support you've shown me.

My writing group, The Rebel Alliance. Stuart White, Sally Doherty, Ellie Lock, Caroline Murphy, Anna Orridge, Lydia Massiah, Emma Dykes & Lorna Riley. You guys are my rock, my lifeline, my cheerleaders and my support group. I could not get through all the hard work without your support and those special gifs.

Team Swag. Too many to name, but you know who you are. The most amazing, kick-ass, sweri, peachy, swaggerific 'banditesse' out there. You guys are my life-line, ready with your shanks to defend my honor – love you all.

My Curtis Brown Creative group. You guys were the

first other writers I met and it's been a pleasure celebrating all your successes and hard work.

Fay – the cover is gorgeous and I couldn't be more pleased! Spot on with the trilogy theme and I can't wait to see what you come up with next.

Hannah Kates, who helped me write The Freedom Song – thank you!

My husband, Neil, for all his cheerleading as I wrote draft after draft.

My kids, Riley, Lucas & Quinn, who have been so supportive and proud of me. You have encouraged me to keep going and stay strong. You are always my first port of call when I get stuck on a plot problem, and you always help!

My parents, Larry and Rita, who read everything I write and have always supported me whatever path I chose to follow.

My early supporters who have given me advice and feedback along the way: Sasha Newell, Kathryn Richards, Michelle Oliver, Nikki & Adrian Kane, Rhia Mitchell, and Mary Bryant.

The amazing writing community on Twitter. I've made a lot of friends there and you have all made my journey less lonely and the rejections easier to deal with. You know who you are. Thank you.

My A-level English teacher, Michael Fox, who taught me to first think for myself and then to defend my ideas.

Last but not least, all of my readers. It is truly a privilege to know that my words are read by you. I wouldn't be here without you and I hope you stick around to discover some of my other books.

www.MarisaNoelle.com

ABOUT THE AUTHOR

Marisa Noelle is the writer of middle grade & young adult novels in the genres of science-fiction, fantasy, horror & mental health including *The Shadow Keepers*, *The Unadjusteds*, *The Mermaid Chronicles – Secrets of the Deep*, and *The Rise of the Altereds*. She is a mentor for the Write Mentor program that helps aspiring MG & YA authors. With dual citizenship, Marisa has lived on both sides of the Atlantic and loves to set her novels in both the USA and UK. When she's not writing or reading or watching movies, she enjoys swimming. In the pool she likes to imagine she could be a mermaid and become part of some of her make-believe words. Despite being an avid bookworm from the time she could hold a book, being an author came as a bit of a surprise to her as she was a bit of a science geek at school. She lives in Woking, UK with her husband and three children. You can find her on Twitter @MarisaNoelle77 or her website www.MarisaNoelle.com

For a sneak peak at *The Reckoning*, the last instalment in *The Unadjusteds* trilogy, read on…

 twitter.com/MarisaNoelle77

The final instalment of The Unadjusteds trilogy…

THE FIGHT IS NOT OVER.

A NEW NEMESIS HAS AWOKEN.

Sinister visions of an evil entity with looming yellow eyes haunt Silver's dreams, threatening to destroy the new world she and her friends have created. The terrifying omens push Silver to experiment with her abilities, but awaken a burgeoning thirst for more power.

As Silver walks a fine line between good and evil, her friends become wary of her intimidating abilities. She finds understanding in a sympathetic newcomer, but their deepening friendship drives an even bigger wedge between Silver and her suspicious friends.

Tragedy strikes during preparations for the final stand, bringing a terrible choice. Grief drives Silver toward reckless actions that may doom the final battle. Can she repair the relationships with her friends and control her powers before her vision becomes reality?

FIND OUT MORE AT: **WWW.
THEUNADJUSTEDS.COM**

Turn over for chapter 1…

THE RECKONING

CHAPTER ONE

THE BATTLE with Earl happened months ago and yet the panic attacks haven't left me alone. I'm dreaming all the time and I can't tell the difference between a vision and a harmless nightmare. I thought my anxiety would go away when we returned to Central City. I envisioned it as salt dissolving in water, hoping it would wash away without any effort. Instead, the salt seems to aggravate the scars I carry, driving me here, to a therapist's office.

Stifling a bitter laugh, I scan the room. It's such a cliché. The big wooden desk, the bookshelves lined with self-help books, the two armchairs facing each other for more intimate conversations. A vase of cheerful, red tulips is arranged on the windowsill. They are my mother's favorite flower and encourage me to bury my hesitation.

The woman behind the desk rises and holds out her hand. "It's nice to meet you, Silver. My name is Deja."

The name surprises me. Deja. Déjà vu. A bit like a vision or an omen. I can't seem to stop reading into things wherever I go.

Although she wears flats, she's an inch or two taller than me. A silk blouse is tucked into a smart pair of trousers and her dark hair is swept up into a messy chignon. Like it matters anymore. But in spite of her formal appearance, her smile is warm and reaches her eyes.

I force a smile onto my lips and take the hand. "I'll be honest, I'm really not sure about this."

She nods, understanding. "Neither was I before I started. Experience of trauma led me to a new career. It helped me and now I like to help others." Her words make sense but that's her life, not mine. I don't hold out much hope that she'll be able to banish my panic attacks.

I shrug.

"Give it a go. For Matt, at least."

Internally, I roll my eyes. He's the one who set all this up. He says he can't stand to listen to my nightmares anymore. The way I cry and scream both of us awake. Not to mention the few objects I've decimated with my lightning power.

"He's worried about you."

"I know."

She gestures to one of the armchairs. "Make yourself comfortable."

I sit on the edge of one of the chairs, an old-fashioned green velvet thing, and cross my ankles. "Is this where I pour out my whole life story, or something?"

Deja sits on the chair opposite. "Actually, I thought we could start with a bit of hypnosis. If you're up for it, I'd like to take you back to the dream."

A flush creeps over my skin. My mouth goes dry. The dream. Vision? No, definitely just a dream. I won't let it be anything else.

"You think you can make it go away?" I ask.

It's Deja's turn to shrug. "I'm not promising anything. But I'd like to try."

I follow Deja's instructions. Listening to her soothing voice, I allow my eyes to close and my thoughts to drift. It's comfy here, safe and warm. Then she takes me back. Back to the dreams I desperately want to forget…

Standing in the valley surrounded by the snow-topped mountains, I admire the way the sunbaked rocks glisten in the evening light. The scattered, leafless trees tremble under the effects of a wintery gust. The cold stings my cheeks and I bury my chin in the top of my jacket.

"*Silver…*"

Turning toward the voice, rough, leathery skin sweeps past my cheek. I startle backward, looking for the attack. Ripping my glove from my hand, I ready my knife, and my black power. But it's just a bat. A lone bat getting an early start on the night's hunt.

"*Silver…*"

I turn again, closing my eyes against the lowering sun and realize I'm facing the doorway, the hole of nightmares.

With a rushing flurry of flapping wings, more bats emerge. Just a handful to begin with, but on their flapping wings they bring the smell of death. A dozen more. Then fifty. A hundred. More. Dozens flap around the entrance to the mountain, haphazardly, seeming to wait for some instruction. Dozens becomes hundreds. Hundreds quickly becomes thousands. A tumultuous flow of bats dart and weave around each other, as though trying desperately to capture the last warmth the sun can offer before it is claimed by the night. The bats, joined by clicking, cackling insects, fly in a chaotic group in a whirlwind of directionless fury. Up down, sideways, seemingly confused as if controlled by some unseen puppet master.

"Silver..."

The wind howls, dislodging the last remaining flakes of winter's blanket from the mountain peaks. The bats and insects fly higher, circling each other in a mad frenzy. The noise of their deafening wings makes me cover my ears. There are thousands of them. More. Tensing, I watch the gaping entrance of the cave. But nothing else emerges.

"Silver..."

Who is that calling my name? It sounds so familiar.

Night descends. Shadows loom, larger than the angle of the sun should allow. The wind whips my hair into my face. After a few chaotic minutes, the bats and insects organize themselves. As one, they join together to form a black wave of power. They come for me, tumbling over each other like the crest of a tidal wave. And they call my name. Other animals appear within the wave, dark animals: the growling mouths of wolves, fangs dripping a hungry saliva; wild-eyed stallions, their hooves clopping skittishly against bare rock; a black bear rears up on its hind legs and emits a tree-cracking roar. Onwards they come, amidst the thousands of bats and beetles and other insects that swarm toward me. A cacophonous clicking noise rises from within them, as though they are an endless mass of glass marbles rolling down a steep hill, eager to reach me.

Spotting the eyes, my knees go weak and I hold my breath. Yellow, inhuman, like liquid pools of fire. They appear in the middle of the sky as though there are the eyes of heaven itself. In the wake of the eyes comes the hulking mass of the body. It's so black it is indistinguishable from the night and the wave, and it seems to absorb the wave, using the mass to add to its own, growing taller, wider, swallowing the night sky.

"*Silver...*"

It calls to me from a mouth that's too large for its face. A mouth with no lips. A mouth that suddenly distorts into a maniacal grin and emits the most horrifying, hair-raising sound I've ever heard. Black hands decorated with crawling beetles reach for me. Fingers that end in razor-sharp claws grab for me. I crouch and roll away. But there is nowhere to go. Everywhere I look, the black wave surrounds me, the yellow eyes loom at me, and those hands, those decay-smelling fingers, creep toward me and encircle my neck, my throat, squeezing. I gasp for breath, choking, feeling the air squeezed out of me. A single tear escapes my eye as I realize this is the moment, this is how it's all going to end.

I scream.

"You're safe! Silver, you're safe!" Deja grabs my arms and stares into my eyes. The yellow eyes glare at me. No, not yellow. Deja has brown eyes. "You're safe."

I can't breathe. I cough and splutter and gasp for air. My hands fly to my neck to wrestle the attacker away. Instead, all I find is the chain of my pendant digging painfully into my skin. Releasing the chain, I suck in a thankful breath.

"You're safe," Deja says again.

Nodding, I wipe the sweat from my brow. The dream. It's the same every time. Waking from a nightmare should put an end to any feelings of terror – for a normal person. Instead my heart pounds faster, my chest tightens, and I'm almost flattened by a dizzy spell. Clutching a pillow, I bury it deep in my ribcage, something to soften the burning acid flashing through my chest.

It is a panic attack. I'm having another goddamn panic attack. I thought I was through with all this crap. Earl is dead. We are safe.

Get over it, Silver.

Cupping my hands over my mouth, I draw in deep, ragged breaths until my heartrate slows and the pain in my chest eases.

"That's it," Deja says.

"I'm so tired." I ache everywhere.

"It's an awful dream. I would be too."

"No, not that. I'm tired of the panic attacks." They're almost daily and have been worsening over the last few weeks. I thought defeating Earl would put an end to my anxiety, but I still have dreams. Visions. Memories. Who knows what they are. The panic attacks won't leave me alone.

Deja pours a glass of water and hands it to me. "If it's any consolation, I get them too. A lot of people do, considering what we've all been through."

"I know I'm not the only one." Sighing, I put the glass on the table. "But I am the only *ultimate weapon*. I am the one who possesses all this power, abilities I don't even know yet, thanks to Earl. I'm the one who has to fight for control of the black power. No one else has to deal with that. I'm the only one who has a catatonic mother who I can't help."

"Silver. That's why we're here. But one problem at a time."

I fist a hand. "I don't have time."

Deja smiles patiently, which irritates me. "Why not? Your mom's not going anywhere. Neither are your abilities. And your dream is just a dream. You said yourself that you recognized Earl's mountain. Well you've already defeated him. There's no reason for you to go back."

I close my eyes. "I'm tired of the pain."

Deja holds my hand. "I know. We're going to work together so you can live with the pain."

Unable to speak, I nod and wipe a tear from under my eye. I wish someone could wave a magic wand and take it all away. Deja has explained countless times that it doesn't work like that. But there might be another option. Not a magic wand, but something equally effective.

FIND OUT MORE AT:

WWW.THEUNADJUSTEDS.COM

CPSIA information can be obtained
at www.ICGtesting.com
Printed in the USA
LVHW090523061220
673447LV00011B/263